Dissolution

Runa Fjord

Dissolution

Book 1 of To Crack A Geode

Production copyright FurPlanet Productions © 2024

Text Copyright © Runa Fjord 2024

Cover Artwork © Shapeless Ink 2024

The Korps Universe © Karen King 2024, and used with permission

Published by FurPlanet Productions
Dallas, Texas
www.FurPlanet.com

Print ISBN 978-1-61450-636-2
Electronic ISBN 978-1-61450-638-6

All characters are © by their creators and are used with permission. All rights reserved. No portion of this work may be reproduced in any form, in any medium, without the expressed permission of the author.

Table of Contents

Foreword
    By Karen King 13

Chapter 1
    Earthfall 17

Chapter 2
    Erosion 31

Chapter 3
    Pressure 39

Chapter 4
    Fault 49

Chapter 5
    Lattice 53

Chapter 6
    Fracture 61

Chapter 7
    Accretion 71

Chapter 8
    Tremor 77

Chapter 9
    Upheaval 83

Chapter 10
    Aggregate 97

Chapter 11
    Collision 109

Chapter 12
- *Shear* — 117

Chapter 13
- *Epoch* — 125

Chapter 14
- *Fissure* — 137

Chapter 15
- *Landslide* — 149

Chapter 16
- *Epicenter* — 159

Chapter 17
- *Earthquake* — 173

Chapter 18
- *Chasm* — 189

Chapter 19
- *Aftershock* — 205

Epilogue

Acknowledgements

Crystallization Chapter 1
- *Accretionary Wedge* — 217

Korps Universe Glossary
- *Common terms in the Korps Universe* — 221

About the Author
- *Runa Fjord* — 230

This book contains depictions of: Violence, Grievous Physical Trauma, Eye Trauma, Neck Trauma, Impalement, Death, Transfeminine Gender Dysphoria, Deadnaming, Homophobia, Slurs, Military Flashbacks, Suicide, Sexual Discussions, Blood, and Police Violence.

To the Monsterfucker Book Club.

I could never have done this without you

Foreword

By Karen King

Nearly seven thousand years ago, an event shook the world. An arrival of something ancient: the merging of humanity with the world of the beast, the eruption of superpowers, and the proliferation of the supernatural. In the modern day, this world appears much like our own but for the pantheon of species that occupy it and the extensive presence of superheroes and supervillains alike. While many states have their own super-powered forces, a vast variety of independent actors exist.

Among the most prominent independent supervillain groups is an organization known as the Korps. As far as most are aware, the Korps is an organization dedicated to world domination, led (in theory) by the shadowy Overlord. This sinister being has tried to wrap their vicious claws around the planet, time after time, since the beginning of recorded history.

The truth, of course, is significantly more complex.

Led by some of the world's strongest superpowered beings, the Korps sees itself not as a state-in-waiting, but a governance method — seeking to depose repressive state-based hierarchies to install systems more capable of effectively distributing resources to those in need. It sees state actors — "Heroes," police, paramilitaries — mete punishment out on innocents, yet go unpunished in turn. It knows, — for all the cartoonish pretensions of the supering world — that this is the true evil. It knows, too, that this cannot go unchallenged.

Operating a number of covert front companies and satellite operations for many decades, the Korps has dedicated a great deal of resources to outpacing the world's greatest scientific, engineering and medical minds. Korps medical technology in particular is extremely advanced, allowing its members to essentially build their preferred body from scratch — and permitting this capacity at scale. The Korps has learned well that monocultures become stagnant without personal expression, which it fiercely encourages in its members — a reality at odds with the widespread public perception that they are nothing more than brainwashed drones.

One of the most useful and distinctive tools at the Korps's disposal are Rose-Coloured Glasses, or "RCGs," a high-capacity communications tool, heads-up display and computer-brain interface so powerful they can be used directly as a VR headset. RCGs can function as an assistive device or therapy tool… but the nature of the technology means they have the power to directly access and even alter one's thoughts. Alternately viewed with relief, mistrust, or fear by the supering world, it is known that wherever they are worn, the Korps is not far behind.

Having emerged in the wake of the Second World War, the Korps has gradually spread its influence, eventually emerging fully into the public consciousness in the 1990s. With increased visibility and emphasis on immediate action, however, comes ever more entanglements…

The Korps began as a big pile of superhero and supervillain tropes that I'd built up a love of through various types of media, like the James Bond movies. While I originally just threw it together as an action playset of stock characters, over time, it began to morph into something very different. Using stock pop culture antagonists to take swings at the injustices unfolding around me began to carry more and more emotional weight.

In an era when information became more and more readily available, we were able, at any time of day, to pull out our phones and view some kind of great injustice unfolding, live in front of the world — to see police forces with the budgets and capacities of small militaries crushing peaceful protestors, to watch the deceptions of nations exposed constantly but slip by unpunished, to see the suffering of those in need, on our feeds, 24/7 …

It became increasingly clear to me, and to many, that the status quo is not a state of normalcy, but something imposed by force. Equally, to many, the concept of rallying the villains — those who challenged the status quo — and giving us a context in which we can, in some sense, strike back against it all… It struck a chord among those of my generation. In a world where fighting back seems so hard, an entity like the Korps is something compelling.

I am now sitting here writing the foreword for an actual, published work about it, and my mind is reeling. Giving the Korps as a set of narrative tools to the wider community feels like it has uncorked a flood: a need to right wrongs, a need to highlight injustices, a need to tell intimately personal stories, stories of love, and stories of redemption... rushing out onto countless pages, from countless perspectives.

All I have ever wanted to do is to help give people a community, and the tools they need to create, and to build the stories they need. It is an honour and a privilege to introduce this story to you — one of love, one of breaking free, one of deep wounds beginning to heal...

— Karen King

Chapter 1

Earthfall

Starshade laughed maniacally as her crowbar popped open the ancient bronze door of yet another safe deposit box. There was no one nearby to hear her cackling, of course, and it was incredibly unlikely that the security cameras had microphones, but it was about *standards*, and she liked to get practice during jobs. One could laugh in the safety of her lair, but it just wasn't the same as in the field. The desert cottontail did *not* want to get into a fight, screw it up, and accidentally giggle like a schoolgirl just because it wasn't an ingrained habit.

Bits of cracked metal had rained on the floor from the shattered lock, but it was the sparkling within that caught her attention. This one was packed with diamonds and emeralds. Eager paws covered in black, shiny gloves scooped the gems rapidly into a nondescript duffle bag. The many that missed the bag fell to the floor, in a rain of rich-people glitter.

The tall, lithe supervillain wasn't particularly bothered by the loss of the precious stones that skittered across the terrazzo floor, joining the detritus of coins, drugs, and paperwork. The goal of this mission wasn't to take the wealth, so much as to hurt the rich assholes who stashed it here; a haphazard mess on the floor was almost better, in its way. The legal wrangling of determining who owned what — and who Didn't-Know-Anything-About-That-We-Swear — would go on for years because of this stunt. Granted, all that would be handled by lawyers and underlings.

"This might be the supervillain equivalent of a flaming paper bag on your asshole neighbor's porch, but I love it." Starshade's thoughts were bright and cheery as she glanced back in the deposit box, to see the paperwork that had been hidden under the pile of gems. "Oh, what's this? Hush money payments to a pregnant housekeeper? Interesting. ROSE, we might be able to use this to cultivate an informant."

[Excellent find, dear. I've relayed it to Recruiting already.]

The soft, feminine thoughts in the back of her head were always calming, while not precisely words so much as *concepts* shaded with emotion and nuance. The mental 'voice' was, above all else, soothing and patient. They helped quiet racing thoughts, and felt like the telepathic equivalent of a warm, safe hug.

Starshade smiled as she took a moment to admire herself in the reflection of the marble. Here she was, a real supervillain, breaking into a bank vault. A little under two meters, she was modestly curvy in all the right places, but lithe. Her long legs were perfectly formed and muscled — sprinter's legs, accentuated by heeled boots to give her even *more* height. Her outfit was all gleaming black, with a subtle hexagonal pattern that perfectly hugged every contour. The material wasn't just for show; though thin and flexible, the suit provided a significant amount of protection. The only visible sign of this was the additional reinforcement of her joints and shoulders. Otherwise, her bodysuit was tailored to show off as much of her curves as possible. It was accented with a big, magenta helix design over her heart to proclaim her allegiance to one of the foremost supervillain organizations in the world: the Korps.

The outfit made her feel powerful and alluring — like a *Villain* — but it was hardly just for show, with the knife strapped to one thigh. Other gear was scattered in hidden pouches or secreted away in the utility belt she habitually wore. She regretted that it broke up the lines of her sexy uniform, but villainy wasn't *completely* about reclaiming your sexuality. Just *mostly*. Her favorite feature, though, was the magenta eyewear; her Rose-Coloured Glasses, or RCGs, glowed in the dim vault. The Korps's signature eyewear came in many varieties, but she favored a sleek-looking visor model. They gave her a heads-up display, and telepathically connected her with the secured communications network for the Korps. Better, they made her look… dangerous. Beguiling. *Real.*

[That's enough, dear; crime awaits.]

Starshade shook herself out of her delightful reverie. ROSE — as the digital assistant running on those RCGs was known — acted as commander, mentor, support, and guide. She also could affect the physiological systems of the wearer, which the uninitiated referred to as "mind control." Contrary to the beliefs of so many, this was not rough mental domination, so much as a tool for self-actualization. ROSE could help quiet racing thoughts or suppress emotions to allow taking needed action. In extreme situations, she could even take over the wearer, temporarily puppeteering their body.

But consent was essential to the Korps, even when it came to mind control, and that power was hardly *ever* used without the full agreement of the agent. In any event, for the time being, it was ROSE that helpfully highlighted the next deposit box to break open. This one apparently belonged to a local high-profile crypto millionaire. One heeled boot crunched down on a Rolex, shattering the face… and then the vault suddenly went dark.

"*ROSE, did the power go out?*" The air suddenly felt still. "*ROSE? ROSE? Are you there…?*"

Only then did it sink in that ROSE was missing. The HUD, the pink glow, the comforting presence in the back of her mind; it was all gone.

Her pawed hand tapped against the side of the RCGs like they were a cheap toy with a bad battery connection, then tapped again, over and over, harder and harder. Her RCGs had never failed like this before, not without massive damage. Still, for the moment… there was nothing… Without the soft magenta light and HUD, the vault was suddenly a dark tomb, littered with all sorts of debris to foul footing or act as caltrops.

Okay, focus, don't panic, the cottontail thought to herself. Starshade quietly set the duffle bag down before turning to see faint light coming in from the bank outside. *No visible lights inside the building, but that ambient light would be from streetlights.* Cautiously, she started walking. *If this is an attack, I don't want to be trapped in that crypt with a single exit.*

Her long ears twitched for any sound as she cautiously peeked her head out from the open maw of the vault. The ancient inventory computer next to the giant door was off, but she could see faint LEDs twinkling on some of the other machines in the office. Swiveling her ears towards the bank offices, she could hear some computer fans from PCs that hadn't quite gone to sleep yet. *So power isn't off to the building.*

Beyond the walls she could hear night traffic in the distance, so no sound of disturbance.

Wait, were those bootsteps?

Glass sprayed in as four windows were simultaneously blasted inwards. Moonlight caught the cold, razor rain to create a glittering star fall. Floodlights clicked on, turning the night into agonizing, disorienting, world-ending light. The roar of automatic weapons fire plunged the world into an unending torrent of sensory pain for the cottontail. Wild rounds peppered the walls, slamming into desks and potted plants. Fake marble tiles exploded from the impact of high-velocity rounds as they zipped and tore through the air, sounding like a hive of hellish, angry bees.

Had Starshade not already been reacting, she would have been torn apart by the military-grade munitions and poor ammo conservation. Dozens of bullets passed through the rabbit-shaped shadow that hung in the air for a moment. Her heeled boot slammed into broken tile a dozen feet away, as she dove for cover.

She felt the impact then. Dull but immediate, as if someone had hit her side with a baseball bat. But no pain, not then. One black glove clamped down on her side and she could feel the slick wetness of blood. The room continued to be ripped apart by munitions, throwing debris into the air to hang suspended in the dizzying confusion of over bright glare and deep shadows cast by poorly aimed spotlights.

The fire slacked a bit as her attackers started to reload. *I have to get out! They are trying to kill me!* She berated herself for the stupid, obvious thoughts, but she had no time. She got her legs under her and...

    LEAPT...

...teleporting away and leaving behind, for just a moment, a fading shadow filled with faint stars.

This time, her paws punched up through the cheap drop ceiling tile, shattering it and giving her the briefest of moments to see her prize. Gloves, one shiny with her own blood, clamped around the fire suppression system pipe.

The impact was too sudden for the poorly installed equipment. The blood-damp glove slipped free as the entire pipe perilously shifted down half a meter before catching, leaving her dangling five meters over the ruined bank interior, with the angry bees still zipping and popping through the air. The fire suppression system itself, however, did not respond kindly to the sudden damage.

Thousands of liters of black, slimy water suddenly started to spray out of the ill-maintained system, coating the hell beneath her in an oily sludge. At this new angle, she was able to glance out the windows and catch her first glimpse of her assailants... and saw the shining gold star of the Dallas Police Department. *Shit, the cops, and they are definitely not taking prisoners.* She hung there a moment, stunned by the chaos of the scene below her, before her training kicked in.

Run, little rabbit, RUN!

The cottontail swung her body, able to catch her other paw on a support beam more solid than the abused piping, and she pulled herself into the space above the drop tiles. When the gunfire finally died, she could hear screams of **"CEASE FIRE!"** from outside, though her ears were ringing more than ever. The space around was dusty, filled with cables and pipes and forgotten tools and... *Yeah, that's asbestos.* She was suddenly *not happy* about the extra scans she would need to get from Nurse O, when she got back to base.

None of it mattered. The acoustic tiles would never support her weight, but she was adept at acrobatics and used the few handholds available to her to scramble through the ceiling. She could hear footsteps as police started to pour into the building from two sides, and the glow between the tiles shifted wildly as barrel-mounted flashlights searched for her... until she put one foot wrong and slipped, her boot punching right through a cheap block of packed foam. Instantly, gunfire roared again; the tiles around where she had been near-instantly disintegrated, as they were torn apart by copper and lead projectiles.

Without even thinking about it, Starshade had...

BLINKED...

...once more, this time to the last place the cops would be focused. She appeared just outside one of the shattered windows, a foot away from an overweight cheetah wearing Lieutenant's bars on his police uniform. She could see the shock forming on his face, even as her fist smashed into it.

Blood sprayed from his muzzle as he went down. Another...

SURGE...

...and she was sprinting down an alleyway. Pain started to rip through her side; her body decided now was the perfect time to let her know that she had been shot, and she urgently needed to *do* something about it. But she had no time.

Few without super-speed could match her stride. She had, quite literally, been designed for this sort of back alley sprint; the rabbit leapt over parked cars and dumpsters, caromed off walls, and slid under trucks. A quick glance showed her the intersection of I-75 and I-30. *That puts me just south of Deep Ellum. If I head East, I should be able to lose them before I hit Fair Park where I can go to ground. I just have to —*

Her thoughts were interrupted as a tall polecat in blue-and-white spandex whipped around a corner, a long pike already lunging through the air towards her. Only her training saved her from an instant death, but she was already tumbling before her brain had processed the threat, sliding millimeters under the steel weapon. In a fluid motion, she pulled a small tube off her belt and brought it up.

PSSSSSHHHH

The distinctive sound of bear mace (and a scream of agony) told her that her instincts had not yet failed her, as the Hero known as Macho Poleax dropped his namesake weapon to claw at his eyes. *Never underestimate the tried and true.* Heroes were trained to deal with pepper spray, making the gambit only a temporary solution, but it still bought her precious seconds.

She could feel her heart pounding; fear and adrenaline, already beginning to drain from her lithe, weary form, suddenly ramped back up. *Shit, if that's Poleax, his team might be here.* As she approached the next intersection, she angled and...

JUMPED...

...planting one boot on the brick wall seven meters above the street, propelling her across the intersection.

This paranoia saved her. A gunshot rang out in the night — the bullet almost seeming to arc up towards her — but it had been aimed too low. She was already throwing a baseball-sized object at the pronghorn sheriff dressed in the dark blue duster. The wasp grenade exploded on impact, peppering the Hero known as Texas Trickshot with dozens of rubber balls. He was screaming as he hit the ground, right hand mangled by too many unlucky impacts.

Keep. Going. Starshade hadn't been idle. She hit the ground with a roll, gritting her teeth as she hit the asphalt too hard from too high, but she would worry about that later. She was already rolling up into a sprint. Every instinct screamed at her that she was in danger. *Why are they after me this hard?* She abruptly pivoted and ran *up* the wall to her left, grabbed a light fixture to swing herself onto the roof, and sprinted across.

That *something* inside her that acted as the source of her abilities was depleting fast. The cottontail had already used her power more in one night than in the past week. She didn't know how many more times she cou —

— Suddenly another figure was falling from the sky at her, roaring with rage; a triceratops with a body of matte-blue metal, a crudely-painted sheriff's star on the bony crest of his skull. ***Impact Crater? He's a Fort Worth Hero!*** Starshade was out of her league, and she knew it. Any of these Heroes was a match for her! She couldn't take multiple *teams* on at once!

She had only a fraction of a second to react, and she…

SPRANG…

…but this time, angled back the way she came, between two AC units, hoping to break pursuit for a moment. The dinosaur Hero impacted the building where she had just been, leveling it and leaving a sizable crater in its place. She saw a hint of confusion in his eyes before she was off, as quietly as she could, running low across the new roof. With a twist and a jump, she was sliding down a rain gutter into an alleyway. She circled back a bit and spotted a white dove with a golden beak kneeling over Trickshot.

Heavenly Dazzler, that bitch!

Fury roared through Starshade as she saw the team healer (and conversion therapist) already pouring golden light into the fallen sharpshooter. Her ear twitched; that was all the warning she had before reflexively launching into a standing backflip *over* the poleax swinging for her. The surprised polecat *almost* reacted quickly enough to save himself, before her heeled boots slammed into his masked face with a sickening crunch. This time she rode the body to the ground and jammed him in one bicep with a small injector. *Walk **that** one off, asshole.*

But she had no time to celebrate. A coral snake in blue spandex was pouring two colored liquids together in glass vials, generating multicolored smoke that was already starting to billow. Given how dangerous Ethicoil's alchemy could be, she had no time. Starshade held her breath, grabbing for another pouch. Even as the wiry snake looked triumphant, she pressed the button, and a blast of wind swept the smoke back into the team's magical support. Whatever the chemical was, the serpent screamed and collapsed to the ground, writhing in agony. The putrid vapor even started to discolor his brilliant-yellow scales into a milky white. She couldn't find it in her to feel sorry for the Hero, who was sponsored by the oil and gas industry.

*That's everyone on that team except Slate! Where is their heavy? And… is the rest of Crater's team here, too? Is… is **she** here too…?* Thoughts raced through her head as she tried to tally up the Dallas Heroes, but there was no time. Two more pairs of boots were approaching up the side alley from the south. *Shit, there's more.* In desperation just this side of blind panic, she…

BOUNDED…

≡

Starshade held her side, trying hard to ignore the tacky wetness soaking her gloves (and entire left side). Her breath panted out in gasps as she limped deeper into the abandoned warehouse. Her shoulder clipped a support beam in the gloom, drawing a pained, muted grunt from deep in her throat and almost knocking the villain over. For the thousandth time, she cursed her RCGs, dark and dead. Panic was well and truly building within her.

The RCGs had *never* failed before. Never. Not like this. Momentary jamming or venturing deep inside shielded vaults might cause her to lose communication, but all the local functions would — *should* — still be in place. Now… nothing. One minute, she was on a classic midnight bank robbery, cleaning out the safe deposit boxes of the rich and soulless; the next, the RCGs had just... died. No impact, no blast, no warning.

Why are they still following me? This was a simple job! There's no reason they should be spending this much effort to stop a crime this small! I was just raiding the lockboxes. The only time they even remember they have these is when their lawyer informs the owners they were robbed. This is the supervillainy equivalent of writing 'loser' on their mailbox...! What is going on?

The young villain railed at the unfairness of the exhausting pursuit. It had gone on for what felt like *hours*. She knew (she *knew!*) that she was failing the first rule of evasion, yet she couldn't stop herself from fleeing as she did — into an unknown, abandoned building, with no extraction, no help, and no plan.

Starshade was rapidly running out of options. She had counted at least three separate teams of the Texas Protectorate Assembly hounding her relentlessly; only a combination of intense training, her incredible speed, and sheer dumb *luck* let her narrowly escape, time and time again, but she could not shake the pursuit. No matter how hard she tried, no matter how clever she had been, she would find that she was falling into yet another trap.

Heartbeat pounding in her chest as she gasped for air, the lithe cottontail finally had a moment to stop and breathe. To *think*. It was so *hard* to think without the RCGs. The focus they gave her was gone; she was suddenly just... herself, again. *Okay, okay, what does ROSE tell you to do at times like this?*

Step one: Take stock of the situation. The cottontail shook her head, trying to clear the exhaustion and desperation. First of all, she was in a dusty warehouse — abandoned, or nearly so. A maze of rusty metal shelves filled with dusty wooden crates, her surroundings all but assured tetanus simply from being in their presence.

No immediate danger meant an opportunity to turn her attention to herself. Absurdly, her first thought was a distressed realization at how her suit had been ruined. Crimson stained fur spilled out of slashes and tears in the armored material. Much of her suit had lost its sheen from abrasions and grime. No longer did she look like, or feel like, the badass techno-ninja.

But Starshade realized that she was stalling and trying not to think about the sticky sheen that coated her torso and leg. She slowly peeled back her fingers from her side, trying to suppress the surge of nausea at the sound of the tacky fluids releasing their hold. Drops of blood rained onto the concrete when the hole in her suit — and in her side — was revealed. *No spurts, no spray; I'm still alive, and I was shot hours ago and miles away. Dangerous, but not immediately lethal. I **need** to get medical help soon, though.*

Almost all of her gear pockets were devoid of their contents, having been used throughout the chase to keep her (barely!) out of the clutches of her pursuers. The remaining supplies were limited, and of no immediately apparent use, unless she wanted to attract more attention.

Step two: Plan. She needed to plan. She had no idea how long she would have before she was found again, and she —

CLOP

One long ear swiveled at the distinctive and heart stopping sound of a metal-shod hoof treading on the cracked concrete. Fear redoubled within her, but with all her reserves drained and more exhausted than she'd ever been, her body was suddenly driven more by instinct than intellect. The cottontail froze solid. Barely breathing, her entire body stood stock-still. A stupid instinct, long obsolete yet fundamentally encoded in the DNA by her ancestors. In her enervated state, critically wounded and deeply afraid, those ancient commands coded into her very *essence* overrode her attempts at rational thought, whispering that *this* was the best way to evade predators. Freeze, and they won't see you.

Another hoof struck concrete, and another. She could feel the life draining between her crimson-stained fingers, dripping silently on the floor while she waited. Only then did her brain *finally* register how they were tracking her. *Stupid, stupid, **stupid**.* Her very *blood* was leading them unerringly to the panicked bunny.

The switch written into her DNA ticked over from 'Freeze' to 'Flee,' and Starshade once again bolted, only to round the corner of a rusted old shelf and find… nothing but wall. She spun drunkenly, finding a massive figure far, far too close. Towering what seemed three meters tall, the gray stallion in the blue-and-white uniform (with that stupid Ranger star on his chest) was the perfect image of Texas Protectorate Assembly muscle.

He loomed over the lithe rabbit, who usually felt so tall, sending all sorts of alarm bells screaming in her head as she suddenly felt tiny. (Although, admittedly, the chiseled form under the barely modest spandex sent *other* instinctive warnings bouncing around the back of her mind too.)

You are about to die! **Stop being horny,** *you stupid fucking bunny!* As had become distressingly common with the deactivation of her RCGs, there would be no soothing of her fractured thoughts, even when trapped by one of the Teepa thugs. She knew this enforcer. The dread eating into the edges of her vision ratcheted up another notch.

Slate. Implacable as the mountains, with the strength and endurance to match. Despite not possessing any particularly spectacular powers, the gray Percheron was dangerous. Moderate super-strength and durability would never put him at the top of the threat list, but unlike many heavies, Slate wasn't prone to anger or distraction. While not flashy, the stallion showed dogged determination and was a tireless foe. Worse, he was famously in complete lockstep with Teepa; the state's official Hero force was known to be deeply corrupt and cruel, but the media worked tirelessly to sanitize their image. In Texas, it was nigh-impossible to escape news of the TPA Heroes being paladins of all that was good and wholesome, showing them rescuing kittens and other such nonsense. All while the supposedly impartial media empires were ruthlessly suppressing any hint of the TPA's abusive — even murderous — conduct.

Starshade took another step back, hyperventilating at the situation. The cottontail's body was reminding her intensely that she simply had nothing left. All her tricks and tools had been spent over the last nightmarish hour of pursuit. If she had even a mote of power, she could have teleported behind the thug and made a dash for safety, but that well was long since dry. She was trapped. *Trapped.* And now this man, this *mountain*, was advancing on her. In the dark.

Her world was narrowing into a cycle of fear. *Not again, not again, not again, not again.* It was a loop of panicked thoughts, stealing her ability to plan. To act. This couldn't be happening. *Not again. Never again. I had sworn I would never be this weak again. Not again.*

It was only after a minute that her thought spiral slowed down enough to realize that Slate wasn't advancing on her anymore. He still blocked her exit, but he had crouched to be more on her level. His hands were open, showing they were empty. And he was... shushing her?

"Shush. Woah there. Easy there. It's okay, little one. I'm not going to hurt you." Starshade's ears, pinned to the back of her skull, pricked up in confusion. She had expected the... *worst* sort of fate. But this? It broke the panic spiral that had been raging. Teepa thugs were never *gentle*. They never worried about anyone, unless it was for a photo op or in the service of some rich kleptocrat.

"What?" Starshade found herself asking the simple question without really registering it. She was just so *confused*. The villain was having trouble squaring this behavior with her expectations of the TPA heavy, and her eyes scanned over his form — that ridiculous gold star on his *perfectly chiseled* chest, the comically tiny cowboy hat, and the *immensely* stupid fake spurs. It was the last item that finally broke the spell. "Why did they make you wear *spurs*? You're a **horse!**"

For once it was Slate's turn to look confused. The conversational turn was too abrupt. After a moment, he barked out a laugh. That single sound sounded like a shotgun blast, and shocked Starshade almost as much. Teepa didn't laugh, not unless it was to be *cruel*. It just didn't happen.

"It's the uniform, Miss. Marketing says a cowboy twist adds a 'folksy charm,' and makes people less scared of a heavy. Now, I long ago gave up on questioning the questionable fashion sense of the Texas Protectorate Assembly, but I am about to question you. Tell me, little varmint, what were you doing in that bank?"

"*I am not a varmint,*" the varmint shouted with heat and fury. How dare he call her that? Of all the nerve! She was going to be damned if she stood there and let this... giant... fucking... stallion... with superstrength... call... The gravity of the situation slowly reasserted itself, as her mind finally started to register the danger again.

But the gray stallion in his *stupid* fucking hat and *stupid* fucking spurs already had his hands up in a placating gesture. "Woah. Woah there. Easy there." The incongruous words did their job again. The anger drained out of her, and the fear, while not quite subsiding, lost a bit of urgency. "Let's try this again, Ma'am. What were you doing in that bank?"

The sense of unfairness was back. Starshade hated how her emotions dashed about the place like a scared... well... *her*. The cottontail longed for the gentle soothing of ROSE, and the clarity and focus that so eluded her now. Perhaps then she could have stopped from admitting a felony to a Hero who had her trapped. "I was raiding billionaires' lockboxes. Stealing their drugs, and baseball cards, and plundered gold! The only people hurt were the innocents that had their futures robbed by all those rich assholes. And that plunder was so meaningless to them that they locked it up and forgot about it! I would bet you everything I took that not a single one of them could remotely say what they even *had* in those boxes!"

It was the wrong thing to say. She knew it, but her mouth was moving, and she was talking like she would with another Korps agent. Not to Teepa. The Percheron looked troubled but shook his head. "I can't just be letting you do that, no matter what you think they've done. And you and I both know you ain't some kid too stupid to know what she's doing is wrong. You're Korps. I'm afraid I'm going to have to take you in."

The fear returned, redoubled. She couldn't be captured. Not like this. The Teepa holding facilities *preyed* upon their victims. Ordinary detainees' civil rights were regularly disregarded. But for a super powered criminal? There weren't any legal protections at *all*. Few of their victims escaped without immense trauma… if they ever left. This was Texas, after all, the state that seemed bent on blatant evil. She was bound to be sent to the *men's* annex — an added cruelty, to brutalize those audacious enough to reject the snap judgment of a doctor made decades ago. The fear disconnected any control between her mind and her mouth. The emotional toll of the day was too much. Fear and pleading overfilled her words as she, to her shame, started to beg. *"No! Please! I don't want to die!"*

The words had the same effect on the Hero as a poleax. He flinched backwards, unable to meet her gaze. After a moment, his shoulders slumped. "I…" But Slate trailed off. His muzzle worked, like he was trying to find an argument or reassurance or refute the cry. After what seemed like an eternity, she watched with incomprehension as he stood up and turned away, saying only, "Okay."

What? Starshade was left blinking. She couldn't quite figure out where this conversation had gone. "What? Okay? What do you mean *okay?*"

The Percheron's shoulders slumped even more. "Just... wait ten minutes. I'll tell them you got away." Without another word or glance, he walked into the gloom, steel-shod hooves clacking like thunder in the darkness... accompanied by the faint jingling of those stupid little spurs, now that she was listening for it.

And so, Starshade was left there. Alone. In the dark. Wondering what happened, and why this Teepa thug had let her go; had *saved her*.

She would find out.

Chapter 2

Erosion

Slate stared at himself in the mirror of the precinct changing room, trying to ignore the smell of sweaty men and mildew... to say nothing of the emasculating jokes and racist ribbing between the other Rangers behind him in the locker room. This was his ritual. When he was new to the force, right out of the military, others tried to make fun of him for this. But he was a giant draft horse with super-strength, and once he told them it was a football superstition to never use a towel — to dry his fur off simply by *waiting* — the others had context. Only then (and when he persistently failed to respond, past his pat explanation) did the jokes slowly fade.

But he watched himself. The figure in the mirror was distorted by condensation from the showers, but he knew that reflection. The massive Percheron stallion. At well over two meters tall and almost as wide, the draft horse was a wall of slate-gray fur and rock-hard muscle, as if an ancient statue chiseled from the very stone of his namesake. The perfect enforcer. The loyal Adonis. Some rumors even circulated that he was an automaton or a mystical construct, literally formed of rock and lacking a will of his own. Or — worse yet — others said that he was little more than a stud farm himbo.

Especially after that stupid TPA Heroes Pinup Calendar, the man thought, near-imperceptibly narrowing his eyes. *So why don't I feel handsome?* He had this thought every day. He stared at the reflection staring back, and it always felt like a... stranger. Here he was, in the body of a god, shaped by innumerable hours of training and by a diet carefully crafted of the finest misery, yet he felt... *nothing. Less* than nothing. The stallion in the mirror stared into his soul, as if mutely deriding him for not appreciating the gift he had been given.

He knew the others preened about their bodies; reveled in them, paraded them about. Used them to pick up women that they either quickly dumped or kept like trophies. But here he was, in a body that made every single man in the local TPA office jealous, and he felt none of that. It was just a further sign that, at some bone-deep level, he must simply be broken.

And he *was*, too. Unsurprisingly, Chief Tulsa had been furious that he had failed to capture the Korps girl. The *entire* op had been for the purpose of capturing one of the Korps's minions who had begun to pop up around Dallas. A trap had been laid and sprung, every resource the TPA could muster in the area had been deployed for one goal: capture a Korps agent. Some new device had been invented, one he had helped carry into the basement of a local police precinct; with it, they could shut down that cursed RCG network for a time. Isolate and capture. He didn't know why. That was above his pay grade, and he hadn't bothered to think about it.

None of them believed that the Korps agent would be so wily, but their easy prey had turned out to be fiendishly difficult to corner. Every time they thought they had her, she managed to escape. Starshade — as she had quickly been identified over comms — was supposed to have very limited teleportation powers that would be exhausted quickly and recharged slowly. She might have had *marginal* super-speed and was suspected of having one or two other minor aura-level powers; she was the definition of a bit player. Even so, she had constantly evaded them, using her powers to perfect tactical effect, narrowly slipping their traps and ambushes again and again... all while bleeding heavily from a gunshot wound.

The Rangers had used every trick in their book to capture one single Korps agent and had failed. *He* had failed. Of course, his boss didn't know he'd *let* her escape. (*Why did I do that...?*) Still, his superiors damn sure knew the draft horse had gone into the warehouse alone, and came out alone, empty-handed. A single minion had made fools of the entire assembled Dallas Protectorate.

He still didn't know why he let her go. That thought chased itself around his brain for long minutes, only finding slow realization. He could picture her there. Tall, in that dark armored catsuit. A dancer's body, or an acrobat's, but with a chest rarely found on a woman so athletic. She had been so… hurt. So *afraid*, and yet, so fearless. That rabbit stood there, while bleeding to death, and sassed him about his spurs. She had stood up to him, even as fear and pain and exhaustion had been etched into the lines of her face. And when he announced he was going to take her in, the raw terror in her had been so… *stark*. She truly feared she was going to die, if she was captured.

In that moment, he found he couldn't argue. Slate was aware of the reputation of the Rangers. He knew that sometimes they went too far, that they hurt people intentionally. He had always chalked it up to a few bad apples, or unprofessional overenthusiasm. But, in that moment, he realized he couldn't assuage her fears. In point of fact, he had a whole speech he used to convince suspects that they would get a fair shake, and that the rumors were false; that if they just came quietly, they'd be protected and taken care of. But there, staring into her dark brown eyes, the words he had used so many times just didn't come. At that moment, he finally, truly *knew* those words had always been a lie.

This was a thought underscored for him by the words of Captain Alamo, carrying clearly across the locker room. The Hero's boastful story sent a wave of quiet over the TPA Protectors, as each group started paying attention to the minor celebrity holding court from one corner. "So, the Korps bitch was holed up in the Remember National Bank, and we were waiting for word to go in and kill that whore, but… they had hostages, or some shit, you know the drill. Same old bullshit. Half those fucks are probably in on the robbery anyway, and the other half are just looking for an excuse to scam you, or shank you. Anyway, we have to wait for *hours*. All the police departments have to show up, *then* there's the pissing match to see who gets jurisdiction. Everybody's got to get their dick wet when there's a hostage situation, right, so they can justify their funding."

The horned lizard on loan from the San Antonio division was lapping up the attention from his story. Everyone was drinking in the tale from this visiting Hero, with laughter on their lips and mirth in their eyes. Everyone, that was, but Slate, who continued to stand frozen, watching the alien reflection in the mirror. "So, people are screaming, 'Help Us, Help Us,' blah blah blah; you know how it is. Finally, *finally*, we're given the green light. We can go in and try to kill this Korps bitch. I mean, officially we're there to capture, but you don't let an opportunity like that slip by, right?"

"So, I burst through a window. Real action star shit, I swear; glass spraying everywhere. Someone starts screaming near me. Must have been in on it, so I punched her right in the gut. She goes down for the count. But the punch felt weird. Only then do I realize the bitch was pregnant. Who sends a pregnant bitch to be a *lookout?* Luckily, she was a mongrel, so it's not like she needed another mouth to feed at home. Bitch probably protested for the right to murder babies. I was just helping her out!"

The other Rangers laughed at the joke. Joke? When had that become a joke? Pain started to shoot through Slate's arm, and it took a moment before he realized he was clenching his fists so hard that he was shaking. "And then this faggot in a dress starts screaming at me. Fake tits and all. Saying something like 'She's an innocent bystander! She was trapped in here! You weren't letting us out!' You know, the same shit all these bastards say to sway a jury later. But I've clocked him, no matter how much he painted himself to look like a whore. Can't hide that Adam's apple and deep voice. I knew he was a rapist right then."

The world was turning red. Slate stood there, a rage filling him with each word of the story. The snickers and laughter of the locker room stoked a deep fury within the mountain of a stallion. "I hear over the radio that the Korps bitch has escaped. But I know I have one of her accomplices, *no fucking way* this faggot isn't in on it. So I grab him by the chest and, no shit, he had fake boobs. This bitch had gotten a boob job so he could sneak into restrooms I bet. Anyway, I ain't about to let this one go. And he's crying, but a light slap stopped that. He couldn't even take a little light grabbing. So I pull him outside and throw him in the wagon."

A strange hopeless pain lanced through Slate's chest. He didn't know for what reason, or where it came from, and he couldn't bear to ask himself *why*. But each word crashed into the equine Hero. "Booked him for resisting arrest. Dropped him at the men's annex, of course. I'm sure that faggot is going to like it, though. You want to know the best part? Some Korps cucks wanted me reprimanded. So the chief came to me, laughing. Gave me a whole *week* paid vacation! And a steep bonus to be 'on loan' to other departments around the state for 'training'! If you *ever* feel overworked, fellas, I'm telling you, find a faggot and rough him u —"

Slate didn't realize he was moving before he was all the way across the locker room. His fist slammed into Captain Alamo's jaw at lightning speed, carrying with it the force of an avalanche. There was a hideous snapping noise as the jawbone *shattered*, and the horned lizard was thrown through two lockers. The Percheron didn't know why he'd done it, but he was already walking down the hall before anyone could react. Radiating fury and barely-contained violence *entirely* uncharacteristic of the normally stoic, laconic warhorse, no one said a word as he stalked, still naked, through the halls of the citadel. Despite being an unstoppable juggernaut that none would dare question, he somehow felt less safe than he had ever been.

TXZJ-CF   March 10, 2023

MEMORANDUM FOR

Commanders, All Divisions
Commanders, Proud Daughters Of Texas Freedom
Directors and Chiefs, Staff Offices, This Headquarters

SUBJECT: Texas Protectorate Assembly Policy Memorandum #13 - Official Language

1. I am the Senior Communications Official for Texas Protectorate Assembly Communications Bureau (TPACB) and Austin Division Headquarters. All personnel within the TPA are responsible for upholding the sanctity and honor of the TPA. Effective communication is essential to protect the image and storied history of this venerable organization. Precise language must be used to avoid creating an unprofessional appearance and diminishing the core values of the TPA.

2. In accordance with Directive 202207-437, it has been determined that the term 'Protector' has a negative connotation among the core recruiting demographic of 10-25 year old males. It has been determined that this tarnish is due to the continued vicious attacks by the biased media. This term is now deprecated.

3. Additionally, several instances of the previously-deprecated term 'Ranger' have been detected in draft communications. Please see Directive 202103-273 for additional details. This term remains deprecated and should no longer be used in any official capacity. This includes during the TPA Luncheon and as part of 'Heroic Field Banter'.

4. Going forward, active members of the Texas Protectorate Assembly should use the new official term of 'Protecteer'. Focus groups have indicated a high engagement with key recruiting and funding demographics. Unlike the now-deprecated 'Protector' and 'Ranger,' or the common term 'Hero,' this bold new alternative has also been successfully trademarked, and is forecast to generate significant funding via enhanced merchandising, licensing and branding opportunities.

5. This department would like to thank the continued support of the image consultants gracefully provided by Travers Media Group.

Larry "Tree Sparrow" Stuffins
Captain, Texas Protectorate Assembly
Commanding

Chapter 3

Pressure

Starshade held herself as she stared down at the disassembled fragments of her RCGs. She felt *naked* without their pink glow. The cottontail had worn them for so long, ever since the Korps had recruited her so many years ago. They soothed her racing mind and helped her focus when she needed it. More than that, they broke her out of thought spirals when the brain weasels threatened to eat her.

The RCGs had started working again somewhere around Waco. She had been safe, inside the dark interior of a random southbound semi, when the device had lit up with that blessed rose-colored glow. When it happened, the relief washing over her had almost caused her to literally faint. Instead, nearly in shock, her cry for help rapidly summoned extraction and medical aid. Starshade had never been more relieved than the moment the ROSE reactivated; she felt that calming silence fill the back of her thoughts, and the pain of her wounds faded away.

But for the moment, she was once again bereft of that comfort and clarity. Her ear flicked to the still form of Nurse O hovering right behind her — a synthetic arctic fox with a pearlescent metallic skin, who was definitely waiting to make sure the bunny didn't collapse. Two sets of arms — one pair clearly mechanical, the other almost, but not quite, realistic — were obviously poised to catch the rabbit if she fell.

She's just doing that to remind me that I should be resting. I'm not THAT weak!

Dressed like a mid-20th century nurse, the synthetic vulpine's uniform was all soft teals and pinks, with a dash of dark blue for accent. What was decidedly not 20th century was the facemask with the LED waveform. The distinctive Korps medical division logo, a caduceus wrapped by a Korps helix, was emblazoned on both her hat and the tunic's left breast.

The 'O-E184' printed beneath the caduceus indicated the unit's particular identification.

Though the rabbit's wounds had been treated, she was not yet healed. The absolutely-still nurse somehow *radiated* disapproval, cross-shaped magenta pupils boring into her. The synth was clearly displeased that Starshade refused to rest while she healed, and was, instead, bouncing energetically on her heels in the engineering bay.

A plague of emotions warred within Starshade, as she looked down at the fragments of her emotional calm. She kept glancing at the engineer working on her goggles, the tiny lion known as Switchboard. Standing at barely a meter and a half, he was dwarfed by the tall cottontail, but he always carried himself with such an air of propriety and *style* that he commanded the room. The model of RCGs he wore were styled as perfectly round glasses, perched on his incongruously mousy face. But the thing that always drove her up the wall was that she could never seem to look him in the eyes; his rose-colored glasses always seemed to be reflecting a nearby light source, or else perfectly casting his eyes in shadow, and over time she realized that she had no idea what his eye color even *was*. For the first month, she was convinced that the RCGs themselves were somehow configured for this nonsense... but then she finally met him in his civilian guise of Adam Pride, wearing *normal* glasses, and it was somehow even worse.

She tried to shake her thoughts back into order. Switchboard had plugged each piece into a different system to run diagnostics. Computer code flashed across a dozen tiny screens faster than she could process them, but the lion seemed to have no issues. *How could a lion look **mousy**?* It felt wrong, somehow, but Adam managed it. His mane was finally growing in, so hopefully that would help.

Focus. You can do this. But there was nothing to focus *on*, for the moment. She was here, hovering over her RCGs like a concerned mother over an injured child, but she wasn't actually helping in any way; she just felt she needed to be there. Just in case. (In case of *what* was unclear, even to her.) *Okay. Okay. I'm just fretting. I need something to **do**. Adam has this. He's the best at this. He's one of only three people on the base rated to work on integrated component-level RCG repairs.*

She had just convinced herself to actually go and do something — or at least rest — for the third time, when a sound pricked her long ears. Then, every hair on the back of her neck stood up; she couldn't help it. That *slithering* sound always sent that primordial part of her brain into pure terror mode. It was her. *Her.*

What is she doing down here…? She never leaves her den — I mean, the command level.

Starshade chided herself for being mean, but something about the base commander made her skin crawl and quickened her pulse. It was harder to keep herself under control without ROSE. She couldn't keep her long ears from standing completely erect, following the sound as it grew louder and approached the door.

Then… there she was. The base commander. Towering over the silver dragon walking beside her, the snake stood three meters tall, not counting the tail that stretched back into the hallway. The cobra was *huge*. Broad shield-like deep-red scales covered her sides and back, while smaller, cream scales covered her front. Her unblinking black eyes were highlighted by her own RCGs, the classic jellybean-shaped visor. Her torso was all obscenely tight black latex and black leather straps, barely containing her evolutionarily (and gravitationally) questionable chest. Lacking legs, a long, muscular tail moved her deceptively quickly and quietly.

"M–M-Mistress Celia?" Starshade squeaked out, proud of her bravery. The base commander was petrifying — sometimes literally. She claimed to be from a race of lamia but had been so distinct and frightening that the public had simply dubbed her 'The Lamia' and knew her by no other name. She claimed she was a high priestess to a goddess of pain, one that no one had ever heard of, the rabbit was sure. And she claimed to be able to turn someone into stone… which was absolutely true, as her office was decorated by the statue-like form of an erstwhile oil company CEO. The cottontail had only ever met the base commander once, during her initial induction; she had felt so tiny compared to the sheer size of the crimson cobra and the almost blinding intensity of her personality.

The snake smiled broadly, showing off enough fang to send a shiver down the cottontail's spine. "Yesss, dear Ssstarssshade. I am glad to sssee you alive. You had usss quite worried when you fell off the grid, and Teepa commsss soon lit up like a Korpsmasss tree. We feared the worssst. Our exxxtraction teamsss were unable to locate you." Mistress Celia's voice was all hissed consonants and sensual whispers, and yet somehow easily understood across the room.

*Of course she hisses all her S's. Of **course** she does. Of all the stupid, stereotypical hackneyed tropes, a giant dominatrix snake that hissed her words had to be the worst one I share a base with. Worse, she just **happens** to press every evolutionary terror button baked into my DNA. And someone wired some of them wrong.* Starshade cursed herself (and her stupid traitorous libido) while subtly trying to press her thighs together, to hide the way her body responded. Apparently, without ROSE to keep her on focus, she reacted to giant dominatrix snakes the same way she responded to giant chiseled stallions: by wanting to do the one thing most likely to get her killed.

A forked tongue — glistening purple in the light of the engineering bay, flicked out of the base commander's mouth — It took a moment before the thought made its way through the storm of confusion in the cottontail's mind. Then she remembered what snakes were doing when they did that; they were tasting the air. And the look in Mistress Celia's eye was devilish. Starshade blushed **hard**.

Her heart was suddenly *racing* as the snake was suddenly *there* in front of her with one warm hand on her cheek, shushing her with far too many s's. "Sssssssshhhh. It'sss okay, little rabbit. You are sssafe. I will not hurt you…" Strangely, the words did have a calming effect, even if the looming snake towering above her was causing a confusing mix of emotions. That was, until Mistress Celia continued the statement. "…unlessss you asssk for it, of *courssse*." The cognitive equivalent of radio static crashed over Starshade, as she failed to adequately process the threat and/or flirting.

The scene was finally interrupted as Switchboard cleared his throat. "Mistress, if you would terribly not mind, could you take a moment away from flustering our poor agent here? I have a report." Starshade stared at the lion, mortified that her… reaction… had been so obvious to everyone. She had barely registered when the silver dragon had entered with Celia, but a quick glance to Karen showed approximately zero sympathy, and an unhealthy level of amusement.

In desperation, she turned back to look at Nurse O, only for the synth to tilt her head slightly, as if to say: 'Of course I noticed. I have a full medical diagnostic suite running at all times. Do you think I wouldn't notice you going into fucking heat over the thought of the base commander, **your boss**, taking you back to her quarters, wrapping you in her scaled coils, and making you scream for twelve hours? Which I do not medically advise because you were shot eight hours ago.'

...Or maybe she was reading into the emotionless expression, just a bit.

Karen was dressed in little more than a leather half-jacket, a prominent collar, fishnet, and villainously utilized electrical tape. The expression on the dragoness's face turned unusually grim as she returned her attention to Switchboard. "I am relaying this to the appropriate parties. As you can imagine, heroes like the TPA having the capacity to fully jam our communications is a critical security risk."

The small lion started pulling up information screens that floated in the air above the worktable to illustrate his points. "I have found no physical component issues that can explain the loss of operations. At this point, we can rule out that as the cause. Similarly, we don't find any evidence that this was a software attack. The RCGs were not hacked, as far as we can tell at this time. There are a number of unusual log entries, however."

Excerpts from log files were displayed next, with some highlighted in red. Some were gibberish characters, with others displaying various error codes, and a few that seemed entirely normal. Starshade was completely out of her depth to understand why any of the latter were of note, but a glance at Karen and Celia showed intense scrutiny. As the briefing continued, the cottontail fidgeted quietly, wishing desperately that Adam had put her RCGs back together first, or that she had gone to get her backup pair. It would have been so *easy* to head back by tram to grab them from her room. and be back in time for this. (Plus, that would have let her swing by the cafeteria in Section 3A on the way back. They had the best carrot cubes in all of RIV, perfectly prepared with a honey bourbon glaze, they were *sinful*. Oh, and if she was lucky, she would run into that beautiful giant red wolf again. Starshade couldn't remember her name, but she seemed so familiar, and she would have to check with ROSE about whether they were single and if —

"...Starshade?"

The rabbit blinked at her name, attention snapping back to see Celia, Karen, and Adam all staring at her. A flush roared across her face and the inside of her ears practically glowed. She had been *daydreaming*, during an absolutely critical briefing. In front of the two most senior, essential members of RIV's command staff. There was nothing for it but to forge ahead, even as the effort drained her normal irrepressible confidence from her posture. "I'm, um, sorry... could you repeat the question?"

The operative flinched, expecting an immediate reprimand, but instead Karen's expression immediately softened, seemingly sympathetic, and her tone filled with concern and support. "Oh, my poor dear. I'm sorry. I know how much it hurts to be without your connection. Please, we just asked you to repeat your report about what happened after the RCGs died. Was there any sound? Anything you noticed? Anything that seemed out of place?"

Starshade quickly glanced at the base commander to gauge her expression. It was impassive as ever, but her body language seemed to be accepting. Even encouraging? Although it was always hard to tell. Half the time Celia seemed to be teasing, and the other half, predatory. Except for all the times that — *Focus. They asked you a question.*

"No, I didn't hear anything. But now that you ask, that's... I wasn't expecting anything? The perimeter was clear, and overwatch drones didn't show anything unusual. I was just breaking through the indicated safety deposit boxes when everything went dark. I stepped out of the vault to see what was going on, and that's when the SWAT team busted through the door, shooting. But... there wasn't... enough time." The operative drifted off for a second as the pressure of being *stared at* faded, thinking through the idea nagging at the back of her mind.

"The overwatch drone never warned me! And ROSE never told me that the drone was offline. There wasn't enough time for a police team to stack up on the front door between when my RCGs went offline, and when the door was blasted open. That setup takes minutes. Not seconds." By this point Karen looked quizzical, Adam looked thoughtful, and Celia looked like a giant snake monster that would eat her soul.

The rabbit started to pace back and forth. She was on the trail of something, and she needed her body moving to help her reach it. The pressure of the important trio staring at her began to recede. She began talking faster and more to herself, an excited edge entering her voice. "I... I do remember something. Or the *lack* of something. Before I went into the vault, I used the ancient bank computer to check records. Old enough that it still used a CRT display. That computer was on when I went into the vault. But when I came out of the vault, that computer was off!"

Starshade looked over at the other three, triumph in her voice. But the expectant expressions of the other three caused her to waver. They didn't quite see yet. "It's an old bank computer." She saw a spark in the lion as Adam started to comprehend but the two leaders still watched her.

The cottontail started to fidget and squirm. She had figured out an important detail, but she wasn't sure how the other women weren't getting it. Doubts started to creep in as she started to wonder if she had been wrong. As Starshade felt her confidence fade a bit under the scrutiny, Celia spoke up, with a calm, reassuring tone. "Go on. Why isss that important?"

The rabbit fumbled for a response. But Switchboard was the one to speak up before she started stuttering. "Because those old computers automatically go to sleep after a set time. When they do, the fan spins down and the screen turns off. The fans tend to be pretty loud. However, this is a bank. During the workday, the tellers need to be in and out of that computer all the time. And they don't want to have to wait for the computer to wake up every time, so they set the sleep timer high. Usually at least 30 minutes."

The lion engineer rapidly pulled up logs, scrolling through them before finding the entry he was looking for. The glare off his glasses was barely distracting to Starshade, now laser-focused in anticipation. She knew she was right. She *knew* it.

"Starshade last touched that computer at 23:47:35. Her RCGs died at 00:05:52. That's only eighteen minutes; that computer should have still been on. So, either whatever happened shut down that computer system too, or Starshade was in that vault a lot longer than we thought." The news was troubling to the other three, but Starshade couldn't help but be excited. She was onto something, and she knew it.

Karen nodded to her, but it was Celia that spoke. "Well done, little Ssstarssshine. That isss an important obsssservatttion." The operative couldn't help but feel that praise from the base commander was confusing, but she was happy she could contribute. *But wait, Starshine? Did she forget my name?* "Now, Ssswitchboard, what isss your assssessssment? What courssse of actttion do you propossse?"

It was the lion's turn to pace. Starshade couldn't help but watch that tufted tail tip lash back and forth. Growing up, authority figures only ever seemed to be screaming and demanding answers. To them, a quick, wrong answer was better than a reasoned, correct answer, no matter how much it cost them. But Celia and Karen — who must have been *dying* for this information — clearly projected calm and patience, as if they would wait forever for the conclusion.

After several minutes, Adam stopped, nodding to himself. "At this time, I think we can rule out the idea that someone got into the system or physically shut them off. Right now, the most plausible explanation is one based around a combination of jamming and powers. Something or *someone* new is out there, and we need to identify it."

Celia and Karen stared at each other for a long moment, maybe communicating through the RCGs, or perhaps just having the silent rapport that came with having worked with each other for a long time. Then, the cobra stood a little taller and fixed her gaze on the smaller cottontail. She felt herself quiver a little at suddenly being the direct focus of the lamia. "Ssshe may have sssimply been a target of opportunity. However, we cannot rule out the possssibility that Ssstarssshade was targeted *ssspecccifically*."

The rabbit winced. *Why would they target me? I barely register as a Korps agent. Am I even in their current database? Is it… it couldn't be because of* **Mom***, could it?* But at least Mistress Celia remembered my name this time.

"Regardlessss, we need to make thisss a high priority. Ssstarssshade, you do not have to go into the field, if you feel at risssk. But I feel our chancccesss of effectively invessstigating thisss unsssettling development would be better if you are on the ground for thisss operatttion. We will have… more *presssent* overwatch for you, going forward."

The rabbit blinked at the comment, and she opened her mouth without thinking. "Of course I want to be on this one! I want to help, and I want to know what happened," she nodded. "And… I want to figure out just what's going on with Slate."

The snake tilted her head at the last comment. "About that… we have reviewed all intelligenccce on him held in our databasssesss. Everything sssaysss he'sss the perfect sssoldier. He ssspent eight yearsss in the Army, three combat toursss. Sssinccce then, he hasss been part of the TPA. Currently he isss the heavy assssigned to the Dallasss-area Hero team, Pegasssusss Phalanxxx. There isss no indicatttion that he isss in anything but in perfect locksssstep with their idealsss. He isss a great danger, and you ssshould exxxerccccissse cauttttion when interacting with him. We don't know their planss, and hisss letting you go may have been a ssstrategic feint."

Starshade immediately bristled at the comment. But there was Karen, stepping forward in her mere suggestion of an outfit, over those striking silver scales. Warm hands cupped around the cottontail's cheeks as she was suddenly there, close to her. Her presence was warmth and sunlight and calm waters. For a moment, Starshade let herself sink into the same sort of mental comfort that Rose so often provided. Her breathing calmed, her mind stilled, and she felt at peace for the first time in *days*.

"Hush now, Starshade. She wasn't giving you a command. She was asking you, the Agent who was on the scene, to use your judgment. She wanted you to remember the essential context of the TPA. It is one of the most corrupt hero organizations in existence, rife with the worst excesses of this world. It is extremely rare that any member is able to be redeemed or recruited. Those that are tend to be very young, or fresh recruits. The TPA has a way of corrupting the soul. You know this. You know this better than anyone, regrettably." Starshade flinched slightly at the memory of her parents, but Karen continued.

"But we also know *you*. You are clever, cunning, and *capable*. You are able to see in ways few others can. We trust you. We simply ask you to remember this context, and that, if our fears are warranted, you must not let him fool you with what you *want* to believe. But we trust you to do what's best. We believe in you, Starling."

Starshade couldn't stop smiling at the warm words with the soothing velvet voice that seemed to reach deep into her soul. She felt a few tears, this time of relief and joy, drop to sparkle on Karen's soft scales. "Thank you."

The dragon finally stepped away with a smile and a happy little bounce. "Now, Nurse O has been very patient with you. You need to get back to the medical bay so you can finish healing. You are needed in the field soon, Starling, but you have enough time to heal properly before you suit up again. Speaking of which, we have a few upgrades planned. And we need to get you another RCG device for the time being. Switchboard needs to run more tests, but I know this pair means a lot to you, and we will make certain they're returned to you when his analysis is complete. And…" Karen trailed off with a smile on her lips and a twinkle in her eye. "Zala is running overwatch for you. And she wants to watch you get suited up."

A giddy thrill went up Starshine's spine at the thought. "She'll be out of the vat in time?"

Karen smirked "Absolutely. I know she'll be eager to see you. And, since it's Zala, even more eager to be seen *by* you."

The cottontail giggled and followed Karen out of the engineering bay with Nurse O following closely behind. A reflexive thrill of fear shot through the agent as she passed the towering cobra, but the feeling had grown distant and muted.

Was she imagining it, or had there been a glint of amusement in the lamia's unblinking gaze…?

Chapter 4

Fault

Slate sat rigidly upright in the cheap plastic chair, posture held at perfect attention. The stallion knew that if he was not extremely careful, his immense weight and strength would overcome what little structural integrity the old industrial extrusion retained; if that happened it would no doubt cause the attempted furniture to fail spectacularly, spraying razor shards of yellowed plastic across the room. (Again.) But the peril that forced him into military attention this time was the figure seated behind the desk in front of him.

The gray squirrel in the immaculate Protecteer dress uniform (complete with far too many ribbons and medals) was the Chief of the Dallas TPA division. The hero known as Manifest Destiny had fought crime for decades but had never been allowed into the ranks of the national organizations. When Texas had decided it needed its own formal state-operated Hero force to deal with situations that were too difficult or delicate to call in outside help, though, Jeremiah Tulsa was on the ground floor.

The decades since had worn away anything that might have once been soft or easy about the man. He was whip-thin, made of wiry, corded muscle, and tall, too; he towered over most average citizens, though nowhere near Slate's own height. The squirrel's now-white hair was kept in a short buzz cut. The man carried himself with all the iron and vinegar of the WWII generals he admired so much. The scowl permanently plastered across his hard face matched his dead black eyes.

This man — voted 'Best Community Leader in Dallas' for eight of the past ten years — was extremely hard on his troops, but always protected them from media attacks. Still, one did *not* want to get on the bad side of the Chief. His voice was full of gravel as he fixed that fierce, unblinking gaze on Slate.

But the Percheron stared straight ahead, unmoving. The perfect soldier, he was stoically unfazed by the steel in that rough voice. "Sergeant Slate." The horse was always uncomfortable that the chief always used his old Army rank but kept the flinch out of his eyes. "I have a report here that says that Captain Alamo, *the decorated hero of the 3rd Battle of the Alamo*, is in the hospital. This venerated officer of the law is going into surgery in —" The squirrel looked pointedly over at a slender, officious rodent in a TPA uniform, his new aide.

"37 seconds, sir," Will Erst, the Ciscaucasia hamster, responded in a cold, precise tone and cruel gleam in his eye.

"36 seconds, to see if they can save his jaw, or if he will *eat through a straw* for the rest of his life."

Slate hadn't known the extent of the injuries, but he couldn't find it within himself to feel guilty for his actions. He felt only… hollow, with a hint of anger flavoring the void that had been filling him since he stared into that pair of large, terrified eyes in the rundown warehouse. The eyes of the villain that saw him as *the bad guy*, as bizarre as the thought seemed.

"I also have a dozen reports from officers who report that *you* assaulted Captain Alamo in the locker room for *no reason*." The words were punctuated with the staccato rhythm of claws, tapping a stack of plain manila envelopes on the otherwise-immaculate wooden desk. "Now, son, you are going to explain to me *why* I have these reports."

"He slipped." The words fell out of the horse's lips unbidden, and a chasm opened up within him. Those same words had been uttered by other officers, talking about injuries to their wives and girlfriends. With a slowly dawning horror, he realized how *often* they had been said within the building in which he sat. He would always frown slightly, say nothing, and forget about it a few moments later… but those memories started cascading through his mind. Just how often had those two words been used to justify horrible actions? Just how often was that lie used to justify — or even *joke* — about the very thing heroes were supposed to stop? When had he stopped noticing? When had it become… *background noise?*

The chief looked incredulous, mouth hanging open. It was the first time Slate had ever seen the chief look anything but grim. "He… *slipped!*"

The apoplectic outburst would normally have cowed the stallion, but today, it made barely a ripple in the roiling storm of emotion hidden deep within the draft horse. "You. *Sergeant Slate*. Are telling *Me*. That *The* Captain Alamo. The *Hero* on loan to us from San Antonio. *Slipped*. And then fell. Through *two* rows of lockers. Shattering his jaw in **seventeen places**. And did it all in such a way that a *dozen trained Heroes* would **swear** that **you** punched him?"

Slate looked back, as impassive as the mountains. "Yes. He slipped." The words were the same simple lie, the obvious fabrication that had somehow become so ingrained in his thoughts that he had no longer consciously considered their vile nature. But he was a draft horse. A soldier. A veteran of Iraq and Afghanistan. He would not let a simple weakness like *emotions* break him, no matter how much it felt like some fundamental bedrock within him had crumbled. He couldn't process this now. *Wouldn't* process this now. But the war inside him meant that he was bereft of a better justification.

Manifest Destiny stared at him, slack-jawed. Finally, he threw the collected papers into the air. "I'm docking you a month's pay. And I'm putting you on shit detail for the next two months. And if I ever, *ever* even think you will assault another member of this division again, they will **never** find your body. Now get the *fuck* out of my office!"

The stallion carefully rose to his feet without another word, sketched a salute, and walked out. Normally, the reaction of the chief would have rattled him. Frightened him, even. But now it didn't seem to register. Two words kept circling in his mind: *He slipped.*

His steps echoed on the linoleum, adding to the collection of permanent hoof marks he constantly left throughout the building. He wasn't sure where he was going, nor was he even capable of coherently forming the concept of a destination. It was only when the old metal door slammed loudly behind him that Slate looked around, and found himself on the roof, of all places. The Dallas sun bore down on him like an angry god of fire, but even the unpredictable Texas spring failed to warm the icy void inside him. Somehow it had replaced the emotional numbness he had fought so hard to forge.

Here, alone in a city of ten million souls, next to a bank of poorly maintained HVAC units, Slate hugged himself. He stared into the distorted image of the blue-and-silver-clad figure reflecting in the cheap metal of the air conditioner. Threatened tears blurred the reflection further, as he finally dared to ask himself the question haunting his soul:

*I'm a Hero. A **Hero**. Why do I feel like the bad guy...?*

Chapter 5

Lattice

Starshade wrapped both paws around the prominently Seize the Beans-branded coffee tumbler. She loved the warmth on her fur, and the incredible aroma of the steaming brew her first sip of coffee each day never failed to elicit small, pleased squeaks from the desert cottontail. And the alertness that joined it was essential, when she had to get up at Oh-dark-thirty, like that particular morning.

If you can call this morning…

Few people were out at the early hour, though RIV, the Korps base located beneath downtown Austin that functioned as their main headquarters in Texas, was never completely quiescent. The Korps agent shivered in pleasure when many of those who were around still gave her appreciative looks or even outright stares. The cottontail was wearing what could *generously* be described as a pair of shorts, and a fur-tight tank top stretched over her chest. She was pleased at the flashiness of the bright pink, and loved the way the twin helix patterns in dark red framed and called attention to the peaks under the thin, soft fabric.

She loved this moment before a mission — when things were still quiet, but that anticipation was growing within her. These were the moments she could show off a little and feel sexy, before things got *dangerous* and *serious* and her brain had to be on overdrive to keep herself and others alive. Starshade spent too many years hating her body, and now she could revel in the lithe, perfectly honed form.

The entrance to the armory in section 4C was an unremarkable door sandwiched between an incredible pizza place and a boutique chocolatier. Armories were secreted through the base in case of attack, or merely for field personnel to gear-up discreetly at their leisure. Starshade loved this one, because it meant she could walk next door and get a *sinfully* delicious pizza (and/or a chocolate-covered strawberry treat) after a mission, without having to go very far.

Stepping into the small entryway, she smiled at Bruin, the older panda sitting behind the desk. He often ran the night shift desk for this Armory, and he always had tiny flowers in little pots scattered about. He liked to grow them for their aesthetic and aromatic qualities; for her part, Starshade thought they were delicious, and if she asked nicely, he was always delighted to give her one. She opened her mouth to do just that when she registered a second figure in the room, standing motionless in the corner.

"Oh, Nurse O. I didn't expect you to be here!" This particular Nurse O was identified as O-E184, according to the stitching below the logo.

"ROSE, this is the same one that joined me in the briefing, right?"

[Yes, it was, dear.]

That's odd... Nurse O usually likes to mess with people through the use of multiple units...

A genuine smile spread across the cottontail's lips. "A pleasure to see you again. Thank you for taking care of me. I know I'm not the best patient."

The synthetic fox curtsied in the same way she did everything; proper, feminine, and perfect. Two hands held her pristine skirt, with the other two arms held out to her sides delicately. "Think nothing of it, Miss Starshade. It is my pleasure to ensure that you get the best possible care under even the most difficult circumstances."

Is... is she sassing me? But the nurse's expression gave no sign. And, after a moment, she had to grudgingly admit that she probably deserved a little sass from the medical staff. Still, it was odd that the same Nurse O was here. *Wait...*

"Nurse O, have you been following me?" Starshade couldn't quite keep a touch of indignant squeak out of her voice.

Eyes bright with immaculate care and a twinkle of glee, the synth clasped both pairs of hands together in delight. "I am dedicated to providing my patients the highest standard of care. Given the frequency at which you follow medical care guidelines, it seemed prudent to ensure my ability to make rapid adjustment to your ongoing recovery efforts should they be needed."

That is… definitely sass.

With ears burning and a long-suffering sigh, she finally changed the topic. "What brings you to the armory? Are you going out on your first field mission?" Though it was played off as a joke, she secretly reveled in the thought of seeing the four-armed synth go into combat.

"Sadly, not today. Mistress Celia requested my final assessment of your healing before you enter the field again. Also, my presence will be required for some of the adjustments to your loadout."

"Wait, what?" Medical signoff after a major injury was common, though she hardly thought a single bullet counted. But why would a Nurse be required for her gear upgrade? A tinge of trepidation started to grow as Starshade thought to herself. *Just what have you done this time, Karen?*

[Come in and find out, dear.] The door to the inner armory buzzed and opened as Bruin ushered her in.

"Damnit, I forgot to ask for a flower."

[Hush, dear. Stop thinking with your stomach; there's crime to be done.]

"Ooooo. Crime."

A flush spread across Starshade's face as she walked through the hallways to the door marked on her HUD. Inside, Karen wore somehow even *less* than the previous time the rabbit had seen her. The Agent suspected that the commander had been in a nearby club and stopped here just long enough to kit up the wayward operative. But there was no doubt about the genuinely delighted smile that spread across those lips.

"Oh, Agent Starshade, I'm delighted that Nurse O cleared you for operations. Bullet wounds are always so difficult to predict." Well, that was a relief to hear she'd already been cleared. *Wait, then why did Nurse O tell me that it needed to be done?* Starshade was starting to suspect that the synths had more of a sense of humor than they let on. Also, that *maybe* she needed to stop being such a bad patient when she was injured.

"So… uh… about this uniform upgrade? Why does Nurse O need to be present for this?" She did not quite trust the devilish smile on Karen's face.

"Well, first, it's not strictly an upgrade. It's a downgrade in a lot of ways." The dragoness walked over the gear laid out on the table, including her infiltrator outfit. It was in its more colorful, Villainous mode, designed to look badass as hell. But far from extensive changes or downgrades, it looked relatively unchanged except that her utility belt was suspiciously absent. It was the RCGs that looked different, and there were some odd-looking bits laid out next to the goggles. She was starting to get a bad feeling about this...

"With modern gear, basically everything is networked through the RCGs. Previous iterations of field wear and accessories were configured with extensive local redundancies, as the network wasn't quite so reliable. These were eventually removed as they added weight and complexity, and reduced reliability; we simply haven't needed them. Anything that could knock out RCGs would rarely leave the local redundancies operable, in any event. Until now, that is."

She quickly laid out how to operate the backup communications gear, including throat mic and radio. There was also backup gear to monitor her vitals, though this did not broadcast; it would only be useful after the operation. Similarly, there was some detection gear designed to record various situational data in case it was of use later on, to detect or counter the threat to the RCGs. As long as she (or her body) got home, the Korps would learn a great deal about whatever had happened.

"Next, our engineers have been hard at work. Your demands for more gear without relying upon the utility belt posed a significant challenge as those items needed to be miniaturized, reconfigured, and still be usable. This particular outfit has dozens more hidden pockets, filled with a variety of useful kit, none of which will break, — and I quote — the 'sexy look of a badass ninja whore.' Though I will concede that at present, many of them won't pass a more tactile examination."

The silver dragoness then began the meticulous catalog and demonstration of dozens of tiny weapons and tools. ROSE helpfully encoded the location and operation of each item deep into her muscle memory. This was one of the more helpful aspects of the RCGs, enabling rapid and deep assimilation of information.

But Karen was conspicuously avoiding any mention of the little triangular pieces laid out near her newest pair of operational RCGs. As she was launching into an in-depth technical specification for the battery layout, and design of a *backup*, backup Geiger counter, Starshade had had enough.

"Okay, Karen, please. *Please*. I'm begging you. Stop stalling."

The dragoness giggled. "I suppose I've kept you waiting long enough." Scaled hands scooped up one of the triangles. It was glossy black and glittered faintly across the surfaces, but there seemed to be a recess on the inner edge. *It looks like a combadge from St* — "Welcome to your new sensor suite. This girl is packed with cameras and sensors of every variety. If you were wondering how all those recording systems got their data, it's from this little thing."

Starshade could definitely appreciate that. But there had to be a catch. She knew she was being strung along, she just didn't know why. "...And?"

"And it will clamp to the tips of your ears, through these seven piercings inside this recess that match those at the end of your ear!"

"But... the tips of my ears aren't pierced." A growing alarm was making itself known within the rabbit.

"Not yet. Which is why I'm so glad you accepted the modification!"

Her sensitive ears twitched in alarm as she started to look between the earnest looking Karen and the positively gleeful looking Nurse O. "But... but I didn't agree to any modification."

A new voice, melodic and feminine, called from the doorway. "That's okay! I accepted for you!" Starshade's head whipped around as a voluptuous black jaguar with blue spots stepped through the door. She had never seen this woman, but she would know her anywhere. And she was suddenly...

THERE...

...in those arms, holding the soft form. "*Zala!* It's *you!*" She buried her head in the cat's cleavage, feeling the warmth and drinking in the intoxicating rose scent in her fur.

Warm arms wrapped around her, pulling her even closer to the form as the high pitch voice laughed with open joy. "Of course, silly, I said I'd be here to see you off! I'm your overwatch!"

After a long moment of closeness, curiosity finally overcame the bunny, and she pulled back to drink in the sight of her friend. Zala was now shorter than her. Maybe 175cm, with a curvy figure. A bit of a belly. She was soft, welcoming, and lovely. Her rosettes were a riot of cerulean, with a touch of sparkle to catch the eye. Golden eyes crinkled with pure joy watched her. Then she spun around, showing off the generous ass.

Starshade couldn't stop grinning. "I heard you were decanting. You didn't tell me you were going in again!"

"The boar was starting to itch!" Her friend Zala was fluid, in every sense. Every few months, they would grow uncomfortable with their form. They would go into Empire Enhancements, the subdivision of Korps medical services dedicated to in-depth body modification, and get a complete overhaul. New species, new gender, completely new settings on the sliders. They would shift between the names Zalen and Zala, depending on their preference for that form. But otherwise, *everything* was likely to change. Zala did have one very minor superpower, a light form of regeneration. It was hardly enough to give her an edge in combat, so she would never join field ops without more training than they were willing to undergo. But... it meant that their recovery time for a complete EE overhaul was measured in days, not months, and they derived endless pleasure from that benefit.

"Did... did you choose this form? Or did your Mistress?"

"This one was MY choice. The next one..." The cat suddenly looked embarrassed, flushing a little.

A slow understanding spread across the rabbit's face. "Wait, wait, wait. The next one?"

The cat radiated joy even if she blushed harder. "Yeah. I... uh... gave her complete control. The level we've been talking about."

Giddiness started to swell within Starshade. Zala and her Mistress, Terra, would often jointly decide her new form. The shifter always got a thrill out of leaving details in the hands of her domme. In the end though, she had always retained veto power and knowledge of what the form would be before she finally entered the vat. But she had often confided an interest in forgoing that one day — thrilling at the idea of waking up in a completely new form, with no idea of its settings or capabilities until she found out through experimentation. A complete submission, with only ROSE to act as a final safeguard.

"For how long?"

A long pause. The cat couldn't quite look at her, but her form radiated a submissive pleasure. "A year."

"A YEAR!" Starshade could not be more shocked. The longest Zala had ever spent in one form since joining the Korps was three months.

She said the only reason she would ever spend that time in one form would be if...

The cottontail *squealed* and wrapped her arms around her voluptuous friend. *It's happening! She's wanted this for so long!* The warmth of happiness bloomed deep within her chest in the pure joy of seeing a dear friend achieving a dream. Together they held each other giggled, sharing that closeness. They both knew what this meant and the journey her friend was about to embark upon. There would be so many delicious details to talk about... *later*. She was eagerly awaiting the opportunity to pry them all out when they had time.

Finally, a light noise from across the room drew her back to the present. It also reminded her of the interrupted discussion. She couldn't help sounding indignant. "Wait, wait. What's this nonsense about *you* agreeing to *my* piercings?"

A devilish grin spread across the jaguar's face, showing a distressingly sinister amount of fang. From... somewhere... Zala drew out a piece of paper. A deep flush burned across Starshade's face and made the room uncomfortably warm. It was her last kink consent form she had signed with Zalen. The one that included minor permanent body modification. "You agreed to let me make these decisions the last time I had you tied up on stage at Val's." That night at Valentine's Bondage Club was one of the best nights of her life, and one of her fondest recent memories.

"That's not fair!" The rabbit protested weakly, embarrassment written in every line of her body. The chorus of giggles redoubled the heat burning across her face.

[*Remember, consent can be withdrawn at any time. None of them would think less of you if you changed your mind now.*]

The calming thought at the back of her head did take the sting off. It helped to be reminded that she did, in fact, have a choice. In the end, she was fine with her friends teasing her, when it was done in good fun.

"Thank you, ROSE." She shook herself, still pink, but able to think again. Also able to give Karen and Zala an almost but not quite affronted glare. "You know, I would have said yes if you asked. You didn't have to go through this... this... *farce*."

The word choice caused another round of giggles, though the curvy kitty managed to respond. "I know. But Karen happened to know that we had that consent contract, and we both thought it would be hilarious. I've never seen you blush so hard! Even when you were tied up and being fu —"

"*Shut up!*" Starshade buried her face in her hands. *How could I have forgotten how much Zala likes to tease?* When she finally looked up, Nurse O was right in front of her with the special piercing tool, the one that would heal the holes near-instantly. With a fall of her shoulders, the rabbit let one ear be gently captured by the synth.

"Zala, you will rue this day. *Rue it,*" the bunny vowed with anticipation.

Chapter 6

Fracture

BOOM. *The world-ending roar was too loud to be called* sound. *A blast wave stole his breath, and battered his form; instantly, his entire world was pain and noise and struggling to breathe. His bruised lungs screamed for air, even as they could not remember how to function. His skin was agony as his uniform melted from the intense heat. His hands were covered in blood and char and fire. An instant eternity of unfeeling agony, and he couldn't* **breathe.**

Pain. The world was pain and confusion. In desperation he looked up to where his squad leader stood in front of him, but what stood there was no longer a man. There were only bloody, skeletal limbs, stripped of flesh but somehow staying upright. Viscera rained to the ground from the still-standing corpse that had been his friend. Then the head swiveled back to stare at him. The jaw was gone, leaving a nightmarish gaping hole. One eye miraculously left in the skull, filled with pain. That desperate orb was filled with such a deep pleading for help that the sight seared itself into his soul. This **thing** *that was his friend was still alive. Oh god, how was it still alive?*

Slate sat bolt upright, screaming. His hoof-nailed hands scrabbled at the floor, and his breath came in ragged gasps through a throat already raw and swollen. Fear crashed through his mind, buffeting him with waves of pain and regret and fury and loss; the present and past had become jumbled all together in a tumble of memory fragments and raw feelings. The Percheron somehow forced himself to lay back on the hard concrete — one hand on the stomach and one on the chest, just like he had been taught.

Breathe in. Breathe out. Breathe in. Breathe out. Breathe in through the nose, out through the mouth…

The air whistling through his mouth slowed as he started to get into the rhythm. Slate squeezed his eyes closed, as if closing them more could help him from seeing the things in his mind.

Slow. Breathe in through the nose. Focus on feeling your stomach expanding. Breathe out. Feel your stomach exhale. Slower… slower…

The tension started to ebb from his form. The stallion could feel the sweat soaking into his fur, wicking into the rough floor.

*It's over. It's **over**. You aren't there any more. It's just a nightmare. It will pass.*

Finally, the storm within him started to subside. His mind slowly began to find purchase, letting go of the maelstrom of jumbled memories and dreams. The horse let out one last, shaking sob and stood up. He frowned at the new furrows in the concrete of his floor; that meant a *particularly* bad night, then. But he was… he was *under control*. He could feel the emotions bleed out of him and could once more be the rock he was named after.

A glance at the digital clock mounted on the wall above the door showed 4:23am. His massive shoulders sagged a bit, as he realized he had actually been able to sleep in; his body clearly needed the rest, if he'd managed almost four hours. Gray eyes closed as he tilted his neck to the side, the vertebrae popping like gunshots. Each little pop sent a bit of relief through him. A full rotation of his head caused a few more snaps while throwing his cropped mane a bit. Slate quashed the familiar pang of regret that regulations required him to keep it so short. He hated the severe, military look that reminded him so much of… before. The black hair was thick and coarse and, when cropped so much, had the consistency of a broom. His old platoon leader said it made him look like a Roman centurion. At least it was a convenient place to clip the ridiculous cowboy hat the Texas Protectorate Assembly insisted that he wear in full uniform.

Another stretch, this time of his complaining back. The Percheron thought fondly of the days he was allowed to have a bed. After he'd kept destroying one with his massive strength, almost every night, he couldn't blame the chain of command when they finally stopped replacing them. That was okay; he had already been used to doing without, from his time on deployment.

Finally, mind cleared enough to be the figurative emotional rock — and with his body starting to limber up — he walked over to the vault that had been repurposed as his wardrobe. The massive door was marred by deep dents from fist and hoof. As it easily swung open for him, he was grateful that he had been able to throw off this morning's episode so quickly, even if it had been particularly bad. With a twinge of shame, he admonished himself that it would not do to walk through the halls naked again at the moment, even *if* the pair of regulation shorts and a workout t-shirt stretched across his chiseled form left nearly as little to the imagination. He regretted not having time to do a proper run (or better yet, go lift weights), but since he was on punishment detail, he was too busy for such luxuries.

Metallic hoofsteps echoed off the halls as Slate worked his way through the labyrinthine basement. The intense feelings of loneliness never felt stronger than when he listened to those steps echo in the silent underground corridors. He regretted not being in the barracks with the other heroes who chose (or were required) to reside in the precinct. But the second time he had punched through a wall in his sleep, they had… kindly… repurposed a disused holding cell in the basement for him. At least it afforded him privacy, and he wasn't a threat to anyone. That it had been far enough away from the others that his screams didn't wake them was a blessing.

He was a Hero. The stalwart defender of freedom and liberty. He saved people. All the pain was worth it. The nightmares, the loneliness, the sacrifice… All of it was worth it because he was a Hero, and a *hero*.

…*I am a hero, right?*

This morning it seemed much harder to kick the black mood that had settled over him. The cafeteria was dark and empty, when he stepped into the room filled with long tables and uncomfortable plastic chairs. At this hour on a Saturday morning, he would have been surprised to find anyone else present. Still, he wished that there had been someone around, just so he wasn't left alone with his thoughts.

He was the only member of the Pegasus Phalanx that ever ate here. The other four all lived off site and refused to set foot in this room, considering it beneath them. In truth, it was meant for the hundreds of support staff that were necessary for operations of the five Dallas TPA

Hero teams. He didn't mind mingling with the crew that kept him alive, though; his humble beginnings were a far cry from the affluent background from which most of the other heroes had hailed.

Without much input, hooves unerringly carried him to the familiar refrigerator stenciled with his name. Inside was his usual breakfast, carefully designed to give him precisely the right amount of every vitamin and mineral his body needed, adjusted based on expected activity level and a host of bloodwork test results. It was only through such maintenance that he had been able to keep his body fat levels approaching negative numbers, and to absolutely maximize his muscle strength. The disciplined diet gave him an edge in combat, to say nothing of a physique that often caused criminals to flee — or surrender — instead of attempting to fight. It kept people *safe*. Even if the gruel had the consistency of wallpaper paste and tasted nearly as good.

He did take joy in sipping the stale coffee. It was warm and full of caffeine, and finally helped to chase some of the ghosts away. The breakfast was to keep him alive. The beloved coffee, no matter how bad, kept him awake and alert.

Finally willing to face the world, Slate pulled out his communicator and checked his schedule. He frowned with resignation at the packed day ahead of him.

The day had been as tediously busy as he had feared. He didn't get nearly as much patrol time as he liked, spending much of his time in monotonous PR stunts, only occasionally interspersed with assisting other Heroes with dangerous missions. Only once the sun had been down for several hours was the day finally over. The halls of the building were strangely deserted, however; even at that time of night, there were usually a few staffers around.

Still, it was a blessing that the locker room was empty, though the stale mildew scent still lingered. He hated the way the smell clung to him all evening as he tried to get to sleep. The harsh, industrial shampoo provided in the dispensers was unscented; the other guys claimed it was because any scent would be gay, though Slate suspected that the committee that chose it to be as cheap as possible had never managed to come to an agreement on anything else.

The stallion showered as he always did: Quickly. Mechanically. Trying to think about anything but the task at hand. Inevitably, his thoughts turned towards recent events and his punishment detail. His days had certainly gotten longer as more assignments were added, leaving him little time for anything other than work.

But the thing that had been troubling Slate was that there didn't... seem... to be anything especially *odious* about these new assignments. They were largely the same, just more of them. Bodyguarding minor politicians during outdoor campaign speeches under the fickle Texas weather, the grunt work of moving equipment, Quick Reaction Force duty during normal sleep hours, first Hero to enter situations where a terrorist or Korps agent might be hostile...

*I thought these were supposed to be the toughest details? The ones **no one** wanted. Unless... have they always been giving me the worst duties...?*

That realization rocked him. He had never complained, and always assumed he was being given an equal share of such jobs. Obedience to orders had been drilled into him at a young age. Moreover, he had been taught to be proud of his heritage; draft horses carried the world without complaint, but he was starting to suspect that the balance of responsibilities on the team might be skewed more than he had realized.

As he stepped out of the shower, his thoughts were interrupted by the door slamming open. The echoey locker room was filled with boisterous voices. The male contingent of his team filed into the locker room. Their loud voices already contained an edge of barely contained excitement. " — Can't believe they waited this long to tell us! This is *bullshit!*"

Macho Poleax was always complaining. The tall, whip-thin polecat was a trained acrobat, and didn't walk so much as *flow*. The dark mask of fur around his black eyes made him look cold, and the cruel gleam in them did nothing to improve Slate's opinion of the hero. He had instinctively hated the polecat and his frat boy mentality from the moment they met, but the warhorse had never done anything to express it. He would be the professional, and one did not let personal feelings about a colleague impact team cohesion.

"If you ask me, this is all Slate's fault. I can't believe that idiot went and punched a *real* Hero like Captain Alamo; now Manifest Destiny's out for all of us. We're lucky we get another shot at that bitch at all." Slate might have assumed that Ethicoil was unaware of his presence in the bathroom, if the coral snake hadn't been looking right at him while talking. With the distinctive red, black, and yellow color bands, the lanky hero wore little more than a speedo and a tank top. He always tried to move with the same natural fluidity as Poleax, but it was clearly a poor imitation of a true acrobat's grace. It was the last part that perked his ears, though. *Wait, what?*

"Y'all quit yer bellyachin', ya hear? I hears we's gots quite the opportunities ahead a' us tonight. I ain't wanna hear yer whining when they's tapped us for a high profile mission, even if'n it *is* at the crack a' dawn, with no warnin'. Y'all know how these things work, they's gots to verify. I bets they told us soon as they was sure."

The pronghorn following the other two was the oldest member of the team, and played it up as their usual field leader, invoking his age and seniority to sneer at any young "whippersnappers" who might criticize him, whether Hero or civilian. Gray fur peppered his head around the base of Texas Trickshot's impressive horns but more eye-catching still were the alternating bands of white and red around the base, which called to mind a bullseye. The antelope loved to play up the whole Texan angle, which Slate thought was just plain tacky. (Also, it secretly bothered him that the gunslinger had grown up in New Jersey and only developed the affectation twelve years prior, when he'd transferred from The Shoresy Boys.)

The pronghorn sniper finally looked over at Slate. "Manifest Destiny wants ta see ya all immediate-like, so ya better get goin' lickity split. He ain't the type you want rustling your trail and he ain't none too happy with you neither."

Without acknowledging their fellow teammate further, the three had all started their various little rituals of showering and preparing with an urgency that they rarely showed, even when lives were on the line. Something big was up. Slate realized with a start that he had already toweled off, the feel of the rough industrial cotton still haunting his skin and leaving his fur a mess. But he was the bedrock of the team, and he did not complain.

As he was suiting up, the horse had a moment to assess the Pegasus Phalanx. Out of the corner of his eye, he watched Texas Trickshot use his miniature tornados — which normally curved the course of his bullets — to redirect the shower spray of water, hitting just the spot he seemed to want. A truly fearsome shot, the buck used his otherwise-minor power to pull off some incredible, crowd-pleasing stunt shooting. However, he'd also long ago stopped taking his physical training seriously and was slowing down.

Across the room, the team alchemist and magical support was trying to sell his latest miracle virility enhancer to Poleax. Ethicoil would inevitably succeed; he'd grown up in a family of oil and gas executives. They had keenly honed his smooth charm and confident demeanor with the expectation that he would one day take a senior leadership role, right up until he very publicly developed powers. When that happened, they'd seized upon the golden PR opportunity that had fallen right in their coils, further tightening their grasp on the Texas economy. Somehow, they'd wormed their way into bankrolling the entire Dallas headquarters — a place on the "Honored Partners in Freedom" plaque in the lobby and all — just to buy the clan scion a spot on a team with the best press. Slate loathed working with a corporate-sponsored Hero, but when the TPA had to choose between the warhorse's quietly voiced ethical concerns, and the lure of an unimaginably wealthy family of oil barons, Slate couldn't exactly blame the Protecteers. Still, it *felt* wrong.

Then there was Macho Poleax, falling for yet another sales pitch. The prominent son of an Austin tech CEO, the polecat always thought he was smarter than everyone around him; somehow, no matter how many times it had blown up in his face (all of their faces, really) to underestimate the team's foes, his callow arrogance persisted. The mustelid kept thinking his power to slow projectiles and finely-honed acrobatic skills made him invincible, and the result was that Slate had had to take more than a few blows to protect his blowhard teammate. There was no denying he was a fierce fighter, and deadly with his extendable poleax, but Slate kept finding himself having to save the masked Hero.

That was the heavy's job, though; he was the big target, tough enough to shrug off the incoming damage, and strong enough to go toe to toe with most villains. Slate would never rival the true juggernauts — those whose powerset or raw destructive force warped the very fabric of society around them — but on this team, at this level, he was essential. Keep the team alive and let them do their flashy work. He could be happy that he was just as essential and valued as they were.

His thoughts had carried him to the front door. Manifest Destiny's office was in the Command Block, a beautifully crafted, exclusive building across the sculpted yard and parade ground. His office was positioned to overlook the rich estate, and to look across the city to the spectacular Saturday night skyline. The giant golf ball of Reunion Tower, just across the river, was scrolling the logo of some big company to the sleepy city.

As the stallion descended the steps, night turned to day.

A figure wrapped in golden light descended slowly from the starless sky. Arms outspread and ankles crossed, the white dove looked beatific, even angelic; some degree of the effect was lost on him, however, for Slate knew she had spent years practicing this entrance for maximum impact. The hero, eschewing the standard blue-and-white uniform of the TPA, was clad in pure white diaphanous silk edged with gold. The rich material was perfectly cut to show off her figure, plainly that of a goddess. Slate hated how he always felt so… *inadequate* next to the radiant figure.

Her golden boots touched the ground, and the light surrounding her dimmed as the angelic soundtrack faded away. Her halo stayed bright as ever, now even more noticeable in the early evening. Her eyes opened to reveal golden orbs of pure light that seemed to bore into the stallion's soul.

"Darling, please tell me you are *ready* to *go*. We need to get going if we are going to catch that Korps whore." In public, Heavenly Dazzler spoke with the voice of the angels; but here, in private, with her teammate, the voice was clipped and annoyed. It always cut Slate deeply, and he never quite knew why. He wasn't religious — not after his second combat tour — but it seemed wrong somehow that this seeming-perfect angel should be so petty and cruel.

"I was just reporting to Manifest Destiny to get the briefing."

"Well, *bless your heart*, God never did give you the sense he gave a horse. An informant just leaked that the bitch who slipped the net last week is holed up in a warehouse over in Garland! If you hurry your lazy self, we can nab her before she can escape like last time. *If. You. **Hurry.**"

Surprise was his first impulse. *Korps agent? The one in the warehouse? **Starshade?** The one I let get away...?* She was so crafty, it was hard to think of her getting caught so easily. She had given the entirety of the Pegasus Phalanx, plus several other teams, the chase of a *lifetime* in trying to run her to ground. But betrayal could do that, and there was no honor among thieves.

Without another word, Slate started to sprint across the grass towards the administrative building. He wondered why he was so conflicted about the idea that a known supervillain was about to be arrested.

Chapter 7

Accretion

Starshade crept slowly through the forgotten warehouse, careful to step around the suspiciously-slimy pools of dark liquid that she chose to believe were collected rainwater. Recent rains were a convenient excuse to keep her from questioning their source too closely, at least; whatever they were, she didn't want their contents on her favorite boots, especially if she suddenly needed to trust her life to their traction.

Not that there seemed any likelihood she would *need* to trust her life to anything, for the moment. The sun had set hours before, but she was still following up on a number of tips they had received about unusual Hero activity around the city. Unless the TPA plan somehow involved weaponizing OSHA violations, she had found no sign of their activity.

Shortly after her encounter with Slate, several of the capes had been seen poking around warehouses in the Garland area. Heroes did that sort of thing regularly as they tried to ferret out villainy, so it wasn't necessarily indicative of anything. However, for lack of any more solid leads, it seemed to her as good a place as any to start trying to unravel the mystery.

"Zala? Are you there?"

The delighted voice came through her RCGs. "*Yes, girl, I'm here. What can your overwatch mistress do for you tonight? Oh, there's a singles night nearby! Do you want me to send you the address? Or better, I could go ahead and set you up ten dates tomorrow and see how many you can get through before anyone catches on.*" The cottontail smiled softly. Zala's teasing was always light; the jaguar liked her, and casual banter made her feel like she was right where she belonged. It never failed to lift her spirits, even if it did occasionally bring a flush to her cheeks.

"*First, no. Half of them would die of fright if an 'Evil Korps Agent' attempted to seduce them. Although now that I think about it, given the quality* of guys that go to those things, that might actually improve the world. I bet you the other half would be Korps chasers, gawking at me to fulfill sick, twisted fantasies."

The air in the warehouse was still and stale, with nearly every surface covered in a thick layer of dust. There *were* a few more recent tracks through the warehouse, left by military-style boots with the familiar TPA logo on the sole, so clearly someone had definitely been on the scene recently. It was increasingly looking like they hadn't stayed, though.

"But don't you **like** fulfilling sick, twisted fantasies?"

"Damn right I do! But not for, like, **investment brokers** who look at me like an object."

"You weren't complaining about being treated like an object last time we went out."

A flush spread across Starshade's cheeks and up her ears. She could quite vividly recall exactly that. The rabbit did not respond for several moments, *definitely* because she was peeking her head into an abandoned warehouse office to look for Teepa goons. Definitely that. Totally not because she wanted her blush to die down and allow her to think of an argument.

Undaunted, she finally tried again. "It's about consent! And standards. I try not to sleep with anyone who thinks I'm an object **all** the time."

"Just some of the time."

"Exactly!"

"Okay, and the second reason you didn't want me to set you up with a collection of soulless assholes?"

"Second, I've been thinking more about Slate. Did we get anything more about him?"

"You really are obsessed with this guy. Girl, I'm telling you. Teepa is bad news. None of them are redeemable."

The rabbit frowned at the response. She didn't understand why the others weren't seeing this as an important detail! Yes, she *knew* the Teepa were pretty much the worst. But there was a reason that the TPA Academy was a fertile ground for recruitment. More than once, a surreptitious Korps recruiter had managed to pull an *amazing* agent out of that abusive hellhole. And another thing, had Zala forgotten that in order to take over the world, they had —

[Calm.]

"I'm not trying to recruit him." The long silence told Starshade exactly what Zala's feelings were on the matter. "I'm not! Listen, Zala, I don't know what's going on with him. He's probably bad news. But he saved me. And I think knowing the answer to **why** is of critical importance to what's going on here. I am **flattered** that you are trying to protect me, but I promise you, I'm not a starry-eyed naïf looking for a knight in shining spurs to save her and then fuck her into the brickwork. So please, trust me to be realistic about this, as much as I trust you to watch my back and tell me if I'm walking into a trap."

Zala's words came back with a touch of warmth and a tinge of apology. "You're right. You're right. I'm sorry, Star. You are important, and I cared more about my fears than your wishes. Hold on a moment while I pull up some files."

The Agent eased open a dusty crate to discover it was full of discarded water bottles containing various unsavory-looking liquids, promotional fast food items that hadn't been available for a decade or more, and half a dozen dead cockroaches. She decided not to list this as an 'important weapons cache of potential extraterrestrial origin' for the extraction team. *I only did that once, and only because Terrorform was being bitchy.*

"Our internal files don't have anything you haven't heard already. Slate. Legal name Slate Johnson. Teepa Heavy. Dallas division. Always in perfect lockstep with the TPA. He's not flashy. Usually in the background. Moderate threat level. Do not engage in melee combat unless you are rated to deal with super-strength. Oh, but we just got an update from Mabel; she got access to the internal Teepa systems."

"Oh! Mabel got this? That's great! How has she been doing lately?"

"She's been causing quite the ruckus of late. Quite the firecracker. When she heard, and I quote, 'That starry-eyed doe with the easy smile' needed some intel, well, she leapt at the chance!"

"I'm… going to hear that nickname more frequently, aren't I?"

"It seems likely."

Even as she silently cursed her, Starshade thought fondly of her newest friend. They had met when the cougar, a recent addition to both RIV and the Korps at large, needed sparring partners. After a bit of a rocky start, they had fallen easily into banter and joking. The thing that had stuck with the cottontail well afterwards was the driven *determination* under the catamount's eager confidence. Here was a girl that had finally been able to find herself, and she was ready to take on the entire world.

"You understand that I will have my revenge, right? It's not wise to mock a supervillain"

"Noted."

"You tell that misty maiden that she has my thanks. And that I look forward to sparring with her on Tuesday."

"I'm certain she's quite eager for it; Mabel wasn't even supposed to be out in the field today. The moment the request went out, she suited up to go out specifically for it. That cat might be a bit overeager."

"I did get that impression, yes. Not like me, though, I'm the model of restraint and careful consideration."

While RCGs didn't transmit a snort of amusement, the echoes of one clearly tinged Zala's response. "The only restraint you show is when someone is pulling you around on a leash."

"Hey!" The familiar burning spread across her face, but fond memories gave lie to the protest.

"Don't even start. You were dripping before we could even get the cameras rolling."

"*Anyway!* About those files? You know, the files that Mabel retrieved through what is no doubt a perilous and legendary operation, in which she almost — but not quite — managed to avoid getting in way too much trouble? Those files…?"

"I would ask how you guessed, but you're an expert in the exact same thing, girl. You should teach a course." Starshade squeaked indignantly but Zala kept going before she could protest more. The teasing slowly died in Zala's tone as it began to be replaced with genuine concern. "Anyway, as I was saying, Mabel got you your files…

"Looks like your little stallion just got himself in a heap of trouble. There's an internal memo she grabbed. Let's see… says here he assaulted a fellow Hero. Docked his pay. Well, that's typical; the only time the Teepa faces consequences is when they assault another supercop, and even then, it's only a slap on the wrist. Sounds like this one might have more anger problems than we thought. You'll need to be careful, Star. He's showing his violent colors."

"Wait, wait, no, go back. He punched a Teepa hero? Who…?" That was odd. The stallion had shown nothing but restraint and concern, even when facing down a sexy, deadly supervillain. (*Ha.*) One who had frustrated his team for *hours* on a chase across South Dallas.

"*Huh.*"

"*…What is it?*" she prompted, after a moment of silence.

"*Says here he punched… Captain Alamo? That can't be right…*"

"*Hah. I thought you said I wasn't supposed to be recruiting.*"

The cottontail looked around the empty, forgotten depot and sighed. Whatever the Teepa had been doing here, they hadn't stayed, and there was no indication they left anything. They must have just been patrolling, Starshade surmised with mild frustration.

"*Holy shit. Captain Alamo is on medical leave. A hometown blog says he might never return to active duty. Slate fucked him **up**.*"

"*He deserves a medal.*"

"*Star, this is serious. You need to be really, really careful with this guy. If he's unhinged enough to do that to one of the Teepa's shining beacons of light, you need to make absolutely sure he can't do the same to you. Promise me you'll be careful around this guy.*"

Starshade tried to square the information coming in with the man she had met in that warehouse. The Hero. Hidden from all cameras and possible negative press, with every reason to be violent, and *no* reason to talk with the Villain he had cornered. She was no fool; the rabbit knew the knives that could hide behind smiles. But something told her that more was going on, that he was something more than just another deranged Teepa abuser.

"*Star? Promise me.*" The prompt brought her back as she dropped the tarp back down over the rusted forklift engine.

"*Zala, I promise; I won't go into this blind. And thank you. For caring. It means a lot to me that you're this worried. I **will** take precautions. And I'll have you there to watch my back, Mistress Overwatch Lady.*"

She could tell from the relief in her voice that the jaguar really was scared for her. That sort of concern meant the world to her.

"*Shit, a drone just pinged us. Teepa team is moving fast, right towards you. And it's Slate's team. You've got about five minutes.*"

Starshade cursed under her breath as she looked around the dusty interior. She always felt she had all the time in the world… until she didn't.

75

76

Chapter 8

Tremor

"Listen up, pardners." Texas Trickshot's drawl over the radio was clear as he issued commands. "Polecat goes in first. This 'un's a wily critter. Each of you take a corner ah the warehouse. When she runs, and ah assure you she will *run*, like a hen in fox season, we'll cut her off. She ain't getting away this time."

Hen in fox season? What does that even mean? How is he getting worse at Texanisms the longer he's here?

The Texas Protectorate Assembly helicopter came in fast and hard; Slate kept his massive fist wrapped around a support column, expecting a tremendous jolt. The TPA pilots were notorious for rough landings when flying a time-sensitive mission. Before they had even impacted, however, Macho Poleax had leapt from the craft. The warhorse was surprised — both at the agility the polecat displayed, in a roll that turned a fall into a sprint, and because he was rarely so eager.

Slate felt wrong, letting him go in alone. It was always, always *his* job to be there; the whole reason he was *on* the team was to go in first, to be the rock that shielded his comrades. But… this was the same Korps agent, and admittedly, she didn't seem very high on the offensive power rating. Reluctantly, he turned his mind to his own mission.

The helicopter slammed into the ground and Slate was out and sprinting —

— *like I did so many times in* — No. No! **Focus!** —

— Metal horseshoes slammed into the asphalt of the rear alley, spraying gravel in every direction. He rounded the side of the warehouse, leaving the near corner for the slower Trickshot. Before he quite realized it, one heavy hoof planted to halt his momentum, and Slate was there, holding steady at his assigned position. His eyes constantly scanned the building as he shifted from moving to searching.

I won't let her get away again. But as the seconds started to stretch out, he was starting to wonder if that was true. *She hurts people… right? That's what the dossier said.*

— *staring into those terrified brown eyes, seeing him as approaching death* —

The memory stopped him. Would he stop her? *Could* he stop her?

— *holding the bullet wound in her side* —

When had she been shot? Had Trickshot done that? No, it must have been before, because Scarlet Retriever had been tracking her blood until her power ran out.

— *every movement of her body screaming panic but she remained defiant* —

That moment haunted him. That moment had shattered the bedrock upon which he had built himself. All his hard fought control was washing away, and raw, confusing emotions roiled within him; the stallion was breaking, and he didn't know what to do.

"Slate!" The sudden yell over the radio from Poleax startled him and let him claw his way back from the spiral. "She's near your corner of the building. If you come in through the wall, we can trap her. Looks like she's all out of teleports!"

His body reacted the way it had been trained. *Follow orders. Save your team. Protect the innocent.* With a crash of rending metal, he was through the wall and into the darkness of the warehouse… and there she was.

The tall, lithe rabbit dressed in that black latex. She was barely standing, holding her bloody side and leaning against a pillar, RCGs now glowing magenta as she stared at him with defiance. A quick glance across the room, staring at the rabbit with undisguised glee, was Poleax. They had her.

He looked back at their prey. A cruel grimace played along the lips of the supervillain who had confounded them all so dearly. She was the picture of defeated menace. There was no meek pleading in this rabbit. This was a woman who had killed and would kill again if they didn't stop her.

Wait… that's not right.

Something was wrong. Slate *looked* again. The rabbit wore an unmistakable Korps uniform, all skin-tight sensuality and magenta goggles and probably too many helixes. But... her build wasn't quite right, she was a *little* too short, and... were the tips of her ears too dark? But it was that grimace, promising ruthless vengeance, that did it. "This... isn't her."

Starshade watched as the helicopter landed half a kilometer away, the blue-clad Heroes spilling out of the Teepa aircraft to surround a warehouse. "Uh, Zala? They aren't... after me. What's going on?"

"We're getting comms intercept now. Scanning... what the fuck...?"

The cottontail started picking her way towards the Hero strike team, staying low and keeping behind cover to avoid being seen. Quickly and quietly, she ran through back alleys at oblique angles to close the distance, only popping out for short peeks. *"Talk with me, Zala."*

"Comms chatter says they have ***you*** *trapped in that warehouse."*

A chill started to spread. Something was very, very wrong. *"I'm going in."* She hurried her next words to stop the impending interruption. *"Listen to me, Zala. I have to go in. I don't know why, but you have to trust me. You do trust me, don't you Zala?"*

There was a long silence, only broken by the soft footfalls of her heeled boots as she reached a closer vantage point. Texas Trickshot was less than a dozen yards away, but he was laser-focused on the warehouse. This was her chance.

"Okay, damn it, yes. I trust you, Star. Please, ***please*** *be careful. I've got you from here. No other units seem to be in the area. Which is odd. Other comms chatter is a lot quieter than it should... wait... Star, I have to go."* Those last words were abrupt and panicked as the connection to Zala was suddenly gone. ROSE?

[*I'm still here, Dear. Zala is okay but occupied.*]

Before she realized she had made the decision to move, Starshade was all-out *sprinting*. Trickshot started to turn just before the rabbit's fist impacted the base of his spine; he was instantly unconscious, his body hitting the ground in a heap. His revolver skittered across the concrete in front of him. Starshade took a gleeful moment to deliver a powerful kick that would have made Scott Norwood openly weep with envy, sending the deadly weapon sailing into the predawn sky. Then she was pressed against the door to the warehouse, long ears straining to hear.

What is going on?

Macho Poleax looked over at him sharply. "What do you mean this isn't her? It's fucking *her*." As emphasis, he extended his pike another foot and pointed at her. "Look at that bitch. She's even been shot. Who the fuck else would she be?"

"It's not her. I'm telling you. Her height is wrong. And she was shot four days ago and didn't get it tended?" Slate watched Poleax start to circle around to get closer to the stallion while remaining steadily focused on the Korps agent. He was certain now. A yawning chasm of dread was starting to open within him. Something was very, very wrong.

"How the fuck can you know what her height was? You barely got close to her the entire fucking chase," the polecat hissed. His nose was twitching like it did when he was starting to get angry. "Wait… Slate, when the fuck were you close enough to see how tall she was?"

There was no mistaking the cold demand that now tinted Poleax's voice. But the stallion's mind went blank. He couldn't think of an excuse. He glanced nervously away from the rabbit to find those hateful orbs of the fellow Hero locked on him. "MD fucking *knew* it. It was *you*. You let that bitch go. We sacrificed everything to give you a shot at catching her, and you fucking let her walk, *didn't you!*" Words brimming with icy rage fell from the masked Hero like bullets; each word, a pronouncement of 'traitor.'

The warhorse turned to face the advancing fencer hands up, trying to calm his teammate down. "I don't know what you're talking about." It was the wrong thing to say, and he knew it. With dawning horror he suddenly realized why so many suspects, when confronted by a Protector, fell upon the phrase like a life raft — even though Heroes reacted to that phrase like a shark to blood in the water.

Any chance of talking down Poleax was gone. Slate's pulse started to race, as he desperately sought a way to calm the situation down... but it was the next words, spoken in a lilting, singsong voice dripping with ill concealed malice that pulled the rug out from under him.

"He *tooold* you. He told you, Slate. If he thought you would hurt another Protecteer again..." It was the rabbit in the Korps outfit speaking, in a haunting, lilting voice that bore no resemblance to the bright, energetic speech of Starshade. She was suddenly standing taller, a deadly confidence infusing her posture. One paw reached up to her RCGs. "... They would *never* find your body." The last was said with such glee that Slate took a step back. With a casual flick of the wrist, the rabbit tossed the RCGs away, revealing not eyes, but orbs of blood. Crimson streaks stained her fur as the gore constantly dripped down her cheeks.

Slate looked with horror at Fatal Thorns, the Fort Worth TPA division chief.

The ground fractured as plant spines like spears exploded from the concrete in front of him. Instincts barely saved him as the two-meter spines — deep green at the base, coming to a blood-red point oozing with scarlet venom — stabbed up from suddenly-ruptured concrete. Then Poleax was on him, his razor namesake singing through the air as it sought his heart.

Starshade's long ears twitched as she started being able to make out the voices within. She was already moving towards the hole ripped in the side of the building even as she listened first with confusion, then growing horror at the conversation within. *They're going to kill him. They are going to **kill him** for saving me. He doesn't realize the danger he's in. I have to stop this.*

The idea that she was aiding an enemy never crossed her mind. This was someone who had saved her life; she would do the same. Higher rational thought and long-term, strategic thinking were beyond the rabbit, as her heart beat a staccato rhythm in her chest. Panic almost broke her as she paused by the hole in the wall, taking a moment to ready herself for a fight instead of just diving in — even as she could hear concrete blasting apart.

But doubts plagued her, even still. *I'm just a scout! I'm no match for a full Teepa team. But… if I don't, who will?*

She couldn't let Slate die. That was the truth the cottontail held to as she took a deep breath, stepping through the hole… into a pitched battle, face-to-face with a *very* surprised Poleax. Her instinctively thrown taser disk suddenly *slowed* before it reached the polecat; it was too late, and he was already holding a paw to his ear, screaming. **"Two Birds! Two Birds!"**

Even as she pulled another weapon, she heard two, urgent voices through her RCGs, both desperately trying to reach her. "*STARSHA* —"

And so, the room — filled with violence, and enemies, and the one Hero who had ever actually been a *hero* for her — was plunged into darkness, as her RCGs died once again.

Chapter 9

Upheaval

Slate registered the new figure entering the combat in some distant part of his brain. Macho Poleax's screams (and a brief flash of magenta) were all noted and filed away for later, but his entire focus was on the rabbit before him. Spines coated in scarlet shot through the concrete, and only years of training and laser-like focus allowed him to predict and dodge the deadly flora.

The stallion kept trying to close with the TPA Chief, but all his efforts were constantly redirected into trying to stay *alive*. He knew, all too well, that the poison on those thorns could incapacitate or kill. In his current predicament, the two concepts were effectively the same.

*Dead! They want me **dead**. Why? Because I punched Captain Alamo? He was bragging about murdering someone! Bragging!* Even the intense focus on preserving his own life couldn't stop the creeping sense of unfairness, of *wrongness* at the situation. *I've been a loyal Protector for years! I've been a Hero! Fatal Thorns is a Hero! Why are they trying to kill me?*

The mortal nature of the peril facing him was slowly sinking in. With it came an overwhelming sense of betrayal; he had sacrificed everything, *everything,* to be the shining beacon of justice. He had humbly and conscientiously lived above and beyond the code of the Hero, even when so many of his fellows had fallen short.

An entirely new sensation trickled through his consciousness. For the first time, in a fight, he could feel *anger* start to fill him. Images flashed through his mind, in time with each dodge. *How dare they?* ***How dare they!*** But he tamped it down, his training exerting itself. He knew that blind fury was the fastest way for a heavy to lose a fight. Hatred could rob the mightiest Hero of the ability to focus and plan.

*Plan... **Plan,** you idiot. You're not acting, you're reacting. Think. **Think!** She assumes you're just like any heavy, and she's fighting you like one. She's pricking you and waiting for you to make a mistake. So, don't fight like a heavy. How do I do that?*

The next time a spine erupted from the concrete — instead of dodging and trying to close, as he had been doing to that point — one hoof-nailed fist closed around the shaft. Immense strength wrenched it to the side, snapping it at the base, and it was instantly hurled at the Hero across the ruined warehouse. He saw a flash of surprise on that lagomorphic face before she was throwing up an arm to deflect.

Her own training saved her — stepping forward into the projectile, so the *flat* of the thorn impacted, instead of the point. He saw a flash of shock and pain cross her bloody expression, and thought he heard a quiet snapping sound. The confident grin faltered and turned into a snarl of fury. Slate only had a moment of triumph before spines, now in tightly-packed clusters, began to seek his heart.

Instinct saved Starshade. The *instant* the glow of magenta died, she was throwing herself to the side, barely keeping the rabbit from being impaled on the pike thrust towards her throat. One paw was already up, triggering a button hidden on the side of her RCGs.

No HUD appeared, and there was no presence of ROSE in the back of her head. The system was still down. Instead, moving objects were suddenly highlighted in magenta, allowing rapid detection and focus in the low-light conditions. Macho Poleax was *unrelenting* in his attack as blade and haft whistled through the air, wielded by an expert who was bending every effort towards her death. Only her own skill, agility, and training kept her alive. But, she knew, she was running out of *time* as her long ears tracked the pounding of boots, converging on the hole rent into the building.

*Three pairs of boots. Trickshot... Trickshot must be back up. **Damnit.** I should have taken more time to make sure. I have to act. Fast. What do I have?*

Starshade locked eyes with Poleax, focusing intently on him. *Willing him to see her intense concentration, willing the veteran fighter to misinterpret it.* Then, she quickly drew out a small sphere, intentionally failing to hide the motion. *There!* She saw the flicker of his eyes catch the motion.

In one fluid movement, she pulled her arm back, pausing a fraction of a heartbeat... until she saw the smirk of triumph on the polecat's face. But it was not at the fencer that she threw the orb; in a moment of dawning horror printed on the Hero's face, she threw her gambit through the hole in the wall.

She had to give Poleax credit for bravery. He tried to hurl himself into the path of the unknown object, but the angle was wrong; the metal device skittered through the improvised exit, just past his bubble of influence. With a distinct *POP*, magenta smoke erupted in all directions just as the other three figures closed on it.

Starshade couldn't help but feel a surge of glee as the Teepa thugs converging on her yelped in surprise and backpedaled from the billowing mist. *They can't know that it's just a smoke bomb. They have to treat it as a chemical weapon. I bought myself some time. Now, to* ***use*** *it.*

It had been too much, clearly, to hope that her acrobatic adversary was still distracted. He was already on his paws, charging at her with a snarl; she dodged his first three attacks, before springing backwards to gain room. Planting her heeled boots on the dusty concrete, she started to sprint forward, right back towards the masked Hero.

The fencer narrowed his beady eyes, assessing her with such confidence that the cottontail knew she was in very real trouble. Then, a crimson thorn, too large to be impeded by the polecat's power, slammed into his side. Starshade wasted no time in exploiting the distraction, as her adversary tensed at the sudden impact. Two gloved hands wrapped around the shaft of the poleax, just below the blade, and she jumped with everything she had.

Strong arms wrenched at the set pike, using it to redirect her body even as it curled into a ball. Then she kicked out with all her might. With the combined force of her jump, her arms, and her powerful legs, two heeled boots slammed *directly* into the groin of the stunned polecat. She felt the protective cup shatter from the immense force, the pulverized shards crushing and tearing the very thing they had been designed to protect.

With a strangled cry of emasculation, the two figures crashed together and tumbled into a heap. Starshade felt her head slam into the concrete before she rolled clear of the confusion; stars flashed across the world, and it took her a moment to focus her eyes, desperate to see if her gambit had worked. A cruel laugh almost escaped her lips as she looked down at the unconscious — and bleeding — Hero.

"Now you are *haft* the man you were, Poleax,*"* she wheezed in victory. The cottontail instantly cringed at her own joke.

Okay, that was awful. Leave the puns to Lawful Neutral.

All thoughts of her horrible wordplay fled, when a screech of hatred greeted her quip. Starshade snapped her head around, to see the source, and *froze*, finally realizing who the other combatant was.

Mother?

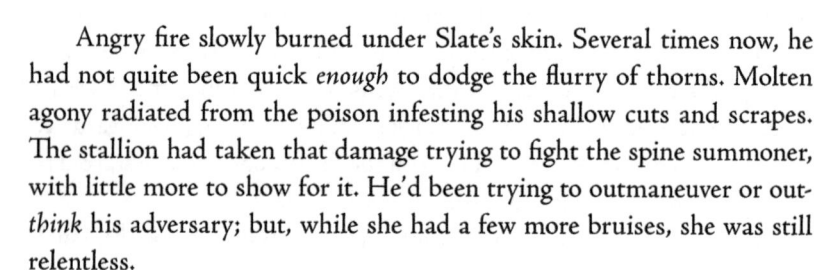

Angry fire slowly burned under Slate's skin. Several times now, he had not quite been quick *enough* to dodge the flurry of thorns. Molten agony radiated from the poison infesting his shallow cuts and scrapes. The stallion had taken that damage trying to fight the spine summoner, with little more to show for it. He'd been trying to outmaneuver or out-*think* his adversary; but, while she had a few more bruises, she was still relentless.

He could hear the combat behind him and felt powerless as the two other capes fought bitterly. A helplessness started to creep into his heart as he struggled. *I don't know what's **right** anymore. Macho Poleax is a Hero and is trying to kill me. Starshade is a supervillain! She could have run at any time. Is she fighting **alongside** me? Or is this just a convenient way to pick off her enemies, while they're distracted? Why is she even here…? And what does it say about **me** that the Protectors I served with are trying to kill me, and the one at my side is the one trying to take over the world?*

It was becoming clear that his earlier confidence in out-thinking Fatal Thorns was not… as *well-founded* as he had hoped. The damage he'd inflicted, and the time he'd lasted, may have been a testament to his skill as a cape, but the outcome was starting to feel inevitable. *Heavies are just too well understood. If I don't change — if I don't **change the situation**, I die.*

Spines exploded from a nearby pillar, metal peeling back from the spikes as they sought his heart. A hasty roll to escape almost cost him his life, as more thorns erupted from the floor right in his expected dodge route. Only punching the floor — with enough force to crater it — launched him into the air, to tumble a hair's breadth over the deadly points.

Slate realized then, as he faced off against the rabbit dressed as a Korps agent, that he was stalling. Because, he knew… the next action he needed to take would be more than simply trying to survive. It would be *choosing a side*. Dread and despair were filling his heavy heart. The choice might have been forced upon him, but he had *never* faltered before, in his endless pursuit to emulate true champions.

The warhorse had spent his entire life working towards being not just a Hero, but *The Hero*. He venerated those shining beacons of light that heralded *freedom* and *safety* and all that was *good*. As a young colt, he had idolized them. As he grew older, and realized he was broken, he knew that he could still carry the world, so others could live happily. He was a draft horse, and he would carry a shield for *all* those in need. Even as each step had become tougher than the last, Slate had stubbornly refused to *fail* those he had sworn to protect.

And as the quill — ripped from the ground — sailed through the air towards the polecat, so too did his dreams go with it. Cast aside, to once more protect a supervillain. This time, no, this time there would be no sweeping it under the rug. No ignoring it, no pretending it had never happened. The impact of that spike shattered any future the Percheron might have had, if he had just been a little stronger and a little less a *coward*.

In a blur of motion, it was over. Slate watched with dumbfounded horror as his choice instantly resulted in the grievous injury of his teammate. That inattention would have cost him his life, if it hadn't also distracted Fatal Thorns. The sheer venom in her screech of fury chilled him to his bones. He had spent the last eternity fighting this abomination, and he knew the signs.

Once more, the veteran warhorse acted as the Hero he had been just a moment before. He sprinted in front of Starshade, as concrete exploded behind him. Six spines slammed into his back and legs, instead of into Starshade's fragile form. Pain *exploded* as the sharp points pierced his tough hide. To his surprise, they did not stab through to his front like he had expected. His flesh was dense enough to stop the hateful plants.

The force of the violently sprouting spines *slamming* into the immovable object of the stallion caused the spikes to shatter like grenades. Six booms echoed like shotgun blasts in the abandoned storehouse, each spraying shards of shattered spine across the room. But the impact *also* forced the entire poison payload from each hateful spire deep into the draft horse. Agony exploded throughout his being, as his body was overwhelmed by the icy burning of venom eating away at his flesh.

Suddenly Starshade was *there*, jumping right at him. At the last minute, her paws reached up, clamping on one shoulder — and, with a powerful shove — *twisted* herself around him, into an accelerated drop kick. Then, she was behind him.

The giant horse, the Hero of a hundred street battles, who had endured *colossal* punishment, fell to his hands and knees. He could feel death coming, as each beat of his heart carried that corruption deeper into him. His great body no longer had the strength to stand, so he knelt there, buffeted by the pain, listening to the voices behind him. His final choice had been made.

It had cost him everything.

Her moment of stunned incomprehension almost ended the story of Starshade. Brown eyes locked on the bloody orbs across the room. Fear and hatred and shock ran rampant through her, and there was no ROSE, no soothing, no *breaking* the *spiral*, no *gentle reassurance*. Just a storm of emotions, too intense to overcome.

But then the mighty horse was *there*, and the spines were slamming into him. Only then, seeing the stallion's sacrifice, did her body *act*, though her mind was still reeling. Once more, her powerful legs propelled her into a jump. She grabbed onto the shoulder of the mountain and *twisted*, adding momentum, kicking straight for the other cottontail's sanguine eyes. Then, she...

SURGED...

...but that other figure was *smiling*. Spines were already erupting in front of and behind the Fort Worth Hero, angled to catch the supervillain in a fatal trap. Only — it was from the *sides* that twin heeled soles slammed into the already-bloody cheek of the elder rabbit. Crimson sprayed from mouth and eyes, and her head was whipped around, crumpling to the ground.

Starshade spun in air to land in a crouch, one leg splayed out, one gloved hand on the grimy floor, and the other high in the air behind her. Her voice was ice and fury, each word a punctuation, as she rose slowly to her feet. "Mother! It hasn't been *nearly* long enough."

The other rabbit sneered back at her, rising to her feet and wiping her mouth though she only managed to leave a crimson smear across her muzzle and throat. There was no mistaking the deranged fury in her own words. "Clint. I see you are still the *failure*."

Each slamming of her heart in her chest filled her ears with a pounding. Waves of fear and anger alternated their assault on her psyche, but her words were steady and as cold as starlight. "I learned it from watching you."

Her mother took a step towards her, every line of her body screaming of a mounting, murderous rage. Her paws in fists at her sides, wearing a copy of her own uniform, the fury radiating off Fatal Thorns felt palpable in the air. "If only you had learned anything else, like how to be a *proper* man instead of this *broken whore*. Then your *perversion* wouldn't. Have. Killed. *Your. Father.*"

Each of those words were spoken with the force of a grenade, detonating deep within Starshade. The ground fell away, and the world narrowed to a single memory...

Standing in the living room, staring at the wood grain in the weathered oak floor. Proud of herself, for being **brave** *enough, even though she was so scared. Just like her parents had said to be. Brave. Looking up at her parents, who had sworn to love her. Telling them she was trans. The expressions of* shock and horror. Her mother, shouting. Her father, standing. Silent disgust and agony on his face. Walking out of the room. The decisive click of the door. The shotgun...

The world narrowed to *pain* and *loss* and *anguish*. Fragments of memories flashed through her mind, filled with doubt, regret, and shame. Starshade distantly felt her knees impacting concrete. Tears streamed down her face as she relived that moment, and a thousand shards of aftermath. It was, all of it, tainted by the knowledge that her mother blamed her. *Hated* her. She couldn't help being who she was.

[*Calm...*]
ROSE!

A surge of relief and desperation shot through the stricken Starshade, fading just as quickly with the realization that there was no telepathic calming. The echo was just a memory of the *last* time ROSE had broken her out of this same, insidious cycle. But it was the crack in the door.

Not my fault. The choices of others are. Not. My. Fault. The phantom ROSE had broken the spiral, and Starshade was finally able to focus on something other than the unending agony.

Dark brown eyes, full of pain and loss, stared up into sanguine orbs filled with nothing but venomous cruelty and murderous joy. It struck her then, as she looked into that bloody gaze, that there was no hint of sadness. Hatred had infused every part of the woman standing over her kneeling form. The woman who had tucked her in at night and read stories to her — who had, once, *loved* her — was gone.

That truth deepened the chasm within her, but it broke the spell. The pain was deep in her bones, but no longer the immediate, mind-shattering panic that had been controlling her. The final acceptance of that heart-rending reality allowed the Villain to finally think instead of freezing. Starshade slowly stood, a grim determination in her expression, as Fatal Thorns warily stepped back. "No, *Linda*. The *only* thing I did was try to live brave, and strong, and true to myself. Like *you* always said I should. But *you* abandoned your oaths long ago. You gleefully hurt those you are charged to protect. You were right all those years ago, though." Each word dripped with an icy acid. "I. Am. **Not.** Your. Son."

A wall of thorns exploded in a ring, encircling the two rabbits. Venom dripped from the cruel barbs even as it dripped from the expression and tone of the older cottontail. "I brought you into this world, *son*. And *now* I am going to take you out of it."

More lances burst from the ruined ground, spearing towards the Korps agent. But she was already sprinting forward, dodging nettles with each step. More erupted in front of her and she...

VANISHED...

Fatal Thorns anticipated the attack, had baited and set a trap for it. A tight circle of spines burst forward around her, skewering anywhere the woman who had never, *ever* been her son might appear.

But Starshade did not appear for the flourish of a flying kick that was her signature move. She did not appear behind her mother for a thrown attack. Instead, she was suddenly wrapping arms around the hateful being who had once been her mother, inside the circle of death, in a cruel parody of a hug. The impact and momentum carried both women back into the wall of poisoned pikes.

Pain wracked Slate as he knelt there on hoof-nailed hands and knees. His ears flicked at the comments, not quite able to process the importance of the words, but seared themselves into his memory all the same. His world was agony. With each beat of his heart, venom coursed through his veins, and static ate at the corners of his vision.

"I. Am. **Not.** Your. Son." The depth of the forlorn savagery in the words cut through to the fog. With titanic effort, the draft horse lifted his head, staring at the twin cottontails facing off. The family resemblance of these women was undeniable, upon inspection, yet in many ways they could not be more different. They were both dressed as Villains. One was hateful and vengeful, spitting vile malice. The other... the other was terrified and furious, yes, but courageous and standing up to protect someone.

One steel-shod hoof slammed into the ground. Fresh waves of pain rebounded up his leg, but now they only spurred him on. With the effort of Atlas, he stood up. Unsteady, and swaying, but *up*. The unbroken colossus once more, he watched as Starshade was replaced with a fading, sparkling shadow. Thorns erupted in all the places she usually appeared, and his heart seized, fearing that he had regained his footing only to watch the smaller rabbit die.

Then she *reappeared*, wrapped around the other cottontail, and both slammed into a briar wall. He was moving then, plowing through the poison spikes in his way. More pierced his skin and pumped their deadly payload into him, but he did not care. He could not get more dead.

In a heartbeat, he was there, pulling the Korps agent out of the wall of thorns. He cradled the rabbit in his arms, looking for injuries. Only a few small bloody holes peppered her arms and legs. He couldn't deny that he was happy to see she had been largely protected. Brown eyes filled with pain and confusion, looked up to his gray eyes. He could see a ghost of thanks haunting the edges of her gaze.

She nestled there for a moment, clearly drawing strength from his grip. He could feel the venom clawing its way through him, and Slate regretted he couldn't hold her much longer. Too much fire was pumping through his veins, and he could feel the last of his strength ebbing.

Then Starshade's face screwed up in concentration. The warhorse worked his muzzle, trying to form a question, but couldn't manage to form the words, or even the thought needed for them. He watched her for a long moment, wishing he could say something. And then she was…

GONE…

…reappearing three feet in front of him. Next to her was a crimson constellation that almost looked like a… replica of an equine circulatory system. Both seemed to hang in the air for a heartbeat; then, the burning pain in him was suddenly *doused* as the venom was teleported out of his veins. The spell was broken.

Starshade crashed to the ground with a pained gasp, next to a waterfall of displaced poison that coated the concrete with a sickly scarlet rain. Slate himself went to one knee, gasping for breath, as the absence of pain was somehow more a burden than its presence. A dull ache remained, from punctures and abused veins, but the sense of advancing, molten doom was gone. The stallion looked dumbfounded as the rabbit slowly forced herself to her feet. *None of her files said she could do that.*

The rabbit swayed, looking back at him with a ghost of a smile hidden in her pain-fogged expression. Just as he was daring to hope this nightmare was over, he heard three pairs of boots sprinting through the open door. Slate cursed his fatigue; slowed reactions meant he could only watch, as Starshade was suddenly pivoting, and throwing something at the trio. The whole scene played out for him as if in slow motion.

Trickshot and Ethicoil dodged easily out of the way. But they had not been the target; the small plastic bag, filled with white powder, impacted perfectly on the golden tip of Heavenly Dazzler's slender beak. The sharp point ripped the thin plastic and the once-contained dust sprayed across her eyes and mouth.

There was a moment of stunned silence before Heavenly Dazzler began clawing at her chest. Desperate wings pulled the dress down as she tried to get air, revealing the pure white feathered expanse of her chest, marred with an old, jagged electrical scar in the shape of a 'V.' With eyes desperately wide, and a strangled cry, the dove's eyes rolled up into her head; the Hero collapsed, unconscious. Her diaphanous white robes splayed out on the ruined, grimy floor of the storehouse. The other two Heroes looked on in shock.

"Fentanyl!" Ethicoil cried out, horrified. He looked down at his uniform, where it had caught the barest splash of the substance. With a squeal of utter terror, the brave Protecteer of the city turned and sprinted out of the building. As for their fearless leader, the pronghorn of a thousand battles, he let out a strangled gasp of horror and — with his sclera showing clearly in the dimness — followed closely behind. Together, the pair vanished, leaving their allies abandoned in the warehouse.

Slate was stunned. Both at their cowardice, and at the monstrous actions of the rabbit he had fought to save. He looked up at her with a stunned betrayal.... only to find the Korps agent wheezing in pained laughter. His voice, though exhausted, carried shock and disgust. "That was *Fentanyl?*"

Somehow the outraged question redoubled her laughter. Before he could find the energy to stand and fight the villain, she was holding up her gloved paw and shaking her head. Tears streamed from her face. "Powdered sugar," she managed in between hysterical giggles.

"...What?"

"It's fucking *powdered sugar*, you idiot. You damn Teepa assholes started to believe your own lies about Fentanyl so much you *panic*."

"Powdered sugar," Slate mouthed, looking bewildered for a long moment.

Finally, with a laugh that was more of a sob, the rabbit's laughter faded. What little mirth present drained from her face, leaving a stony mask. After a long, long moment of staring at each other, Starshade finally turned around. Her gaze pulled inexorably towards the wall of thorns, and the still form still hanging within.

The Korps agent's shoulders sagged and shook, as she took slow step after slow step. With a massive effort, the exhausted warhorse forced himself onto his hooves and followed the smaller woman. A cascade of emotions played through him, all muted by fatigue and shock, but he couldn't help but feel for his companion.

The bloody form of Fatal Thorns was suspended in the air, spines pierced clear through her arms, legs, and torso. Her bloody eyes were closed and her head hung limp; Slate couldn't see her breathing, not that that always mattered in his line of work. What *did* matter was the woman sinking to her knees in front of him.

Silent, wracking sobs shook the smaller form. She buried her face in her hands and wept. Whether it was for the death of her mother, that her mother had tried to kill her, a thousand could've-beens, or even just adrenaline withdrawal, the warhorse couldn't say. Whatever the reason for the rabbit's anguish, the unlikely pair couldn't stay there. The fled Heroes might return. Backup *would*, eventually, arrive.

Slate couldn't find anything to say. Nothing seemed adequate, and he didn't know this Starshade well enough even to know where to start. But... she was clearly hurting, and hurting so *badly*, his heart ached more for her than for his own shattered future. Without saying a word, he placed one powerful hand on her back.

The contact caused her to tense momentarily, only to begin weeping harder and pressing back against his touch. Making a decision, he bent low and scooped her into his arms. The cottontail buried her face in his chest, and he felt the wetness of tears soaking his uniform. It was only then, looking down, that he realized his badge had been torn off at some point during the fight.

The draft horse started to walk to the hole ripped in the wall of the storehouse. A faint glint caught his eye; there, next to the fallen form of Macho Poleax, was his badge, dented and spattered in grime. He paused, looking at the tarnished gold shield for a long moment. The symbolism was not lost on the Percheron.

The thin metal crunched under his hoof and the once-Hero walked into the night, carrying the villain away to safety.

Chapter 10

Aggregate

Celia stared grimly at the displays in the command center. Red symbols flashed all around the map of the Lone Star State, indicating areas of combat. Updates and key information scrolled across her HUD as the situation changed every moment. The TPA had launched a statewide, coordinated strike; not directly on RIV, thankfully, as that would turn this cursed cold war very, *very* hot. But the Hero teams were targeting known informants and allies, and even just Korps-friendly neighborhoods. The Quick Reaction Force and all other available Korps personnel — activating even local combat-rated civilian members — were engaged in small battles across all of Texas, trying to protect the most vulnerable.

Bastards.

The crimson snake looked over at Karen, standing grimly next to her and staring at the same bleak situation. The silver dragoness, always so patient and warm and kind, was now stony. A glance around showed that the overwatch agents, in frantic communication with their teams, looked shocked or grim. The drones, at least, were drones, and carried on with their tasks in the same bliss as always.

The command center had always felt a little like her throne room, all dark chrome and obsidian. In a way, that was exactly as intended. The Korps helix logo, in magenta, was splashed everywhere; on banners, on the obsidian tilework, and in four large sculptures in each corner of the room. Giant flatscreen displays and workstations ringed a central point, allowing immediate access to the most essential of all resources: information. The fact that it clearly screamed who was in charge, to anyone daring to assault the room, was also quite intentional.

Celia grimaced as the markers flashed in a constellation across Texas. She did not let herself forget: these were not bloodless pieces in a board game. Each represented agents and minions fighting against TPA Heroes in private dances of violence, in alleys and buildings and even one rural highway pursuit. So far, the media was silent and civilians were unaware of the extent of the conflict. A special set of symbols indicated the presence of Manifest Destiny, or at least one of his duplicates. The fact that he was in the field himself was very worrying, though his Prime had not yet been identified.

A quick mental command activated a privacy field. Karen finally spoke, in a grave voice. "The Overlord has denied your request for reinforcements. We will not be sending in units from outside the state, nor is Arcane Research and Control authorized for further summoning. You are also instructed not to activate any more reserve personnel."

Celia stared at the readouts, scaled lips pressed together in frustration. "We are *barely* fending off thisss assssault. If thisss goesss wrong, the mossst vulnerable are at risssk. Every asssset we have available isss engaged. If they launch another attack, or if thisss goes badly, RIV itssself could be threatened."

"But you *are* fending it off. The Teepa badly underestimated our strength; they expected to walk over us. However, because of that, the Bradley Group leadership is assessing the situation. And the PHL is watching too, of course, with new leadership in the Prairie League and Cascade Group, far more amenable to Rockwell's brand of aggression. If the Korps commits any more forces to this… *upheaval,* it may be the spark that ignites the powder keg."

Celia hissed in frustration as another wave of reports rolled in, including a confirmation of yet another Manifest Destiny, this time in Waco. "We losssst contact with Ssstarssshade again. I need more, to sssend her backup or exxxtractttion. I'm ccccertain that *thisss,*" her hand swept across the air to encompass the entire map, "Isss a diversssion. There isss *sssomething* more going on here than the ssstate of Texxxasss onccce more sssseeking to ssset the world aflame."

The dragoness grimaced, not unkindly. "If we send in more forces, then *we* may start the war. And if we're at war, Texas is *not* the place those forces will be needed. I'm sorry."

"Karen, I underssstand the deccccisssion. I even agree with the reasssoning. But, asss bassse commander, it isss my duty to put the needsss of RIV above all elsssе, jussst asss it isss your job, and the job of the Overlord, to look at more than my little backwater. I accccept the orderssss, even as I lament them."

A hand on her hip sent a wave of calm through the massive snake woman. She lowered her torso, and Karen placed her other warm palm on her cheek. Even in the midst of watching a tense battle unfold, the soothing of the dragoness and her welcoming mind made her feel at home. It was easy to sink into that feeling and lose herself.

The two women smiled at each other in a soft, knowing moment. They had worked together for a long time and shared a deep understanding of — and respect for — one another. "We trust you. You are not forgotten. Each member here is important to me, and to the Overlord."

Celia nuzzled softly into that hand, her tongue wrapping gently around the silver scales of Karen's wrist. "That, I assssure you, I ssshall never doubt." But her expression, though difficult for so many to read, turned pensive. She withdrew, looking down at the kind woman. "But there isss one more asssset that hasss not been deployed. One that isss not activating ressservesss, nor deploying outssside forcccesss."

Karen frowned, concern flashing through her eyes. "You haven't been in the field for a mission like this in years. And your presence is needed *here*."

But the large snake was already shaking her head. "Unlike cccertain opponentsss of oursss, I have not *ssslackened* in my training sssimply becausssе I am no longer ssslithering through dark alleywaysss or dank ssswampsss. And no, Karen, it isss not my presssencccе that isss required here. I am but a figurehead; it isss you who direct operatttionsss, and give orderssss. I sssimply handle adminisssstrative tasssksss, and ssshow the world what they exxxpect to sssee."

"It is a major risk. If you are killed, or captured, it would be a great blow to the... region."

"Yesss, it would. I am aware of the risssk. I am aware that luring me out may be exxxactly the outcome that the Teepa desssiresss. But I feel in my sssscalesss that I mussst go. My Goddesss hasss given me no sssign that thisss coursssе of action isss againssst Her will. *Pleassse*, Karen. I will ssstay if ordered, but I feel thisss to be...*important*."

The silver dragoness stared at her for a long moment, worry etching creases in those delicate scales. Celia wasn't sure if her friend was assessing her, or communicating with the Overlord, although it was probably both.

[*Yes, my dear friend, both,*] came whispering across her mind.

Finally, with a small, worried sigh, Karen relented. "The Overlord has agreed with your request. And, though I worry about you, I do too."

Lamia swallowed and nodded. While she was glad her request was accepted, she shared the worry of her friend. This *was* a risk. In the end, however, she couldn't shake the feeling that the target of all this was one lone operative, lost in Dallas. She worried about Starshade, as she worried about all agents under her command. But she also couldn't shake the building dread that *something* more nefarious was at play, and that the Korps itself might be in more peril than they believed.

"Would you sssee fit to help me sssuit up? It hasss been a while sssinccce I have been in full missssion gear, though I'm cccertain you have kept it prepared for thisss day."

A soft smile slowly curved scaled lips. Then the light rekindled in Karen's eyes even in the dire situation. "It would be my pleasure."

Ethicoil cursed and punched the hospital's helipad door, denting the flimsy metal. He could hear the medevac helicopter disappearing into the distance. The pre-dawn air was chilly, and cut right through his thin uniform, stealing what little warmth could be found under his cool scales. Dallas weather in March was always so fickle, and he hated how sluggish the cold made him.

For the moment, however, it was difficult to dwell on the chill, or the torpor it threatened. He was so… *frustrated*, and fury flashed within him.

*We had them. We **had them**, and then we let them walk away. I can't fucking **believe** Heavenly Dazzler, being so stupid to assume Fentanyl, and just… working herself up into a panic attack and passing out. And… and Texas Trickshot, he just fucking ran! **Fools.** How could I have trusted them?*

Or maybe, the coral snake seethed, *he* was the fool. He knew better. He *knew* better. Fentanyl wasn't nearly as deadly or dangerous as it was made out to be — but in that moment, seeing their healer seemingly dead on the floor, and watching his leader running in blind panic, he had been caught up in the very same.

But the worst part... he had realized the dumb mistake for what it was. A moment of his own alchemy had shown it to be but spun sugar. His attempts to retrieve Trickshot had been too slow. By the time he had returned, the traitor and the Korps drone had escaped.

Ethicoil shuddered at the memory of the ruin that was the Fort Worth Division's chief. Fatal Thorns had been a mangled husk, mutilated by her own spines. He still had no idea if she was alive, or if the paramedics were simply lying about an obvious corpse to stave off any chance of the Hero Revenge Rage that so commonly ruined operating rooms and recovery wards. He had tried, *begged*, the paramedics to realize the truth — that there was no dreaded Fentanyl, that it was paranoia and panic alone that had felled his team.

They had listened patiently, thanked him for the report, and then calmly, boredly explained to him that *of course* they were taking no risks, and that the drug was every bit as deadly as the lie they themselves had created. That they would take no chances with his team who were so valued and honored. That they hadn't believed him.

The doctors hadn't believed him either, saying they had to wait for tests that would take *hours* yet. Texas Trickshot was awake, if having difficulty breathing; no doubt psychosomatic, another case of believing their own propaganda, the Hero sneered to himself. The pronghorn hadn't believed him either. *No one* would believe him.

And so, he was alone on the roof; his team leader was being treated for nothing, their healer and chaplain unconscious from nothing but the ghost of fear. Both unable to avenge the unspeakable injury that Poleax had suffered.

Better dead than suffer... that, the snake shuddered. And then, of course, there was the matter of the traitor. *How could Slate* **do** *this? He was always dumb, but to betray us, to let a Korps agent* **go**? *It doesn't make sense...!*

But the universe did not care about his protests. Their heavy was gone. Defected, corrupted, *probably* already brainwashed and droned. All by the murderous bastards who had killed his grandfather.

Fury raged within him. His grandfather had been an upstanding citizen, a CEO of wealth and power who had *earned* his fortune, after fleeing the communists that seized his estates with nothing more than the clothes on his back. His life had been snuffed out by a monster in a marsh near Miami, years before Ethicoil had been born; though he'd never had the opportunity to know the man, family stories showed a kind and intelligent patriarch, whose savvy and entrepreneurial spirit had carried them all to the riches that were their due. They *deserved* their life of luxury.

Peasants are so blind to the opportunity all around them. Anyone can achieve wealth and power, if they're worthy.

And now, once again, he was surrounded by fools. How could they not see? How could they not *understand?* He had explained that they were wrong, and yet they could not grasp the truth. Did not *believe* him. *Him.* The scion of Pegasus Oil, and *Hero* besides.

Fools, blind fools, all of them. Now, for their folly, the traitor and the drone were free in the city, and none of their team was left to stop them… except for Ethicoil.

The coral snake gazed up into the spring night sky and hissed in rage. "You're just a *heavy*, Slate. More brawn than brains. The *most* replaceable part of any team. How dare you betray me? How *dare* you join **them***!*"

No one was around to listen to the man's ranting. No one was around to watch him punch the door. And no one was around to watch the Hero disappear into the night, with murder in his eyes.

Celia slithered past her office, and the hapless coral snake statue that had once been the CEO of Pegasus Oil. He had *also* once been the man who killed a little boy, a fledgling Hero who had been so overjoyed to go on his first real mission with The Florida Men, Junior Division. This week, the granite statue was wearing a bright pink baseball cap emblazoned with the words "TWERK QUEEN."

I sssussspect it isss Volta'sss week to choossse the hat.

The commander ducked through the door into her private armory, just down the hall from the operations center. A dizzying variety of glittering weapons graced the walls. As she would act as the last line of defense against any all-out attack on RIV, she had to be prepared for anything. Karen, in her distributed, pseudo-AI role as ROSE, was the essential command network of the Korps. In a lot of ways, the role of base commander was a fiction.

She definitely spent a lot of time directing operations. Taking care of agents. Ensuring that the stronghold was expanding and operating. She did give orders, which were expected to be followed, and she was to be treated like the Overlord's chosen captain. But at the end of the day, she was a smokescreen; the Heroes generally did not know that Karen was the heart of the Korps's vast command and control network, and they were certainly not aware of the extent of that truth. They expected to see high-value, powerful henches and trusted, scheming advisors in charge of operations and facilities. So, Celia played the part, to keep them from guessing the silver dragon behind her was the true prize.

If the worst ever came — if war broke out, and the Heroes descended upon this stronghold in full force — then Celia would be the field commander. It would be the gigantic, petrifying Lamia who would be visibly shouting orders, and planning the defense and evacuation. And while most of those shouted orders would be those dictated to her by ROSE, she would be there to act as the focus of the enemy.

If that horrible day ever came, and RIV was lost, it was unlikely she would survive. She would sell her life dearly to give her people (and especially Karen) the most time to escape. And, if — worse still — she was captured, with no chance of rescue, the last thing she knew might be ROSE quietly deleting all that she *was*, to protect the secrets that could be used against the Korps — against her comrades, her friends, her *family*. All this she had long accepted. In truth, it comforted her greatly that, if that dark day ever came, ROSE would be there for her. Few could say they had a beloved companion to usher them into the arms of a Goddess.

Updates scrolled across her RCGs, feeding her the latest updates. She could feel the telepathic link imprinting those essential details upon her mind, without the need for constant concentration. The more pressing number was the countdown to when the next transport would be available, to ferry her to Dallas. Both showed she had a bit of time. The situation was relatively stable, but it wouldn't do to tarry, just in case something big changed.

That treasured friend walked in behind her, tapping her chin and looking around. After a moment of consideration, Karen stepped forward to one of the many large gear lockers, mission-specific caches stocked for out for any eventuality, and pressed a button. With a soft hiss of air, the crate unsealed to show the outfit hidden within — or, rather, the *lack* of outfit.

Celia slowly, deliberately, turned her head to stare at Karen to gauge if it was a joke. Where *usually* these crates contained a full outfit top and gear, this one looked to contain nothing but some random accessories and two nipple cups. For her part, the silver dragoness stared back innocently.

After a long moment, during which she could *feel* the smug anticipation radiating off her friend, Celia finally couldn't take it. "Isss thisss… all?"

A delighted giggle burst from Karen. "Yes. You're going to love it. If we had more time, I would delight in this process more, but we don't. So, strip and try it on. *Trust me.* You'll soon agree this is the best gear you've ever worn."

Lamia pursed her lips. If it were anyone else, she would demand more explanation, or suspect a prank, but this was her friend. She might take a deep delight out of this, but the dragoness wouldn't lead her wrong. After a heartbeat, Celia grabbed the hem of her shiny latex top and pulled it off, cursing slightly as she felt something tear from her haste. She tossed it to the side, where she had no doubt a maintenance drone would happily take it to the vast laundry wing of the Facilities sector for careful mending.

Scaled hands plucked one of the caps from the velvet case. They were thick with seams and lines that hinted at a complex mechanism, and the bars passing through the interior cup obviously matched up with her piercings. A glance up at Karen showed a beatific smile. "So they're *highly* secure yet easy to remove, of course."

Celia was certain that it had *nothing* to do with her friend's knowledge of her enjoyment of nipple chastisement, or the fact that it would serve as a constant reminder of their presence. *Certain.* But, ultimately, she trusted her friend. With deft fingers, her thick rings clinked together as they were tossed into the equipment case for later.

Then the caps were set in place, and twin bolts shot forward automatically with unerring precision. A soft gasp of mingled pain and pleasure escaped her at the sudden sensation. She shivered lightly as she could feel herself stretched and tugged by the two suddenly-secure cups that were *technically* covering her, but offered approximately zero modesty. "Karen, I've played your game. How isss thisss a field uniform?"

[*Allow me.*]

An arrow drew her attention to the full mirror wall next to her. Only when ROSE detected she was watching herself did a small icon highlight on her RCG HUD; without waiting for any further input, the icon activated. Her sensitive peaks felt like they were bathed in ice water. Then, an explosion of heat replaced the cold, but not stopping at the edges of those caps.

She watched, fascinated, as her scales turned black and shiny, like each had been instantly coated in perfectly-polished latex. The wave of ebony washed over her entire body, turning her into some sort of serpent fetish statue. Then, a magenta glow began to show between the gaps in her scales; with each movement, the light rippled and moved, creating a mesmerizing, dangerous effect. Finally, in true Korps fashion, a magenta helix logo flared to life over her heart.

Celia preened in the mirror, *incredibly* satisfied at the gear's aesthetic qualities, her confusion at its logistical utility momentarily forgotten; she wasn't quite sure what to say. Karen started to speak, with ROSE giving a gentle nudge to make sure she was fully processing the gear description.

"Consider this a gift from one of our brightest engineers. One whom you think doesn't even know your name. Yes, that *is* all the hint you are going to get. She was considering your... unique physical qualities, and she realized that there might be an opportunity here. A nanite mesh is used as a focal grid for a transmutative alchemical magical core built into each cup. Utilizing that nano-weave, the core temporarily converts the outermost layer of your scales into a super-hard material, anchored into the nanite lattice. In this mode, you will shrug off any small arms fire. You were tough before, but with this, it'll take anti-materiel weaponry to do serious damage."

Celia was beyond impressed. It was difficult to integrate magic and nanotechnology at the best of times; only a handful of inventors in the entire world could manage the necessary precision, and mastery of each discipline. She suspected it was only possible because of her own origin. But, she had no luxury for introspection, as the transport fueled up and Karen's rundown continued.

"There is also a stealth mode." The icon flashed again, this time with a little cloud around it. The magenta glow between the scales vanished in a rippling wave from her chest. The scales lost much of their shine and turned a deep mottled blue instead of black. "No glowing lights obviously, as charming as they are, so much easier to hide. The blue is designed to break up your outline and blend into deep shadows; it doesn't draw the eye like an artificial black. This will also suppress your heat signature, meaning you won't light up on thermals. All this comes at a cost, though. With no way for your body to regulate temperature, due to the thermal enclosure, you'll start to overheat. The more you exert yourself, the faster you'll reach your limit. You have at most a few hours of operation before it becomes debilitating, but I don't recommend fighting in it for long."

The base commander nodded at the standard warning for stealth gear. "There's a standard internal battery onboard, and all of the functions *do* require constant power to maintain; it should last for about a day with active use, or up to five if kept on standby mode. However, there are two small supplementary power packs that can be swapped out for weeks of additional field activity." Scaled fingers tapped two of the small packs still in the gear case. "You have a number of hidden gear pouches along the spine of your tail, just past your hips. The two at the base just below your hips are designed for these packs."

Karen then quickly covered a number of important points about how to use, wear, and deactivate the suit. Not covered by the technical specs was that the change in the texture of her scales made them feel tingly, and a lot more sensitive, *distractingly* so. But Celia was a professional, and merely made a note to test out the nano-weave suit for *non*-field work purposes in the near future.

Finally, with the last of the gear stowed, Celia slithered over to the counter where she kept her most precious weapons. A long, low box awaited her mental command, slowly springing open with a thought to expose the two wickedly curved sabers nestled in velvet-lined indentations. Made of a metal that matched the shiny black of her new scales, these blades were nigh-indestructible; the glowing magenta edge kept the blades monomolecular and self-sharpening. They clamped perfectly onto the small contact patches on her back. Upon being stowed, the nanites that sharpened the blade reformed into a cover to protect the blade, and to protect her from it.

With that, she was ready. It was time.

Karen stood between the massive snake woman and the door. Sensitive to the time pressure, the base commander nevertheless took a moment to really look at her companion. As with any field operation, this could be her last time to see a dear friend. The silver scales, perfectly buffed to shimmer in the light. The naughty clubbing outfit she had been wearing while relaxing before everything went wrong. The pensive, sad smile that was so alien on her face. It was Celia's turn to slither forward and cup her hands around Karen's muzzle. She drew close, putting their foreheads together.

No words were spoken or needed, nothing more than sharing a quiet, private moment together. They felt each other's warmth and closeness, letting each other know how much the other cared for them.

Then, a ping beeped from Celia's RCGs; she needed to get moving, or she would delay needed supplies. Without another word, the Lamia — infamous terror of Heroes — glided out of the armory, leaving a pensive dragoness behind to worry.

Chapter 11

Collision

Starshade came back to herself slowly; her first coherent thought was to wonder just where she was *now*, but a quick glance showed it was a warehouse. (Another one.) She was seeing a lot of those lately. Maybe she, like this empty storehouse, should take stock.

The cottontail hadn't fallen asleep, exactly. Fragmented memories of being carried — for some time, it seemed? — floated across her mind but failed to really stick. The stress and distress had simply been too much for her. More than anything, she had needed time to be held and carried and to cry herself out. Having found her center again, though echoes still remained, Starshade was finally able to process the world around her.

Okay, I'm in a warehouse. That means that Slate didn't arrest me and take me back to a TPA holding cell. They were trying to kill him. I need to assume he's gone rogue. Starshade fell into the pattern of analysis easily; her field work instructors had been thorough. *Rogue doesn't mean ally... but it doesn't always mean enemy, either.*

The Korps agent turned to herself for answers. *Okay... I have a number of wounds. I still have my gear on, including my knife and other obvious weapons, so he isn't treating me like a prisoner.* She grimaced at the filthy mess that was her outfit. Much of it was tacky with drying blood and coated in the grime. *Oh shit... that smell is **me**. Looks like the self cleaning mechanisms are tied into ROSE, which seems inconvenient. Then again, someone can live a few hours being icky. And if the network is down longer than that, we have bigger problems than how fresh-smelling the field agents are.*

...Oh, right, wounds. Wounds were an important thing I should have paused on.

She cursed herself for running right past that point. Luckily, she didn't feel any of her moth — Lin — *Fatal Thorns*' hateful poison burning in her veins. The rabbit's mind shied away from thinking too much about that topic, not ready to reopen *those* wounds just yet. Her deft paws pulled a small medkit out of a tiny pouch hidden between her shoulder blades. *Very impractical if I'm wounded, but extremely easy to miss if I'm ever searched. Luckily, Empire Enhancements made sure of my flexibility.* A tiny part of her felt smug about the fact — and the *primary* purpose — of that, even in a dire situation.

Quick paws started pulling tiny applicators out of the small pouch. The distinctive sound of steel horseshoes on concrete echoed through the room, signaling the return of her erstwhile savior. Starshade was methodically hitting each puncture with a tiny spray as Slate emerged from what she suspected was the warehouse office. Relief washed through her as the misted nanites began to do their work, cleansing any infection and knitting the flesh back together.

She watched the massive draft horse out of the corner of her eye. He looked like hell. Though he wore his signature stony expression, red-ringed eyes and damp fur betrayed his turmoil. His calm demeanor — clearly a strenuous mask — was further undermined by a uniform shredded and caked with drying crimson, some brighter spots indicating fresher blood. But it was the haunted expression that most concerned the cottontail.

Definitely a fragile mental state, which tracks, for someone who just went rogue. I need to be very careful. Keep him calm, be soothing and reasonable. She did not speak, waiting for the Hero to carefully take a seat on a crate nearby, not quite able to meet her eyes. *That's adorable. He's trying not to spook me.* She let quiet be her ally as she watched him and waited for the tiny terrors to wipe away her more concerning wounds.

Finally, the stallion broke the silence with a hesitant and evasive tone. "So… uh… You're Starshade, right?"

Starshade could see the Hero grasping for the script he had so carefully thought through moments before walking out here, only for it to vanish like dew when confronted by the *interaction* itself. The rabbit had been there so, so many times herself. She would spend hours obsessing over every little detail and wild tangent, following tiny, tessellating thought spirals down wildly unrealistic conversational warrens, just in case they came up. Then, when the moment finally came —

The stallion shifted uneasily.

"Yes!" Starshade squeaked, forcefully, with a touch of panic, causing them both to jump from the sudden noise of the response. She felt the insides of her ears redden as she tried to calm her breathing. "Sorry. Yes. I'm Starshade. You're Slate, right?" *First I get distracted and forget to answer him, now I'm yelling and asking him blindingly obvious questions. SO much for being soothing and reasonable.*

Slate scratched the back of his neck. "I suppose I was."

Was. *I was right on the mark; someone's just lost their sense of self. I know what that's like.* "Wait! I remember, you were in last year's TPA Heroes Pinup Calendar! You were August, the hottest month!"

Starshade was surprised to catch a flinch in Slate's eyes at the comment. *Wait, what? Most guys would be preening about that. Oh. Oh no.* But she was making things worse, and she couldn't let herself fall down the rabbit hole of speculation. Not now. She had to get things under control.

With a calming breath, Starshade tried very hard to let the tension and urgency drain from her posture and tone, if not from her mind. Her voice steadied and she sounded much more like the reasonable, capable Korps agent she struggled to be without ROSE.

"Hey, it's okay. We have a bit of time. Actually, what time is it, anyway?"

The draft horse blinked at the question then looked around. "About 0300. It's been about an hour, Miss. I was rather expecting you to ask where you were."

Starshade grimaced. "Where am I? I'm in a warehouse. I'm *always* in a warehouse. In the last week I've bled in more Dallas warehouses than I knew existed. I've been mauled in so many of these damn things that I'm afraid I'm going to turn into a bungalow during the next full moon."

Slate's expression was a blank one, evidently confused.

Exasperated, she tried to explain the joke. "Because, see, I'd be a… *were-house…*" When the horse did not, in fact, burst into gales of laughter, the cottontail grumbled. "Okay, note to self. Humor is not part of the TPA's standard duty equipment."

"No, it's issued for special assignments only. You have to complete the qualification requirements, and then get admin approval. For general field use, we are instead allotted a limited amount of Witty Banter™, but that's mostly military surplus from the 70s, so I don't rely upon it if I don't have to."

The entire statement was made in such a deadpan, matter-of-fact tone that the Korps agent just stared, with her mouth slightly agape, not entirely convinced it *was* a joke. Then she smiled and gave a weak Evil Laugh™. "You *fool*. With this intel, we shall be unstoppable." She was gratified at the tiny upturn of Slate's lips.

Starshade took a moment to let the levity hover. She tossed the tiny healing kit to Slate without a word, though was secretly hurt when the fallen Hero gave it a suspicious glance and set it aside. *Not that I can blame them for not trusting strange medical sprays.* But she needed to start getting answers, so the mirth faded to a ghost as she turned to more serious matters.

"Slate… do you know what happened to my RCGs?"

The Hero shifted. They were normally so impassive, so to see even tiny cracks in the facade spoke volumes about the horse's inner turmoil. The silence stretched as she watched them struggle with how — and whether — to answer. Starshade was not blind to the gravity of the question; she was Korps, and the sworn enemy of the TPA. Giving her information about the TPA was tantamount to treason. Even if there had been an even more overt act hours ago, that didn't mean that this Hero was truly willing to betray their sworn duty further.

She was starting to think she had pushed too far, too fast, when she saw broad equine shoulders fall wearily. Slate then took a breath and deflated further. "We… there was a new device brought in. Sent by the Steel Magnolias, out of Biloxi. One of their new recruits, some techie whiz-kid, claimed he had a new toy that could stop the Korps threat. But the group didn't have the resources to manage it themselves. Some department squabble or other. Reached out to see if the TPA was interested. To make this plan work, the initial phase was to capture a specific Korps minion." The mountain looked distinctly uncomfortable and couldn't meet her eyes. "You."

Dread welled up within her, but she nodded, trying to keep it from showing on her face. She had convinced herself that she was just a convenient opportunity. The idea that the whole operation had been planned to take her, specifically, was chilling. "But... you said capture. Those cops were trying to *kill* me. So was Macho Poleax. Impact Crater leveled a *building!*"

The Percheron looked distinctly uncomfortable. "I have recently begun to realize that not everyone interprets the word 'capture' the same way." Mighty fists clenched and lines of deep anger and sorrow briefly etched themselves into their posture, but it didn't seem directed at her and faded, quickly replaced with discomfort. "The plan didn't necessarily require you to be... *alive*. What they really needed was your RCGs."

Her eyes widened, both at the admission and at the implications. "Wait, don't you guys capture RCGs all the time? Either off the street, or even from the occasional Korps minion or agent? Fatal Thorns was wearing a deactivated pair *herself* earlier!" Her heart twinged at the thought, but she ruthlessly quashed it.

The response was less than helpful though, as Slate shrugged. "I don't know. Just had to be yours. They didn't exactly *tell* me this, so much as they complained about it in my presence while I was carrying heavy equipment around."

The cottontail bit her lip. She knew the next question she needed to ask. It took her a moment to build up the courage. "Slate... Why did you let me go?"

In retrospect, she should have expected the tears. She knew that this TPA heavy had been on the brink, and had been torn up inside, but they still seemed so powerful, so *tough*. Her heart broke in sympathy as the horse shied away.

"I... don't know. I've been asking myself that question for days. But you were there, and you were so hurt, so exhausted, but so *brave*. You showed courage that few Heroes could ever aspire to! We had only barely managed to run you to ground, and only caught you at the last hurdle. It was only luck that I saw you duck into that warehouse." When Starshade moved, the massive super flinched and shrank back. The words were heavy with distress and almost tumbled over each other.

"Every other Hero was out of position. The cops were useless. If I hadn't caught sight of you, you would have escaped. So I followed. You were cornered, and clearly had nothing left, and yet — *yet* — you still sassed me about my spurs. It wasn't bravado, or an unfeeling hive mind, or whatever. What I saw right there was *you*, stripped to the core. You were tough, and brave, and I was there threatening to take it all away from you."

The rabbit flinched at the sound of cracking wood. Splinters fell from the edge of the crate on which Slate was sitting, as they squeezed it so hard that the entire side panel was disintegrating. The Hero didn't even seem to notice, nor were they making even the pretense of meeting her gaze.

"And when I said I was going to take you in... you were... *scared*. Deeply, truly terrified. Even still, you remained defiant. Seeking a way out. Here you were, a supervillain, more vibrant and brave and *alive* than any Hero I've ever met. And there I was, trying to take all that from you. And... I couldn't. I felt so small and weak and cowardly. I looked at you and I felt *evil*. I couldn't. I just couldn't do it. So... I walked away."

Starshade started to respond but Slate held up a hand in silent pleading even as tears fell like rain. "I told myself it was a simple moment of weakness. The other Heroes make terrible decisions all the time, and it wasn't like I was the only person you escaped that night. No one would ever know.

"Except you *did* steal something that night. You stole my blinders. I suddenly couldn't stop... *seeing*. I suddenly couldn't ignore all of the ways that we fail to live up to our ideals. The *brutality* so casually deployed and dismissed. How all of the jokes seem to make fun of anyone *different*. I... I joined the TPA to be a *Hero*. To *help* people. And without even saying a word, you showed me that I had not only failed to live up to my ideals, I had become a *monster*."

Face buried in powerful hands and wracked by powerful sobs, Slate could summon no more words. Starshade's heart broke as she looked at the hunched figure, looking so small despite the enormous frame. She couldn't bear it. Swiftly crossing the distance, the cottontail wrapped arms around the larger horse, pulling herself close, offering support the only way she knew how.

The tears ebbed quicker than the Korps agent expected. A moment more and she could feel Slate pulling away and composing themself. She politely stepped back, giving them a moment of composure. It was time to call all this back, after all.

From a small pocket concealed under one of her large breasts, she withdrew a small, nondescript flip phone she had brought just for this occasion. She had just flipped it open when it was *slapped* out of her hand. The phone hit the floor and was crushed under one steel shod hoof. Fear and confusion spiked in Starshade as she…

LEAPT…

…back across the room, knife drawn to defend herself.

Slate already had their hands up and was speaking before she could get the enraged words out. "Woah. *Woah*. I'm not trying to stop you from contacting your friends."

Unconvinced, and with the distinct knowledge that Slate was a horse-shaped emotional minefield at the moment, she did not ease her combat stance. Her response was clipped as she growled, "Explain."

"Two years ago, the TPA seized a trailer full of those phones from a smuggling operation. We… the TPA… had a top secret program to install a variety of very subtle monitoring tools in the phones. Since then, we've been seeding them around Texas. Pawn shops and secondhand stores, even replacing stock in retail shops. Never trust that model of phone."

The knife slowly dipped as she considered. The Korps didn't use phones much. While it might have been clean, if it *were* compromised and the Korps had missed it, she could have just given them away. After a long moment, she sheathed the knife. But there was steel in her tone to replace her hidden blade. "I have a radio. I'm going into the office to call in. I've been out of contact for too long."

She searched those gray eyes for any sign of deception. Zala's warnings flashed through her mind. The seconds ticked by as the silence stretched. When she finally turned to walk away, Slate made no protest.

Chapter 12

Shear

Slate held his head in his hands, ear twitching as he heard indistinct voices muzzled by office walls and echoing acoustics. He kept trying to find that emotional center he had relied upon for so many years. But for once, the cool, calm waters of his serene armor did not come.

What am I going to do?

That was the real question, wasn't it? He was a wanted criminal now. He had thrown his life away.

— the wicked grin of the polecat, eager for the kill —

He was a traitor who had helped a villain kill a storied Hero.

— bloody orbs instead of eyes, filled with malice —

Maybe she's not dead? Even now a spark of hope guttered within him.

— the unmoving body, covered in crimson, suspended by impaling spikes —

SLAP

The sound echoed within the hollow room, and he could feel the impact of his own hand on his cheek burning from the impact.

*Get a **hold** of yourself. You are a Hero.*

Were…

Are! *Are a Hero. You acted to save lives. Being a hero is about sacrificing yourself for others. You did that. Now how do you **keep** doing that?*

And that was the question. Half-formed ideas flickered through his mind as he thought about avenues to escape his fate. But the ghosts of ideas simply chased each other through his mind, never quite connecting into each other. Nothing concrete had formed when the door to the office was flung open and Starshade *stalked* out with a dangerous glint in her eye.

"Did. You. *Know?*" Each word was filled with ice and fury well beyond anything he had heard from the tall bunny. But just as quickly, the passion faded slightly as her deep mahogany eyes searched the confusion on his face.

Not one to hide from danger, Slate asked, calmly and with concern. "Know what?"

There was icy steel in her tone, but it wasn't as intense or as targeted towards him now. "Your friends in the TPA are attacking. Did you know?"

A chill when settled over him. An all-out assault on the Korps would be war… And while all the Heroes bragged about how they would easily stomp out the Korps, that was not how War — *Real* War — worked. He had seen that firsthand, in mountains and deserts and choked city streets. The idea of going to War, *again,* was terrifying.

"Attacking the… Korps?"

The response was hissed. "Worse. Our dependents." Each word was devoid of any of the heat that so often filled her words. He listened with growing horror. "There are TPA Heroes roughing up friends and lovers. They are arresting *children* for the 'crime' of living in neighborhoods that don't hate the Korps. The Heroes that have pretended for *so* long to be the shining beacons of good are roughing up non-combatants. *Right. Now.*"

Slate opened his mouth but no words came out. *Was this it? Has it finally happened? What have those damn fools done?*

"So I'm going to ask you this question again. And *you* are going to tell me the truth. The *truth.*"

"Did." She stepped forward, a dangerous glint in her eye.

"You." An accusatory claw poked hard into his chest.

"*Know?*" Her eyes drilled into his.

He was speechless for a moment. Fear and confusion circled within him. Finally, he shook his head emphatically. "No! No. No, I didn't. I… I'm a hero. I don't attack civilians."

"Well, *Hero*. The Teepa is. They are doing that *right now*. As *Heroes*. So I need to go. I need to try to stop it." The cottontail stepped back, checking her gear with practice ease. Though her movements were stiff with anger and terror, they were, to his weathered eye, the movements of someone filled by… *ridden* by… the need to *protect*.

She looks like a hero.

She was clearly planning to walk out into the night. "Wait…!"

He saw her pause, that limber body going stiff at the surprisingly hoarse word.

"Wait. Is it... war?"

Starshade sighed, the hiss full of barely-contained panic and frustration. "Not yet. It's just Texas. Just Teepa. For now."

Slate almost sighed with the sudden wave of relief. But swallowed it down at the last minute. It would be insensitive and the situation was still horrible. Just... not War. *Yet.*

"I..." He trailed off. His mouth had started to speak before he considered his words. Their implications. A heavy weight started to settle into his heart. A spike of selfish frustration shot through him. *Each time I take a step, I'm forced to take another.* But the voice was small and distant, and the impulse died under the weight of fury and fear.

His silence stretched out as they both waited to see what he would say. The room was utterly still as if the universe held its breath to see which future would unfurl. As if all reality narrowed to this one decision in this forgotten warehouse.

"Not far from here is the brand-new headquarters of the Richardson Police Department."

The cottontail turned around. Her expression was still guarded. Still wary, still searching to see if he was the enemy. That last stung, but he didn't blame her. *Couldn't* blame her. "So?"

"So, it's a brand new building. A headquarters. Which means it has offices of all of the important senior officers. And what do commanders like to see?"

With narrowed eyes and venomed words, she asked, "Minorities in chains?"

He flinched at the barbed comment. "*Trophies.* Things that they can show off and say 'Hey, look at this.' And when the Heroes you work with come to you and say 'We have this extremely important thing we need you to hide, and it might win the war, and everyone nearby will be covered in glory when the histories are written?' Where do you think they keep it?"

Finally, he saw the Korps agent start to look thoughtful. "They should hide it in an abandoned building no one thinks about."

The horse shook his head. "They *should* do that. But it's not their weapon. They aren't *invested* yet. They keep it nearby. So they can rub themselves in glory."

"Did that one star Backchannel?"

The Percheron squinted, confused. "What?"

Starshade looked nonplussed. "Never mind."

Shaking himself a bit to pick the thread back up, the draft horse continued. "So, if you handed the police force a weapon that could, say, shut down the RCG network for a time? Where do you think that might be?"

Finally, he saw the spark of understanding light up those brown orbs. "Oh. Oh! Okay, yes. Yes!"

"And so *many* of their units will have been called away. Plus, at this hour, the place will be practically deserted."

"*Yes!* Perfect! I'll go there!"

"*We.*" The bottom dropped out from his stomach as he said that one, terrible word.

Her enthusiasm was pulled up short with surprise. "We...?"

"I'm going with you."

"But... you betrayed the Teepa. They are going to be looking for you. You might have to fight them."

Swallowing, he nodded. "Yes." One word. Firm and final and a portent of doom.

She searched his eyes again then. No longer the hostile visage of an enemy seeking answers, he saw surprised concern in her expression. And a bit of... admiration?

"Are you sure?"

Another nod, this one slow and sure and as steady as the mountains. Slate could feel his center. He had found his emotional touchstone once more. "Yes."

"But... why?" The bewilderment was rich in her voice. She clearly wanted his help. And he secretly thought she *needed* his help. But she would risk losing an ally during an assault on an enemy stronghold, just to double check on him. *Like a hero.*

"Because... because I'm a *hero.*"

And with that, he strode out into the night, leading her towards Richardson. Towards their fate. And, perhaps, towards a small detour first...

Slate stepped out of the rear door of the Party Metro costume store, to find Starshade staring at him in confusion. "Slate? Did you... did you break into a party store, and steal a licensed copy of your own uniform...?" The mix of shock and pride in her voice was... *unnerving*.

He rubbed the back of his neck and looked down at his brand new uniform, complete with stupid fucking *spurs* and stupid fucking *miniature cowboy hat*. The only thing missing was his badge.

"Not... exactly."

"Explain." The rabbit was not going to let him dodge this.

I've done worse tonight than spill some classified, if dumb, information. "So... Hero uniforms — at least, in the quality the TPA tenders for — are durable, but not immune to damage."

Starshade nodded and gestured for him to get to the point.

"We tend to break them. A lot."

Starshade looked like she was going to shove one of his stupid fucking spurs somewhere unpleasant if he didn't get on with it.

"The Teepa ..." he stumbled for a moment when he realized he had, for the first time ever, used the slang word for the TPA, but he continued. "The Teepa find it unseemly for a Hero to be wandering around the city, flopping out of their uniform because they didn't bring spare clothing."

"One of the perks of joining the Korps, frankly," Starshade mumbled with a pointed sniff.

A blush threatened to creep across his face, but he ruthlessly squashed it. "So, we have partnerships with costume companies, like this one, to keep a small selection of real uniforms in their stock rooms for us, if we need to quickly privately, change into something less... *indiscreet*, and more Heroic."

Starshade stared at him. Then she smiled. Then she *grinned*. Then, Slate found himself beginning to be *unsettled* by the glee radiating from the bunny. "Oh, this intel is going to be *fun*."

He really, *really*, did not like the manic mayhem in her tone.

"Also, I... made a phone call."

The delight instantly died, replaced with alarm. "To... who?"

He swallowed and hoped he would live long enough to explain.

"The Richardson PD."

Ice, with a touch of impending murder, began to fill her voice. "Explain."

He already had his hands up in a placating gesture. "They hadn't heard of my... impropriety yet. To them, I'm still one of the key Dallas Heroes. Which means that when I requested all available units to join me on a stakeout at UTD... well, they were all too happy to accommodate a request from an esteemed Hero. So that also means there may be less than a dozen people left in the entire HQ complex right now."

She pursed her lips in distaste, then slowly huffed out through clenched teeth and nodded. "I don't like that you took that risk without telling me. But... okay. If it works, it makes our lives easier."

They started walking through the night, with its chill bite. The headquarters weren't that far away, all told, and it would be easier to walk than find transport. But he could see the tension building within his smaller companion. He'd seen that before; someone getting so wound up with impending combat that they got trapped inside their own heads. He needed to distract her. And... he had some burning inquiries, at that.

"Starshade... may I ask you a question?"

She looked at him, searching his face for a hint, but finding nothing in his once more stony expression. Then she nodded.

"So, you're, um... transsexual?" He didn't know why he had suddenly asked *that*, of all questions. Part of him had been dying to ask it since he met her, admittedly, but the reason continued to escape him.

The Korps agent pursed her lips and he saw her shoulders tense. But, with an effort, she relaxed. "First, the term is *transgender*. Or just trans. Second, yes; is that a problem?" The latter words, he said in a tone that suggested that an affirmative might have bloody consequences.

Slate was silent for a long time, looking away. Honestly searching himself for the answer, and then, hesitantly, answering: "No. I... don't think that it is."

She took a while to respond, the silence turning curious. "Why do you ask...?"

Slate grasped the air, as if trying to capture the question he wasn't sure how to form. "How," he began, but it wasn't right. "Why..." The question fragments hung helplessly; he did not even know how to form what he wanted to know into *thoughts*, much less words. Finally, his shoulders slumped, and he shrugged.

For her part, Starshade seemed to take pity on him. Her words were filled with patience, and the educational tone of a teacher. "For me, I knew at a young age. Or rather, I knew there was something *wrong* with my body. It didn't look right. It didn't feel right. When I stared into the mirror, it was like a stranger staring back. I felt ugly and wrong. It was worse when others called me handsome, because I felt like they were pitying me. Or worse, that I had fooled them. I could see what I really looked like."

Each word stabbed into some part of Slate he didn't understand and tried to ignore. But... he could empathize with her, at least. He nodded and stayed silent, except for soft noises to signal that he remained listening.

"But it wasn't just my appearance. I didn't get along well with the boys; I kept wanting to do other things, things that I *couldn't*, because everyone — my parents, my teachers, my peers — thought they were too 'girly.' Or too 'gay.' I couldn't explain *why* I wanted to do those things, but it hurt to be excluded. I couldn't repress any of it for long, though, and soon enough I was an outcast. I was isolated."

"But I had the internet. My parents were never good at it, and I got around their content restrictions easily. Turns out the filters were keyword-based and only used English words, so when I started learning Spanish from classmates, well, fluency was suddenly a burning goal. And then I started to learn that what I was feeling wasn't something wrong with *me*. I wasn't ugly, and I wasn't *broken*; I was trans. When... when I accepted that, everything finally clicked. Suddenly, I had context. I could *understand*."

"And... yeah, maybe I make it sound so simple, but it wasn't. I had my doubts. Heck, I *still* sometimes doubt. But when I started to embrace myself, I had a rush of euphoria. I was a *desert* and when I soaked up that tiny bit of rain, I bloomed with life. Being trans isn't all about dysphoria."

At his confused expression, she quickly explained. "Dysphoria is not feeling right in your own body." Slate frowned uneasily but nodded and she continued. "Being trans is often about euphoria. About the joy of embracing. Of being. Of loving your gender, and yourself. It's the greatest thing in the world when you realize yourself. And sometimes, *sometimes*, it makes all the pain worth it."

The stallion wasn't sure how to respond to that. He wasn't sure how to understand the massive wall he felt inside himself, or how the words felt too big for the inside of his head. The thought hadn't completely formed when he opened his muzzle to ask, "Do you think...?"

But the question died when they turned the corner, and the Police station was suddenly *right there*. The time for distracting conversation was over. All he could feel now was the enormity of his actions crashing over him and washing away all frivolous thoughts.

Chapter 13

Epoch

The edifice loomed in the night. Even early in the morning, with no one around, innumerable lamps were carefully positioned to light up and show off the imposing structure: a fortress of glass and tan stone, brand-new and expensive. With a jaded eye, she looked around, seeing the older buildings and shops. "Slate, is this whole area Middle Eastern?"

The horse blinked at her. "And Chinese. There's a wonderful Asian mall just north of here, with a lot of restaurants; best ramen in the city, too."

The Korps rabbit looked back at the Police department. "Fucking typical. Racist bastards."

Out of the corner of her eye, she saw the Percheron flinch at the word. "Uh… what do you mean?"

She took a moment to eye them, a frown tightening her lips. She took a moment to remind herself that the Hero might not actually understand. "Look around, Slate. Worn, but solid, buildings, hosting beloved shops. Lifelines to their community." She gestured sharply to demonstrate her point. "Look at the signage. I see writing in Arabic, Chinese, and Japanese. And here, *right here*, is where they decided to put… *this*. This Western, expensive, *imposing* police headquarters, with nonsense corporate art out front?"

"They just replaced the previous building," her companion offered weakly, a troubled look in the horse's eyes. "They already had the land…"

Starshade snarled and stared up into those gray eyes, "*Even worse.* The building that doesn't match the cultural heritage or history of the people around it. They *just* built this, and it makes no effort to fit into the neighborhood. Not even a little bit of *inspiration* from the architecture and no attempt to *connect* with those under its watchful gaze. Do you know why?"

She didn't give the fallen Hero time to respond, throwing her arm wide to encompass the headquarters. Though she kept her voice low, her words were quick and filled with restrained righteous fury. "Because *this* isn't about helping the community. It's not about protection. It's about *projection*. It's about telling a vulnerable population 'We. Are. *Watching*. You.' That's the whole point. *That's* why they built this."

A clawed finger poked into that broad chest for emphasis, causing the giant superhero to flinch back. "You don't build *this* in the middle of someone's life by accident. This was intentional bigotry, the worst kind. The kind where upstanding citizens of the *right* background won't see anything wrong with it, but the targets of the message read it loud and clear. Slate, *this* is what you upheld. *This* is what you protected."

Slate was clearly taken aback by the tirade. She watched them look at the structure with new eyes, searching for a rebuttal. The horse, breathing quickly, swallowed and opened their mouth to speak. But after a moment of seeking a counter-argument that never came, those massive shoulders sagged. She searched gray eyes intently for a long moment as the fallen Hero squirmed. She desperately wished she knew the direction of those thoughts, but she finally had to let it go for now.

After a long moment of uncomfortable silence, Slate gestured, changing the subject to the task at hand. "We need to circle around. The loading dock is back that way; easiest way to get in. We'll be seen on camera, but it's not like we're trying to keep our identities secret, and it's unlikely to be actively monitored closely enough to alert anyone in time."

They walked in silence as they skirted the edge of the station, using the nearby buildings to screen their approach. No one appeared to be around at the early hour, but they were taking basic precautions against casual observation. Starshade was pleased that Slate seemed to be considering her words, and she noted the massive Percheron was looking thoughtfully — perhaps with fresh eyes — at the surrounding buildings.

For her part, Starshade could feel a growing anticipation from the fact that so many of their answers lay inside. As they ducked through a residential area along the back of the station, she started activating systems of her suit. A desperate longing surged within her for ROSE, or even a late-model smartphone, that could have tied her systems together and given more integration, but she would make do. Her goggles stayed dark, but a primitive HUD appeared, showing basic statistics about the area. Some of the basic adaptive armor features were functional, though in a manually-toggled, bare-bones state, and she prayed she wouldn't need them. Simple metrics about her own body were displayed too. Without ROSE, she had to monitor these things herself, but at least she had *some* data.

Deft hands checked her gear, mentally cataloging her remaining tricks. Pouches were half-opened to allow secure storage but quick access. The small radio, her last precious connection to the Korps, securely and discreetly stowed on her side. The throat mic was hidden under her suit, but she hated the earbud and stretchy cord she was forced to use. A frown grew as she realized how few throwing weapons she had remaining, but she would just have to be careful and creative. She patted the trusty dagger on her thigh, more for comfort than any fear it was missing.

The facility was ringed by a high privacy fence. *Because Overlord forbid anyone be allowed to watch what the police get up to.* It was there that they paused, backs against the wall. As Slate started to peek over, she put a paw on their bicep to stop them. With a flick of a hidden switch on her dark RCGs, the tips of her ears warmed slightly under their metal caps. Video feeds sprung to life in the corner of her vision, a disorienting riot of color and movement at first, until her brain could resolve the new information. Then she let her ears stand up, the tips just barely above the concrete. Now, with no more than the tips exposed, she could peer into the station motor pool.

Starshade's bright teeth flashed at the new capability. *Zala will still rue her treachery, but this is cool as hell.* After a few moments of toggling through camera modes, she tapped her companion's meaty forearm to signal that the coast was clear. With the casual ease of trained athletes and capes, both leapt over the barrier and into the empty yard.

Then they were both running. She was quiet and swift, trained operative as she was. But she winced with frustration each time a heavy metal horseshoe impacted asphalt behind her. She knew that Slate was running as quietly as possible, but the Teepa uniform was not designed for stealth. Heroes did not hide. *Not with those stupid fucking spurs, they don't.*

But no one was around to see them, dashing across the open lot to reach the loading bays. As they neared their destination, the horse motioned her to the side of the doorway. At the last moment, she pirouetted to press her back to the wall next to the heavy fire door, as the horse mirrored her motions on the other side. Then those gray eyes were looking at her, waiting for her signal. Starshade was quietly thrilled that they had fallen into working together so naturally.

She took a moment to listen through the door; there was nothing, and she nodded to her companion that the coast was clear. She started to reach for the tiny lockpick set, but as she did so, the Percheron clearly misunderstood the plan for how to get through the locked door. Slate reached up, grabbed the top hinge, and — with a loud pop of metal — casually pulled the door out of the frame.

Starshade stared for a moment, mouth agape, while her companion casually propped the warped scrap metal against the wall next to them. *Dear sweet Overlord, I forgot how strong they are. I'd love to watch them bench press a car, see how those incredible muscles ripple...* She shook her head, trying to clear the tantalizing image while the needs of the mission called. **Stop daydreaming***, you stupid, slutty bunny.*

Embarrassed at the track of her thoughts, she refocused on listening, trying to hear if anyone had overheard that little living ballistic-breaching-maneuver stunt. Then one ear dropped to the side, giving her a peek into the cargo receiving room. Clear. *This place must really be empty, if no one was around to hear that.* As much as she hated to admit it, Slate had made the right decision with that call.

At her signal, her equine companion cautiously entered the building, scanning for trouble. The cottontail quickly followed, setting her ear cameras to a 360-degree view in thermal vision. She found that mode wasn't quite as disorienting, and the sharp color difference alerted her quickly to body heat. Without a word, the disgraced Hero gestured for her to proceed down a hallway to the right.

The corridor was all new concrete and fresh, unworn paint in bland colors, all overlit by too many fluorescent lights. The whole design set her fur on end, and the buzzing of the overhead glowing bulbs drove a deep discomfort within her. Everything about this place screamed *oppression* and *control* and she hated it.

Turning a corner, Slate paused and gestured at the end of the corridor. The hallway ended in a T-intersection, with a door directly in front of them. In a low voice, her companion rumbled: "In there."

Excitement and urgency ramped up until Starshade couldn't take it anymore; this place was getting to her, she had too much energy, and she just had to *run*. Moderating herself only through sheer force of will, she started jogging ahead. Heeled boots made little noise on the concrete floor from her stealthy stride. She was just so ready to have this nightmare *over*.

As she neared the intersection, a hamster in blue and silver spandex stepped around the corner. She barely had time to register the leveled barrel of a shotgun with the muzzle that yawned about twelve kilometers wide. Then her world was pain as the world-ending *BOOM* assaulted her ears and her chest exploded in agony.

═══

Slate smiled to himself as the young rabbit started to jog ahead. He could sense her eagerness, and he too was glad they were almost at their goal.

But then the bottom dropped out of his stomach as the figure stepped around the corner. It all happened so *fast*. The boom of the 12-gauge echoed painfully in the hallway. The horror of seeing the Korps agent stumbling from the impact. She staggered from the blow. A second blast roared and Starshade… stopped. All movement just… ceased. She hung there, in the air, suspended at the moment of impact. That horrible moment stretched as the rabbit was trapped as if in amber. Frozen in time.

His focus snapped back to the hamster, and his mad grin. Gone was the officious bureaucratic sniveling of Manifest Destiny's new assistant. The shotgun, and that feral rictus, turned upon him next. "Hello, Slate. I don't think we've been properly introduced. I'm Erstwhile. And this is what happens to *traitors*."

A third report deafened him, this time it was accompanied by pain as 8 lead balls slammed into his chest. Slate reacted with little more than a grimace and looked darkly at the Ciscaucasia hamster. With a deadly calmness, he casually reached up and brushed himself off, showing how little impact that blast had on the super. He was the one that was supposed to take damage for others, after all.

Confronted by this nondescript rodent and finally given a name, a few details started to flood back. From the El Paso division, the Hero could fill an area with time spheres. Anyone touching them would be encased in a bubble of slowed time that would entrap them for a while. Slate would have to be very, very careful.

"Who are you again? I don't seem to recall." He noted with satisfaction the rodent's eye twitch at the casual disregard.

The hamster growled in agitation. "Erstwhile! I just told you that."

Slate affected a casual shrug while watching his opponent's estimation of his intelligence fall. It was a tactic he had used many times to play into the low opinion so many had for heavies. He had to be careful to hide his true assessment, lest a shrewd gaze give the game away.

He was trying not to think about his companion. He couldn't help her now. Worse, if he himself was bubbled, there would be no help for either of them. But Slate was nothing if not a veteran of many fights, some with far higher stakes. He schooled his expression, adopting the emotionless professional mask he had worn for so long. He knew it was working when Erstwhile was suddenly nervously glancing over the shotgun that had done so little. The aide was clearly off-balance, as the situation started to deviate from his expectations.

The horse slowly began to reach both hands straight up. He forced down the impulse to smirk when he saw the spark of hope in the hamster's expression; the bureaucrat was desperate to believe Slate was simply surrendering, and such fantasies flashed plainly across the tan, fuzzy face of evil. But his hands instead plunged through the drop ceiling tile above. Powerful hands pulled it apart as white fragments and dust rain down around him.

"You think you have all the cards. Starshade trapped. A corridor in front of me filled with your little mines. A shotgun that makes you feel so *tough* even after its limited impact. Up against little more than one big, dumb horse. But, you see, I've learned a little something from that rabbit."

Will Erst looked confused. Super fights usually followed a script, and Slate was breaking all the rules. *Like a supervillain,* he acknowledged to himself. A real veteran of the business, someone who was out on the streets, would have learned to adapt and prepare. Real cape fights were *filled* with the unexpected. But this Ciscaucasia hamster was clearly a bureaucrat and a pencil pusher; he would have received a combat rating, probably trained occasionally, would fight — mostly when called in to join a roster of dozens, for larger operations, no doubt — but did so as a bully, and never *seriously* enough to understand how to adapt. Slate was not fool enough to think that made the hamster harmless; far from it, there was great danger in the foolish and half-trained. But it did mean that he had walked into Slate's verbal trap.

"What's that?" he asked.

"*Throw shit.*" His arms shot forward, throwing fistfuls of pulverized tile dust in wide arcs in front of him. The dust filled the hallway, catching in those little pockets of time. Then Slate was *charging,* dodging past the first few time traps, suddenly plainly visible from their coat of ivory powder.

For his part, Erstwhile recovered quickly. The shotgun came up and barked twice more. The first blast snapped through the air as it barely missed the horse's head; the second should have taken him in the face, had the pellets not hit a time bubble and hung as a suspended lead constellation in the air.

Now, the Percheron utilized the *real* lesson he had learned from Starshade. One massive hoof planted, cracking the brand new concrete, and he changed direction. Suddenly he was slamming his shoulder into the wall, crashing right through it; drywall, shattered timber, and several electrical cables blasted into the next room. The structural supports failed to even slow the gigantic horse.

Slate barely registered the dark server room he had begun charging through. The tiny green and red LEDs acted as beacons to guide his steps. Two more deafening blasts punched tight clusters of holes through the panel between him and his target, as the hamster blindly fired.

Slate bunched his legs and *leapt.* Though nowhere near as skilled or acrobatic as his counterpart, super-strength made up the difference. When his gray form punched through the wall once more, it was near the ceiling, above the hastily-deployed time spheres that caught the falling debris. He sailed above the panicked, snapped shot from the hamster.

The fallen member of the Pegasus Phalanx knew that if the hamster had been a veteran of super fights, he would have changed position the moment Slate broke contact. He would have held his power in reserve and used that to try to counter the inevitable attack. But Erstwhile was not the badass he had always assumed he was. His inexperience left him unable to avoid the sickening **CRUNCH** as nearly a ton of super-strong draft horse crashed into the bureaucrat.

Starshade stumbled back in pain from the second impact. But Slate was suddenly there, catching her and lowering her gently to the floor; confusion reigned, as she tried to figure out what just happened. Paws came up to her belly, frantically searching for blood. Only then did she register the shushing noise.

Wild-eyed, she searched the Percheron's face, hovering close to her own. Seeing reassurance and calm, she relaxed enough to finally understand the words she was hearing. " — little one. It's okay. *It's okay.* You're fine. Your armor stopped the shot. You're fine. *Woah* there." By centimeters, slowly, she let herself relax.

Her ribs *ached* and she could only imagine the bruise now spreading under her fur. Under control enough to think, she finally looked around. There, kneeling on the floor three meters away was the asshole who had shot her. Only... both his arms were visibly broken, and his wrists were tied together, with a... mangled and twisted shotgun...?

"What... What the fuck happened?" she squeaked out in what she figured was a perfectly reasonable tone of voice.

"Easy there." Slate tried again, unconvinced about the reasonableness of her tone of voice. Two strong hands gently cupped her cheeks and turned her face back to look into those gray eyes. "One thing at a time." He held her gaze for a moment, then spoke clearly and succinctly. "Time manipulator. Has the ability to create temporal mines. Touch one, and you get frozen in place, pulled out of time for about fifteen minutes."

"Time..." She blinked. *Fuck.* But with difficulty she got herself under control. *ROSE, I wish you were here.* "Okay. Okay. So I've been *out*, basically?"

"For about fifteen minutes. Asshole behind me is Erstwhile. He shot you, twice. Your armor stopped it." All that tracked and she tried to nod, and failed, because the pony holding her face was roughly as immovable as a mountain.

She was getting her breathing under control now. "Okay. What else?"

"Please, don't kill him."

She wanted to protest that she wasn't going to... but now that she had been told not to, she really *did* want to. With effort, she pushed down her instant contrarian impulse and decided it would hard to explain to Slate that she wouldn't really have done so, even though she really wanted to, and —

"...Please, Starshade."

Right, I need to answer. "I won't kill him. I'm not that kind of villain."

— *bloody thorns piercing an unmoving body* —

Or maybe I am. But she wrenched herself out of that line of thinking, lest she lose herself completely. Then Slate stood up and, with the gentle, implacable strength she had come to know, drew her inexorably to her feet. It took a moment of wobbling, and a silent thanks to the draft horse for the moment to steady herself on those tall heels, before she finally had her balance back.

Should I reconsider high heels for combat? No. No, I should not.

When she finally felt steady, she turned to scowl down at the Teepa thug. "Asshole." She didn't have *time* for this. She had to get into that room. It was right there, and they had lost so much time.

"We almost had you, bitch."

Starshade stopped in her tracks and slowly turned to face Erstwhile. Her tone was ice and she started to clip her words. "What did you say, you fascist piece of shit?"

The Ciscaucasia hamster sneered up at her, his teeth covered in his own blood. "In the bank. You were so easy to lure there. And you fell into the trap so easily. If you hadn't gotten lucky, your bullet-riddled corpse would have been one of my fondest memories."

And there, in that hallway, staring into the manic eyes of that hateful TPA agent, it suddenly clicked.

— *Stepping out of the vault, carefully. Cautiously. A sudden silence and bootsteps and explosions and glass and gunfire* —

"You ..." She started but didn't need to finish. With sudden clarity, she understood. *The lost time. This asshole was* **there**. *He filled the bank with those time mines. I stepped into one, so they had time to get everyone in position. That's why the computer fan stopped. That's why...*

"I heard bootsteps. But... those weren't the first steps ..." A chill ran down her spine, a dawning realization of just how desperately narrow her escape had been. "Those were the last." Had the cops been two seconds faster, she would have had no warning.

Two seconds faster, and Erstwhile would have had his fondest moment.

Fury and terror and *grief* crashed through her and jumbled together into an indistinct mass of internal pain. Slate's arm was suddenly wrapped around her chest, holding her firmly, anticipating the need to stop her. He needn't have bothered. Even in the midst of this internal maelstrom, she wasn't going to give the hamster the satisfaction. Her words were as barbed and cruel as her mother's thorns. "You *failed*. You had this whole private army of oppression, and you *failed* to stop one, lone cottontail." A cold rage suffused her words further. "There are a thousand of me, and more every day. You won't stop us. You *can't* stop us."

That infuriating smirk remained on his face, as if the threat were expected. But Starshade wasn't done. "And don't forget, when all this is over and your bosses want someone to blame, they are going to look for the *first* person to fail. Like the one person who couldn't catch... One. Single. *Bunny*."

Then she spat in his face, and it was the most satisfying thing she had ever done.

Ten Minutes Earlier

Slate stared at the frozen form of the Korps agent. Her expression of shock and pain was clear. But he couldn't *do* anything. Not yet. He had gotten as close as he dared to the time bubble and it didn't *look* like the pellets had penetrated, but three still hadn't impacted and it was so hard to tell with her black bodysuit.

The figure kneeling at his feet must have been in severe pain, with two broken arms that had still been brutally tied together with the twisted remnants of his shotgun. His expression showed none of that, however. He was calm. Almost... smug. The look in his eyes unnerved the hero.

Another minute passed and the unease grew. All he could do was wait and fret and hope. The silence was jarringly broken by a soft, mad chuckle that escaped his prisoner. The urge to scream 'what' surged within him, but Slate was made of sterner stuff and he didn't snap or quickly react. Calmly, after a moment, he asked his question. "Have something to say?"

"Slate dies on the roof." Five simple words, said with barely suppressed mirth, drove a spike of fear through his heart.

"What?"

"I know what happens next. Slate dies on the roof." The words were said so calmly. So... *happily*. And a cold chill gripped his heart.

"What... roof? When?"

The hamster smiled at him with malice and glee. "Soon. You'll see."

"I don't believe you," Slate lied.

"Yes, you do." The refutation was as calm as it was unnerving.

There was a moment of silence as Slate tried to process this sudden omen of doom. He watched the lackey's face intently, searching for some hint that this was a fabrication, finding none. For his part, the aide turned his attention to Starshade.

"They will offer you three choices."

The change in topic was sudden and the details were important here. "Who? Starshade?"

"The Korps. If you take the wrong path, they will offer you three choices."

His mouth ran dry. "If? That might not happen?"

A dry chuckle filled the hallway. "It might not. If you die first."

Not as comforting as he had hoped. "What are these three choices?"

The hamster smirked at him. "That would be telling." The horse growled in terror and anger, but it had little impact on Erstwhile. Nevertheless, he seemed to relent after a moment.

"If you believe them, if you accept their offer... they will hypnotize you. They will bind you. They will mutilate you. They will torture you. You will suffer humiliations that you can't even imagine." Slate tried to speak but could find no words to respond to the calm recitation of his fate. "And Slate dies on the roof."

The Percheron stared with open terror at the hamster kneeling below him. Both of his arms were mangled wrecks forced together by twisted iron. But it was the horse that felt no control over the situation and no escape from this casual pronouncement. The words echoed in his head.

"The bubble is about to pop. Time to go to her like the poor, doomed traitor you are."

Slate could find no words as he numbly turned to catch a falling star.

Chapter 14

Fissure

Starshade carefully stepped over the battered door, following the large mustang into the dark room. She could tell from body language that it was not good news, but it wasn't until she saw that the room was empty that the bottom dropped out of her. *Empty.*

The device wasn't there. The small room was completely bare. There was no RCG jammer, no obvious, giant, clearly-labeled red self-destruct button, no conveniently logged-in computer terminal that could access the root OS. Just an empty room.

Fuck, fuck, fuck, fuck. The refrain ran through her head. Frustration circled distress within her. The rabbit held her breath, forcefully wrenching her thoughts out of the spiral. *Okay, get it together. It's not here. It's important to track it down. You know better than to assume everything goes to plan. So, stop panicking, and focus on adapting.*

Starshade exhaled weakly. "Slate… we need to find where this thing went."

For their part, the horse had remained silent. "The officer in charge when I delivered this thing was Lt. Jordan Travers. Kind of an asshole, always barking orders even when they were clearly wrong." The horse tapped their chin in thought. "A lieutenant would have his office upstairs with the rest. Bet you he does all his work there, to appear *important.*"

Starshade nodded. It was a good place to start. *I need to check in.* She hated checking in without much to report. Her instinct was to wait until she *had* something. But this was still a police headquarters and so much could still go wrong. The Korps *needed* to know the weapon was missing, even if they didn't know where it was. Even if it felt like she had *failed.*

She held up a finger to Slate and reached up to activate her throat mic. For the second time in as many minutes, there was… nothing.

No, please no.

No click. No beep. No faint electric static that accompanied a living radio connection. Just… nothing.

Frantic paws reached for the tiny radio module clipped to her side and found only plastic shards. With trembling hands, she pulled the mangled device off her suit and stared at it with dawning horror. This had been her last communications link to the Korps. This had been her last way to get help, or to warn them. Once again, she was alone.

Alone.

Tears suddenly threatened to overtake her. Her heart ached, as the ruined radio slipped through nerveless fingers —

— And then she was enveloped by the massive horse. Incredibly strong arms enfolded her gently into the massive form, holding her. She hugged back fiercely, thankful for the unexpected support.

They held that pose for a few moments before her brain kicked in again. Reluctantly, she pulled away. The Percheron looked faintly embarrassed, but she could see a hint of moisture in those gray eyes, and suspected the fallen Hero might have just had their first real hug in… too long.

She steadied her voice. "Okay, radio's dead. If we can't find a way to communicate, it's all on us. We need to stop this. And we need to know what *this* even *is*." At some point she had moved to simply assuming that Slate was in for the long haul. *And it's working so far. I don't want to give them the chance to challenge that assumption, in case they realize they have a choice in the matter. I can't do this alone.*

The draft horse nodded. "We've taken too much time and made too much noise. It's a miracle we haven't been discovered yet. We need to be careful, and we need to be quiet."

"Says the pony with the *stupid fucking spurs*."

Starshade gave the grumbling horse a smile, though one still ringed with frustration and urgency and just a touch of desperation. With an overly courteous wave, she gestured for her companion to lead the way to the offices.

The heavy horse stepped out of the stairwell onto the top floor. His metal hoofbeats, muffled as they were by the industrial carpeting, seemed to carry him forward without his input. Vinyl tiles were left crushed and deformed behind him with each pace. For once, Slate didn't feel bad about ruining new flooring. He even reveled a bit in that tiny feeling of rebellion. He had spent so much time struggling to live up to his own impossible standard that he had never really asked himself *why*.

His thoughts trended darker as he realized that he had spent so much time turning away from the suffering of others, suffering *he* caused, simply because he wanted… *needed* to be a hero. A *Hero*. So much of his life had been a struggle to uphold duty and honor, because that was the only way he knew to be… *good*. And to be *good* had been all he had ever wanted.

But over the last few hours, his worldview had been challenged so many times. This bright and impulsive disaster bunny kept finding new ways to reveal the world to him. Reality felt… tilted, and fragile, as if his entire self were on the edge of shattering. But the entire evening had been a series of frantic moments, with too little time in between to really think; each moment seemed to lead into the next.

His gaze fell upon the display cases peppered around the room, heralding their approach to the offices of the *important* cops. Each glass and wood enclosure was filled with trinkets and the physical detritus of institutional memory. Stormy thoughts swirled through Slate as he began to wonder just how many of these trophies represented dark realities. He couldn't shake the dawning horror that much of his own past — his own triumphs — were instead deeply shameful moments.

Then he stopped dead in his tracks as his gaze fixed on a small, unassuming amulet with a faint green glow. Slate gazed dumbly at the object that should not have existed, trying to make sense of why something so dangerous was casually on display. The brass plaque blandly stated that it was on loan from the Texas Protectorate Assembly, with no details to indicate what it was, or why.

Starshade took a few more steps before turning back, clearly wondering what had distracted her companion. She opened her mouth to ask when an office door opened across the room. Badly startled, Slate froze, turning to staring across the room filled with trophy display cases at the startled armadillo in the RPD uniform. He searched for a quick way to keep the officer from sounding the alarm that didn't involve hurling a display case through him. The armored mammal was already reaching for the radio clipped to his chest, when Starshade was suddenly...

THERE...

...with her arm wrapped around his throat, and her heeled boots clamped around his thighs. They both went over backwards with a thud and a choked gurgle.

Slate didn't know what to do, or how to feel, as he watched the cottontail choking out an officer of the law. He gave rapt attention to her intense, desperate expression as she focused utterly on the task, and the obvious, trained strength of her honed body as she controlled the panicked struggles. The ineffective way the cop pulled at her elbow to dislodge it from his neck, and the cold, professional — but not cruel — look in her eyes, as she simply did what had to be done. It was over in moments as she expertly cut off the sergeant's blood supply.

The old warhorse was troubled by what he watched. Except... as he slowly came to realize, he wasn't. Instead, what bothered him was that it *didn't* trouble him. *It was actually... kinda hot.*

That last thought was confusing, and he didn't know what to do with it, so he buried it, deep down, and moved along.

He didn't have to ask if Starshade's prey was still alive. The fact that she had rolled the body off her (and was immediately tying his limbs with his own zip ties) was answer enough. Jaw set, Slate shoveled complicated feelings away for later consideration, then pragmatically walked across the room and casually picked up the trussed form of one Sergeant Stokesberry. The cottontail grinned at him with pride as he unceremoniously tossed the bound cop in his own office. The Korps gremlin was already holding a key that she had somehow gotten from *somewhere*, and locked the door.

They looked at each other for a moment. Slate was still troubled, but the rabbit flashed him a bright and happy look before turning to head into the office labeled 'Lt. Travers.'

Starshade nervously glanced out the office window, grimacing at the lightening of the sky. While sunrise was some time yet to come, the world was going to start waking up soon... and they could be found at any time. Only the early hour, Slate's subterfuge, and a heavy dose of luck had kept them alive this long. *I have to hurry*, her thoughts urged, but she reined in her panic.

The computer was unhelpfully off. *Too much to wish he was still logged in.* A claw poked the small button on the side of the PC. She nearly jumped out of her fur at the loud Windows startup sound, and glared with dark hatred at the cheap plastic speaker that had betrayed her. The off button was right there; she could have simply pressed it and silenced it, or even turned down the volume. But such treachery deserved no such mercy.

As the monitor scrolled the random computer gibberish all systems displayed during bootup, her gloved hand wrapped around the offending speaker. She pulled it off the desk and, with large, sharp teeth, cleanly *bit* through the long cable. She was sorely tempted to dismantle the plastic scrap, but tossed it in the trash bin instead. The screen was displaying a simple page asking for the disk encryption code.

The whole point of this code was that no one without it could even *reach* the operating system, let alone enter it. The disk drive was protected against anyone accessing the files if they didn't have the PIN. But, helpfully, it was written on the quarter-size Post-it note and pasted to the monitor, and the cottontail suppressed a snort.

Honestly, I have never seen this size of Post-it *used* **except** *by system administrators writing down encryption keys.*

Slate kept nervously looking into the open area beyond the door, and back to the screen. For her own part, Starshade wanted to scream at the computer to move faster. This whole 'waiting for a system to boot during the middle of a high-stakes infiltration where too much had already gone wrong' thing was a nightmare. *I bet this is why Backchannel retired*, she mused.

Sorely missing ROSE, it was up to her to calm herself. *Getting nervous doesn't make systems respond. Well, except maybe for Steve.* She had met the mouse technician once, during her time at KDS. He acted as tech support for the entire base and was occasionally sent to other sites when demand was high enough. Codenamed Tier 4, his superpower was that he could solve any coding or system problem, but *only* if another engineer called him over for help once they had tried everything themselves. Then, while the harried rodent stood over them, they just had to try the same thing they had just been trying and it would, bizarrely, work. This understandably made him of immense value to the Korps, and especially to synth personnel.

As such, Steve's day largely consisted of frantically sprinting between engineers across the entire base, showing up just long enough to 'fix' a problem. Rumor was that his nervous demeanor was necessary for his power to work, and that ROSE kept him at a constant state of almost-but-not-quite-breakdown; of course, ROSE refused to corroborate this persistent rumor. *She's just mad that we figured her out.*

Just as Starshade was about to start carving profanities into the cheap laminate desk (but before she had decided on what to start writing) the username and password prompt popped up. The username field was helpfully populated with '*jtravers*'. She then lifted the keyboard to check for a hidden sticky note there, too, finding nothing. *That would be too easy.*

She glanced around the desk and caught sight of the picture — a wedding photo between two tall, lanky red wolves; the woman was in a traditional, modest wedding gown with a dour expression, with the man in a police dress uniform, looking stern. *Delightful couple.* Her thumb touched paper on the back of the frame. *Ah, here's the note I was expecting.*

1488

She groaned in frustration, causing Slate to look over in alarm. "Are you not able to get in?"

The desert cottontail sighed heavily and brandished the sticky note. "Oh, I got it. I should have guessed, the bigoted piece of shit." When her companion looked blank, she groaned again. "1488."

The Percheron clearly had no idea what she was talking about. "What happened in 1488? It's a common number, I guess, but I never got the reference."

She shook her head. "It's not a year, it's —" she started, but stopped herself. "Okay, we do *not* have time for this. But you *seriously* need to look this shit up when all this is over."

Slate clearly wanted to ask more questions, but stopped with a troubled, thoughtful look. Finally, they nodded to the door. "I'm going to keep watch. Hurry. Be ready to run if we are discovered." Then the large horse was through the door, leaving her alone in the office to try her luck with an informed guess:

> Username: jtravers
> Password: password1488
> The Username or Password is incorrect. Try again.
> Username: jtravers
> Password: Password1488

On the second try, she was greeted by access to the operating system. *There's no such thing as security for people who believe that rules don't apply to them. Even when those rules are there to protect them.* The desktop background showed a poorly photoshopped image that included a busty bald eagle wearing an American flag bikini, while holding an AR-15, and wearing a red armband, several stylized skulls, and a frankly *tacky* number of thin blue line flags. Her claws bit into the desk at the panoply.

Before she could start planning violence, however, the email client loaded and filled the screen with open emails. The first few were unrelated, but the words 'Operation Magpie' caught her attention.

Let's see… Operation Magpie… There. She caught the keyword RCGs. This particular email was just a sparse status update. Her claws tapped out a quick search for emails, seeking out the oldest emails on 'Operation Magpie' and… there.

The full details of the program. Her eyes scanned the PDF, seeking out the inevitable Executive Summary. A chill spread through her heart as she started skimming the text, trusting her backup recording system was getting the details.

A weapon developed to shut down the RCG network for a short time… I already knew that. But it says here that disruption is… Phase One.

Phase One. The loss of the network had been terrifying for Starshade. She had been cut off from help and support. It had almost killed her several times and kept threatening to do so. To say nothing about how… *alone* she felt. The idea that it was just the *first* part of the plan scared her.

Developed by a Doctor Chad Shottington out of Biloxi…

Starshade snatched the picture frame from the desk and *twisted* until the frame snapped. She snatched the image from the debris as the shattered glass and cheap metal fell to the floor of the office. She *could* have used the stack of notepaper next to her on the desk, but she was not feeling that generous. She snatched a pen and started scribbling details on the back of the wedding photo.

Hero name is… let's see… Shotgun Surgeon. Inventor, gadgeteer type, relatively new. Kind of a mixed message with the name there. He's not even a medical doctor. Does he even use a shotgun? He's… Wait, stop. Focus. He's not important right now.

Her eyes scanned further down the page. *Where is Phase Two… There.*

Starshade's blood, already cold, filled with ice.

Phase Two: Eavesdropping The Korps Network

> If the correct asset can be obtained, we will be able to use the initial communication patterns observed during the reconnection to the network from a compromised pair of RCGs to create a backdoor into the network. While an attempt to make changes would risk detection, this will allow us to monitor ROSE communication with agents across a wide geographic area, resulting in the identification and tracking of the Korps infiltration network.

The Korps agent stared in stunned silence. *That… can't be true? … Can it?* She felt numb. The thought of the TPA being able to listen in on her communication with ROSE, that in *itself* was terrifying beyond words. It would allow the jackbooted thugs of the organization, and all their law enforcement partners, to listen to her innermost thoughts. *And if the Bradley Group or the PHL got this information… It would be a disaster.* Her breath came quick and shallow, fear riding her. She sat there longer than she wanted to admit, the untold misery unfolding in her mind. Then her fist slammed into her bruised stomach. Tears suddenly filled the corners of her vision, but the pain broke the cycle of panic.

Asset. It says they needed the right asset. I have to know what that is.

She quickly scanned more of the document, but didn't see details. A few searches in the email inbox, however, pulled up a bit more.

> Asset has been identified. Target is CODENAME Starshade. Genetic and psychic match to existing TPA Personnel. Profile is close enough to delay system rejection long enough for Phase Two to commence. Starshade's RCGs must be captured while BLACKOUT is still in effect. Fate of Starshade is irrelevant per the order of the Fort Worth Division Chief. Target risk assessed as low.

The Korps cottontail brooded on the words glowing before her. Her mood had darkened with pain tempered with the glowing embers of rage and fear. *They needed **my** RCGs? Because... genetic match... oh. Because Linda thought she could use me to destroy the Korps. She couldn't have me, so she would break me and anyone who dared support me. Even if it meant killing me. **Especially** if it meant killing me, I bet.*

She fumed bitterly at the evidence that her mother wanted her dead, but she already knew that. A chasm yawned within her, with the dawning dread that the fight in the warehouse hadn't just been a momentary rage. The email had been weeks before. *Planned.* Her mother had hated her so much that she held planning meetings with her coworkers about her daughter's murder.

Numbly, she scanned through detail after detail about Operation Magpie. Everything was so coldly bureaucratic, entirely bereft of any consideration about the fact that they were discussing the fate of a person. Of Fatal Thorns' *daughter*. Contingencies were laid out in stark detail describing the TPA's plans in case she was captured, or killed, without her RCGs.

Instincts screamed that she should simply run away. If she could run fast enough and far enough, she would deny the Teepa the chance to seize her and her RCGs. But doing so would doom too many of her comrades, because that vile damper, used at the right moment, could be disastrous; she had to act, to do whatever she could to thwart the TPA's war. Doing so would require every advantage, including the essential combat information her primitive, ROSE-less RCGs provided, no matter the long term risk.

Feeling a cold bitterness seeping into her, she glanced at the system clock. She could *feel* herself running out of time. *One last task.* She double-clicked on the remote server connection and ignored the watery distortion around the edge of the screen.

Starshade had expected some additional security but all that came back was a UNIX command prompt. The banner welcomed her into the Project Magpie Central Repository. She was no expert, but she did know enough to cause a little mayhem in a corporate system if the need arose on a mission.

First, to check my permissions.
jtravers@magpie:~$ su -
root@magpie:~#:

Starshade stared, her muzzle hanging open in shock. She now had complete and total access to the entire system. The security was *beyond* sloppy; there hadn't even been a prompt for a password! A quick scan showed hundreds of files relating to the project, most of which were code and documentation.

A loud **CRUNCH**, followed by a musical cascade from the room outside — the telltale tinkle that accompanied raining shards of glass — sent her leaping out of the chair, knife already in her paw. The muffled voice of Slate called out: "Hurry up, we need to *go!*" The infiltrator in her dearly longed to download these files… but there was no time. Sheathing her knife as she sat once more, she quickly checked to see what backups were configured… and was greeted by the backup configuration wizard.

Starshade was salivating now. It took moments to start the server purging itself. Assuming there were no backups, her actions might well have ended any hope of recreating the research. *And if the Korps can find and deal with the creator, this threat may be ended… if we can ruin the jammer that's out there right now.*

A blaring alarm deafened her. Red lights started flashing. *Out of time.* Damn.

But as she was about to spring to her feet, an open browser tab caught her eye. The Twitter icon was plainly visible as the second tab. She was out of moments, but she took the risk. Claws pounded the keyboard and she sent the DM.

@thinbluelupine: @magicmabelle TPA Dallas Headquarters. Send help. -Starshade. PS: The password to this account is Password1488.

She hoped it would get through in time. But time was up, and she just had to hope a single unsolicited twitter DM to her friend Mabel would be enough. With that, she closed all the windows she had opened, then her fingers found the key shortcut to lock the computer.

Suddenly, the massive form of Slate hurdled through the door, snapping the cheap wood in two. The obstacle hadn't even slowed down the draft horse's headlong run, as they stuffed something small and glowing green into the pocket of their hat. Gray eyes locked on hers as the Hero slammed into the office window... and went right through, in a rain of glass.

Two gunshots rang out, deafening in the tight confines of the office. A quick glance showed two uniformed officers brandishing sidearms at her and shouting something, but then she was...

SPRINTING...

...across the parking lot, with a wild horse right behind her.

Chapter 15

Landslide

Slate's hooves *slammed* into the concrete three stories below, cracks radiating from the impact that drove him to one knee. The blow barely slowed him down, as his immense strength pushed him through the momentum, with cement pulverizing to dust as he forced himself up and forward to race after the Korps cottontail. The chirp of an unlocked car, accompanied by the flash of brake lights, showed their destination to be a gigantic black pickup truck poorly parked in the visitor spots. Starshade was a blur as she sprinted towards their destination. Not even bothering to adjust course, she simply jumped and slid across the hood of a police SUV in her way.

That cruiser is positioned for quick pursuit...

Instead of following her, the Percheron planted one hoof, and ground to a halt. His fists plunged through the side windows of the vehicle, smashing through the armored glass that posed no impediment to the behemoth. Powerful hands wrapped around the reinforced frame, deforming the metal slightly, and ignoring the jagged shards that tried in vain to slash preternaturally tough flesh. A heartbeat passed as Slate centered himself, then every muscle in his herculean form tensed as he hissed out breath, straining... and *hurled* the Chevy Tahoe.

The SUV sailed through the air for twenty meters to slam into the corporate sculpture near the entrance. Moments before, the 'art' had been a bright blue steel monolith, evoking both a sunburst and a police badge. It crunched nicely as three metric tons of armored cruiser slammed into it. Debris and various toxic fluids rained down, but the deformed and ruined sculpture somehow stayed upright, holding its captive victim suspended in the air.

The fallen Hero had no time to revel in, or be horrified by, his actions. Shots started to ring out from the jagged hole he had jumped through moments before; pain blossomed from impacts, as several rounds slammed into his back. But he was sprinting again, sparks flying from his horseshoes with each thunderous step. Ahead of him, the rabbit was already in the driver's seat and throwing the truck into gear.

Powerful thighs bunched and, with a great leap, he was in the bed of the truck, rocking the pickup with the impact and deforming the corrugated metal. The customary two slaps on the roof proved unnecessary, as Starshade was already flooring it. Tires squealed for a moment as the heavy wheels spun for purchase, then the entire vehicle *shuddered* as the Ford F-250 surged forward to leap over the curve like a startled bull. Slate braced himself as best he could, thrown about by the bouncing as his ride smashed through the decorative topiary. Then they were on the deserted streets and speeding into the night.

Slate looked around the old parking lot as he hopped out of the bed of the truck. The dim light of old lamps struggled to push back the evening gloom. Most of the signs nestled against the grocery store were in Korean, but the shops clearly offered groceries and food. However, while the pair had quickly evaded the police, being a giant stallion wearing a TPA uniform — barely bracing himself in the bed of a pickup truck — was not the greatest way to keep a low profile.

He knew time was of the essence and was glad that Starshade had anticipated the need for a quick stop. The rabbit was clearly young and inexperienced, but she knew this business well already. The TPA knew little about her, classifying her as one of many low-level criminal operatives. He always hated that the Heroes seemed to only care about the strongest and flashiest of their opponents, disregarding those it ranked as low-power, as if such threats were to be easily brushed aside and forgotten about.

Moving quickly, he leapt over the side of the bed and, under Starshade's curious gaze, pulled open the passenger door to stare into the cab. The unmistakable scent of fresh leather and new car washed over him. While the average person might find the interior of the massively oversized truck incredibly roomy, Slate found no such comfort. The screeching protest of twisting metal provided a mock fanfare as he *ripped* the front passenger seat out of the truck. The former Hero of Dallas unceremoniously discarded the ruined luxury upholstery as he twisted himself into the cab, cramming himself into the backseat and awkwardly pulling the door shut. He glanced up to see the rabbit staring at him wide-eyed.

"What? I needed space."

"Actually, this is pretty common in the Korps. I'm just surprised to see *you* casually defacing the personal property of an *honored* member of law enforcement."

Slate snorted in a mixture of laughter and shame even as he tried to find his balance on his shattered emotional ground. "Where did this truck even come from?"

Starshade grinned devilishly. He could swear that she had pointed teeth in that mischievous grin. "Sergeant Stokesberry was kind enough to donate to the cause."

The horse looked at her blankly. "Who...?" he started, but the question slowly died on his lips. "Oh... that officer you choked out."

"That's him!" she confirmed with demonic glee.

The fallen Hero stared. "When did you...?" But the twinkle in her eye told him that she had stolen the keys while he watched her cuff the hapless armadillo. With a sigh, he let the matter drop and turned his attention to the streetlights passing by. Traffic was still light at this early hour, but more cars were on the road.

After a moment, he turned back to her, quizzical. "Where are we going?"

A grim line set on her muzzle and quiet determination filled her voice. "To destroy that jammer they've created."

"You know where it is?"

She cast a dark but inscrutable look at him. "Exactly where you think it is."

He looked at her, confusion written in his expression. "What?"

The rabbit sighed as she turned onto the service road. "If this was a story, where would it end? Where would the climactic final battle be?"

"Uh..."

"We're headed to the Dallas TPA Headquarters. We're headed home."

Slate stared at her. His muzzle fell open. He stared some more. Unperturbed by his desperate confusion, the shiny black pickup truck accelerated smoothly onto US-75 South. "But that's where…"

"Where all the Heroes are? No, actually. Remember? *They're* all out attacking innocent civilians. The place will have a token defense force *at best*. That's where they have the jammer. There was no way the TPA was going to let it languish in the basement of a Police Department, instead of having it on hand during their moment of glory."

The horse watched the sparse headlights pass as the truck roared its way down the highway. His thoughts turned back to Erstwhile, and the hamster's warning. He wanted to dismiss it, but he found the prediction still eating at his heart. Fear. The pronouncement had been made with such calm… such certainty…

"Starshade, can I ask you something? About the Korps?" Slate found himself asking the question before he even realized he was going to. But he forged on, heedless of his own surprise. "Are you really trying to take over the world?"

The Korps agent smirked at him. "Hell yeah we are." Her voice was tinged with pride and approximately zero shame.

He stared in horror. Starshade continued to lack anything resembling remorse.

"You… admit it?"

Laughter greeted his incredulous query. "Fuck yeah. Are you really telling me that *this* shit is the best possible way our world can be run? Basically everyone suffers, every single *day*, all so a few assholes can have more zeroes in their bank account. Soulless monsters who take everything, and are never satisfied."

Slate wasn't sure how to respond, but his response didn't appear to be necessary as the agent continued on. With each word, she became more passionate and more bitter.

"The government does worse than nothing. The whole *purpose* of the government is *supposed* to be to use limited resources to best serve the needs of everyone. Does that *sound* like our government to you? When was the last time you remember the government solving a problem? At all? No, their 'solutions' only ever make the problems worse, and every single time their plans seem to involve massive kickbacks to those same rich assholes!

"When was the last time you felt the government was not only supporting, but standing up for a minority? *Any* minority? When was the last time you felt the government was stepping in to stop people from being hurt or killed? Fuck, Slate, every year we are bombarded with reports about tech companies having cultures of sexual harassment so toxic that it's killing their employees. Name *one* where the government stepped in with a criminal investigation!"

Slate opened his mouth but his contribution was no longer required for this conversation.

"Even when they *do* investigate — which is extremely fucking rare, and requires massive civil rights violations — the most they ever do is levy a fine small enough that the company is still *profitable*. The *bastards* who made the choices, the choices that got people killed, are never inconvenienced in any way. There's no *accountability* for those in charge and there's no *help* for those that are hurt! *That's* what you were defending, with your stupid fucking hat. You're really going to tell me that this country is some… 'shining beacon of freedom' in the face of that? *Really?*"

Slate looked away first. He didn't like to *think* about the pain around him. He had seen it in a thousand places, and in a thousand faces. Far too often, the criminals and villains he fought had been driven to it by circumstance, and it had always bothered him; time and again, he had consoled himself with the hope that by simply being the most stalwart of Heroes, he was somehow making it better. But after his experiences with Starshade… he felt helpless. Hardly a net positive for anyone, he was far too aware that the only reliable result of his actions had been to increase the net amount of *misery* in the world. The shards of his righteousness ate at him as he stared at the city passing by above the vehicle.

It was only when he saw the sign for them to exit onto Spur 366 that he realized he had run out of time. He had to ask the next question immediately, before they crossed the Bridge To Nowhere and reached the TPA Headquarters. There never seemed to be enough *time*.

Slowly, hesitantly, he started to voice a question that had been troubling him since he let the agent go… so very long ago. "Starshade…"

he started before trailing off. She glanced at him with a touch of concern, her eyes dark behind the faintly glowing visor, but she remained silent. "The Korps... mind-controls people. I've seen Korps drones. They lack anything resembling free will. How... how can you support that?"

The truck swerved a little as the rabbit whipped her head over to stare at him briefly before turning her attention back to the road. He saw her chew at her lip for a moment. Finally, Starshade blew out a breath at the question, the sound filled with too many emotions.

"Oh... you should really be having this conversation with someone who can explain it better..."

— *They will hypnotize you* —

But Slate was shaking his head, granite entering his voice as he pressed. "This can't wait. And you don't seem to be a mind-controlled drone. Your connection to the... hive, or whatever, is down. But you're still fighting. I need to know *why*. I need to know how the Korps isn't *worse* than the TPA. And I need to know. *Right. Now.*"

The rabbit swallowed, clearly nervous. She slowed down a bit and fumbled to activate cruise control. Slate suspected this was to buy herself time as much as it was to devote more attention to the conversation. For a moment, the only noise was the distant sound of the truck smoothly gliding over asphalt.

"Okay... okay. So..." she started before trailing off.

The cottontail pursed her lips in clear frustration, but he steeled himself, waiting for her to continue. The difficulty the supervillain had in answering was driving that fear deeper. But he schooled his expression to stay implacable, patient as a mountain.

"It's complicated. The Korps does use hypnosis, and even mind control. But... the most important part of that is consent." The confusion must have been evident on his face as she continued. "Slate... the Korps doesn't do that without their permission. We don't strip people of identity and free will."

"But —"

"Let me finish. *Yes*. There are drones, a lot of them. They are completely devoid of those very things. But *we* didn't do that to them. They *chose* that. That was by *choice*."

"How could... why would...?" Slate was shocked enough he couldn't form the thoughts necessary to ask the question. It didn't make sense. Did it...?

"Because they wanted it. They want the safety of not having to make choices. They want the pleasure of serving. They want to be directed, and shaped, and to be of *use*. And drones don't just start at full drone! The Korps builds up to it with *lots* of opportunities for them to back out. And *plenty* of safeguards built in."

"But... why would anyone...?"

"Because some people just want to stop being themselves!" She gestured wildly out the windshield at the towering buildings around them. "The world has broken them so much and so deeply that they can't have peace, even in their own head! The only way they can be happy is to surrender their will to another! For others, it's because they can't get horrible thoughts, memories of past events, out of their skull —"

— One eye miraculously left in the skull, filled with pain —

"— Or because it makes them fucking horny as hell! It doesn't matter. It was *their* choice. And the most fundamental part of the Korps? The reason we exist? The reason we keep attracting so many willing to fight? Is because we offer *choice!* We offer the only damn place in this world that seems to care about *consent* anymore!" Slate couldn't remember when Starshade started shouting, but her voice was so full of frustration, echoing with a much deeper pain, that he wanted to hug her.

"Slate... that's why I'm with the Korps. That's why I'm out here fighting. And that hypnosis stuff? It's not just something that happens to *other* people. ROSE... the RCGs are in my mind, when they're active. They calm my thoughts if they race out of control. I have an AI that is more a mother to me than **Linda** ever was. I have my *best friend* in my head. She's there to calm me and soothe me and take care of me. She brings out the *best* in me. I will do *anything* to protect her. Not because she controls or forces me to do her bidding; I serve because I *care* about her enough that it's the *least* I can do.

"That's what these Teepa assholes have *taken* from me, Slate! This jammer? It's not just something that breaks a command and control net so I can't speak to my *boss*, or the next henchmen up the chain. They took my peace of mind from me, Slate. They took my *friend* from me! And they want to do that to fucking *everyone!*" She finally lapsed into silence, breathing a bit heavy. He stared at her as a flush started to tinge her ears as it so often seemed to.

"Sorry," she mumbled, the single word filled with regret and suffering and apology.

Slate held his breath at the outburst, not sure how he felt about her explanation… but he knew, in any event, that his companion was hurting. He just wasn't sure what to do about the pain and passion that radiated from her. They lapsed into an awkward silence as they crossed the single-arch suspension bridge.

As he stared at the imposing edifice of the TPA Dallas Division Headquarters, he tried to square her passionate words with his experience with the Korps, and with that ominous warning from Erstwhile.

Then a terrifying rictus of glee spread across Starshade's face.

"What are you doing?" Slate asked with alarm, as he was sharply reminded that he was trapped in a truck with a supervillain, no matter how young and earnest she was. Starshade's only response was a mad twinkle in her eye.

"Starshade, no!"

The desperate plea was all he managed before the rabbit slammed one high-heeled boot on the pedal. The engine roared as it started to accelerate. Gloved paws spun the wheel hard to the right. The vehicle lurched over the curb with a shudder, the Ford pickup gaining just enough air as they sailed off the side of the bridge to clear the protective bollards around the compound. *Almost.* Slate felt the jarring impact as the rear bumper was ripped off, catching at the top of the pillar.

Starshade continued to hold down on the gas, and the tires spun impotently in the air. There was a tremendous *jolt* as the pickup slammed into the ground. Something important-sounding snapped somewhere deep under his braced hooves, but it was not enough to slay the mechanical beast. The truck's tires spun as they hit the grass, kicking up massive clods of dirt, then — with a deep tremor that popped trim panels in the cab — found traction. The pickup hurdled forward across the manicured parade ground between the two main buildings. Then, with a maniacal laugh, the supervillain jerked the wheel to the right and the vehicle spun out. They corkscrewed across the perfectly-tended lawn, the wheels tearing into the soft grass and ruining the turf.

The black Ford wreck spiraled out of control, and all Slate could do was to hang on. Beside him, Starshade giggled with manic glee. The moment of chaos seemed to hang in the air… right up until the vehicle slammed into the topiary carved in the shape of Manifest Destiny, snapping the imposing sculpture and sending leaves flying.

The impact was jarring, but did not dislodge the stallion braced with his immense strength. The rabbit looked back at him. He had never seen her so happy and it, frankly, scared him more than anything else in the past day. "*Whatthehellwasthat?*" he panted out, in a rush of bewilderment, as he tried to conquer the dizziness.

"Fuck grass," was all she said. Then she was…

RUNNING…

…across the utterly *devastated* lawn.

Chapter 16

Epicenter

Starshade raced across the ruined parade ground. She wasn't sure where she was going, but she was a capable Korps agent, and she could figure this out — a feeling that persisted until she reached the front door of the larger building and discovered the door was locked. No amount of frustrated tugging budged the door. She glared at the little sign that read 'DOOR TO REMAIN UNLOCKED DURING BUSINESS HOURS,' as if it had personally slighted her. Still, she was just glad that she had schooled her expression like the professional she was, and wasn't *pouting*.

Steelshod hooves on the concrete heralded Slate finally catching up to her. "No need to pout," they said warmly.

... *Damnit*.

"Good instinct on the building though. Listen, before we get into this, we need to prepare. We might need to face Manifest Destiny."

She stared, uncertain if she had heard the horse right. "Wait... what?"

"If we're lucky, we get in, find the device, smash it, and get out. But... it's unlikely that we'll find it completely unguarded. And when the TPA is spread so thin they don't even have a receptionist on duty, who do you think that's going to be?"

The mirth drained out of Starshade as she considered the implications. "But... he's a *major* hero. He went toe-to-toe with *Madam Maximum* in his heyday. The only reason he didn't go national is that he was too bigoted for *the Bradley Group*."

"His duplicates are spread across the state, so there's a good chance he's here too." The Percheron's words were grim, though not as hopeless as she was starting to feel.

Starshade stared at the horse for several long moments. "How do you even fight the guy who can make endless copies of himself?"

"Here's the thing: they *aren't* endless. No matter what the media says. All the reports about his inexhaustible power? It's a lie."

"Wait, what?"

"Don't get too excited. While it's not as bad as it sounds, it's also worse that it sounds."

One paw rubbed her face with a frustrated groan. She looked at them, already exhausted by the pace of this conversation. "Slate, we do *not* have time for this twenty questions bullshit. Spit it out."

Slate looked sheepish, with a hit of apology, and urgency, entering their tone. "Sorry, this is just highly classified… and… so… *anyway*. During the Christmas party, he got drunk with our team. See, the thing is, he *does* have to tap a power source to create a duplicate. It's just not his *own* power source."

The rabbit blinked. "…What?"

The horse sighed but continued, more succinctly. "Ok, here's the deal. Manifest Destiny can tap the power reserves of *other people*. He uses *your* power to duplicate."

"And that's better *how?* He can sap your strength and I can't teleport!" She could not find any good news here and she was trying to keep that spark of alarm from spreading into a blaze of panic.

"Because, forgive me for saying, but you don't exactly have the biggest pool to start with. And he told me, after way too many Palomas at the big holiday bash, that he couldn't tap me at all. I'm a heavy. I don't *have* a power pool. My powers are just passive, always on, like Macho Poleax. There's nothing for him to use. So…?" Slate prompted.

"So he can't duplicate *much*. And even less, if I drain my own reserves!"

Even she could hear the growing excitement in her voice as a look of intense concentration crossed her face. *Do I drain them to zero so he can't feed off of me at all? Or do I leave a little bit for an early fight jump? What if it's not Manifest Destiny we fight? Then I'll have sacrificed my biggest weapon. Do I instead preserve my power and just resolve to rapidly jump if we do encounter that asshole?*

"If we do fight Manifest Destiny, if I can find the Prime, I can shut him down." Starshade wanted to ask how, but the pony continued on before she had a chance to ask follow-up questions. "There's been a lot of misinformation spread about him. That's been very intentional. He didn't want the Korps or even other hero groups to know the details. So forgive me if I say something you already know."

Slate was clearly embarrassed to explain the powerset of one of Texas' most famous heroes. But they didn't have the luxury of assumptions. *Something I should have learned long ago.* "First, he duplicates. Obviously. All his gear is duplicated as well. Here's the thing though. Those clones are not perfect. All the clones lack blood. They run on some caustic chemical instead."

"Wait, *only* the clones have that?"

"Exactly. The Prime bleeds. That's how we find him."

The rabbit nodded. "Making someone bleed is… dangerous. Even in a fight like this. What happens if something… happens to the Prime? Do the clones vanish? Wait, never mind. If that had ever happened, we wouldn't be having this conversation. I'm an idiot… Sorry." Starshade felt her ears burning at the dumb question.

"Actually, we do know. If Manifest Destiny Prime dies, one of the clones becomes the Prime."

The rabbit blinked in surprise. "Oh."

"But *only* if he dies. He can't voluntarily change which one of him is Prime. Oh, and one last thing: no one is quite clear if all his clones share one consciousness or if they are all partially independent, but they do have some kind of telepathic connection to share knowledge between them."

The rabbit nodded, clearly thinking through the implications. But as she pondered, it really did seem like they might have a chance. With limited clones, it would be a much more even fight.

She could feel a growing sense of excitement swelling in her heart. *We might have a chance to take down one of the biggest pieces of shit in the TPA. Not permanently, since he has clones already out there, but a big 'L' in his column would be a massive accomplishment. And getting to see the look on Zala's face when I tell her what she missed…* "Anything else?"

In response, Slate casually punched the entryway, which exploded inwards in a rain of splintered glass and shattered metal. The caved-in wrecks that had once been double doors bounced and skittered across the imported marble. "After you, Miss." There was a strange pause as Slate looked much more somber than they had a moment ago. "Our quarry is on the roof."

"Our quarry is on the roof." Slate said this with a heavy heart. Though he composed his expression and held a tight rein on his tone, he knew what this meant. Deep in his bones he knew that the roof was where all of this would end.

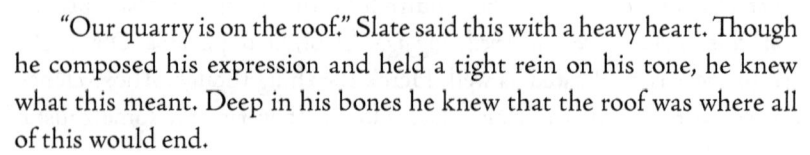

— *Slate dies on the roof* —

There was no point in searching the building, or hacking computer systems, or beating up a random graveyard-shift security guard. No matter what route they took, they would end up on the roof.

He had thought hard about not offering up this information. Delaying it while she figured it out somehow. He had briefly considered telling her to go up alone. He had even been sorely tempted to simply walk away. The weight of the moment bore down on his shoulders like an oil tanker. But, in the end, a hero did not turn away from danger... even if that danger was both certain, and fatal. Erstwhile had been certain of it, after all, but the job of a hero was to risk their lives so others may live. He might no longer be a Hero, but he would never stop being a *hero*.

Or... well... I guess I stop being a hero pretty soon, won't I?

— *Slate dies on the roof* —

Those five words haunted him. Doomed him. The roof would be his death. He just hoped it wasn't a futile one... that he could manage to save this impulsive cottontail. Or, at least, stop the jammer she feared so much. He wasn't sure he was convinced by her plea that the network, or even the Korps, was good. But he had been convinced the TPA was evil. Opposing that was... that was *enough*. Even if it meant he would never see the sun rise again.

Not that it's exactly a rich life worth saving.

His horseshoes rang with each step up the concrete stairs. He took them three at a time; his long stride and indefatigable nature meant the floors rapidly fell away from him. Each step was a step closer to death, but he had faced death before. In mountains and deserts and choked city streets, that specter had chased him. For her part the rabbit...

BOUNCED...

UP...

THE...

STAIRS...

...to burn out her energy, and to keep herself fresh for the fight to come. She couldn't know for certain it was a fight, though *he* was certain she suspected that was the inexorable conclusion to their harried night. But *he* knew. There was no *way* there wasn't something waiting for them. Not when...

— *Slate dies on the roof* —

Then they were at the thin metal door at the top of the stairwell. He tried to shake off his dark mood but couldn't. It had never been so... *certain* before. Starshade looked back at him with a question in her eyes, but he answered it, whatever it was, with a flawless Sparta kick. The crumpled metal bounced and skidded across the roof for a good ten meters, before bouncing over the edge of the building.

And there, as he expected... as he *feared*, was the expectant form of Manifest Destiny. The gray squirrel in the blue and silver uniform looked singularly unimpressed, from where he stood next to the empty helipad. The old hero's chest was decked with rows of pointless ribbons, proclaiming his overinflated valor in a hundred forgotten scuffles. He stood in the cool spring air, soulless black eyes boring into the horse. Slate was surprised to see a new addition to Manifest Destiny's gear — some kind of high-tech bracers graced his forearms — but he didn't have time to speculate.

"Took you long enough." The gravel in the voice seemed to grate across his soul.

Starshade gasped in pain and staggered as six more copies of the Teepa squirrel popped into existence, each with a cruel grin. One of the new clones spoke this time, "Thank you, Slate."

"You did your job well," another said.

"Your infiltration was a success."

"We couldn't have captured this Korps whore without your help."

Slate bit his lip at the words. He kept looking at each new speaker, with a growing sense of worry. He knew immediately his boss was trying to sow doubt and discord. It was a canny ploy, designed to drive a sharp wedge between the shakiest of allies. But the worst part was that the Percheron wasn't sure how he could convince Starshade that he hadn't betrayed her. Apprehension ate at him even as he furiously tried to marshal his defense… hoping to find *some* way to show her that Manifest Destiny was lying, but his reverie was shattered when Starshade just laughed.

The sound was gloriously maniacal and almost completely hid the fear he knew it covered. "Oh, *please*, you fucking *dumbass*. Slate isn't a double agent. There's *zero* chance you'd risk sending a girl with *that* much dysphoria to try to double-cross *the Korps*. With an egg like her, there's no *way* that doesn't blow up in your face."

Slate whipped his head around to stare at the rabbit. *What…? What is she…? How is…? What?* Even as the statement made no sense at all to him, he couldn't process why it caused the growing sense of unease to spread within him. His thoughts felt… *fragmented* as he tried to understand the statement.

He felt like a spectator, head swiveling simply to stare at the nearest noise, when one of the Manifests Destiny shrugged indifferently, sneering in disgust. "I knew he was a fag when all of the Dallas Cheerleaders were hanging off him, and he didn't even notice."

Wait, what? The conversation was moving too fast, and it felt like his thoughts were trapped in amber. *At least I'll get to be in the next Jurassic World movie.* His first complete thought in an eternity was not the most helpful.

One of Starshade's ears had swiveled back, tracking the sound of boots on the stairwell he only now registered. But she scoffed, her tone dripping with scorn as she continued her banter. "Give me a *break*. With the way she was studiously and respectfully *not* staring at my ass all the way up the stairs, she is *definitely* gay."

Slate stared in open-mouthed mortification and confusion as his thoughts were scattered to the four winds once more.

Unaware of his fractured mental state, she continued on blithely. "I *suspect* the only reason she wasn't ravishing the entire squad was because *no* woman could stay aroused around you. Just ask your wife." It was the wrong thing to say.

The squirrels snarled in fury. Manifest Destiny was charging up the stairs towards them, with more figures behind. As the ones on the roof began to surge forward, Slate's thought spiral abruptly died; combat instincts, honed over years, kicked in and shut down extraneous considerations. Even as Starshade shuddered, and more duplicates appeared, he was already charging forward to meet the first of the gray squirrels.

Starshade cursed herself for the banter misstep. She had been trying to stall for time, to see if she could identify the Prime in some way. She was usually so good at confusing and bewildering opponents just enough to stretch things out and put them on the wrong foot.

She had been so afraid, facing down one of the local terrors, but that laugh had given her confidence. *Thank the Overlord I practiced the laugh.* Once she had gotten through that first moment, she had felt almost giddy. The rush of sassing a bigot of the highest order and seeing the confusion and impotent rage on his face had been a potent drug. Slate's befuddlement had been even better in its way; it was damn well time she figured it out.

But she had gone too far. She couldn't help it. The idea had popped into her head, and it was past her lips before she could consider that it might be a bridge too far. As delightful as it had been to watch Manifest Destiny almost have an aneurysm in stereo, she was now faced with several charging heroes intent on murdering her and taking her goggles.

Quickly, she scanned the roof and spotted her next jump point. Just as she prepared to use the last of her power, *something* was ripping it away from her. She instantly felt cold and sick as the very core of her being was drained by the hateful bigot. The rabbit staggered from the feeling of wrongness, and the sudden realization that she didn't have her usual escape route.

The first Manifest Destiny had almost reached her. Time seemed to slow as the cottontail felt her thoughts turbocharge to analyze the situation. The squirrel was about her height, but bulkier — both in terms of muscle, and in the fact that he had *clearly* long since stopped following a strict Teepa diet. His bushy tail flicked back and forth to distract and confuse, but the Korps agent forced herself to focus purely on the torso. She swayed back, pulling the knife from the sheath on her leg in one fluid movement. Then she was springing forward, out of the grasping paws of the version behind her.

That knife glinted in the lights of the roof as she ducked down and to the left, sliding easily under his punch. The blade came up and drew a long, ragged line down across the underside of his bicep. Instead of blood, a caustic ivory powder poured out. Even though she was past in an instant, just being near it made her eyes water and her fur itch.

A second clone was to her left, swinging a baton at her head. She tucked down and rolled forward, feeling the grit of the gravel roof crunch under her bodysuit. She had no time to score that one as she rolled back to her feet and was jumping over a third aiming for a low tackle. Her dagger flashed, drawing a long, bloodless line down his back and spilling more of that cursed white chemical.

She could taste it at the back of her throat. It reminded her of harsh soap and industrial cleaners. Every instinct screamed at her to stay away from the poison sand, but she didn't necessarily get to make that choice.

The first Manifest Destiny with the 'bleeding' arm was pressing forward again. Even with one limb hanging limp, the squirrel didn't seem deterred. Instead, he slammed into her with that shoulder, knocking her back. Only training let her keep her grip on the blade, as she barely managed to spin away from the impact. In a panic at the pace of the action, she stabbed out, only for the razor steel to slam home into the neck of the next squirrel.

Wild eyes stared at her from centimeters away, showing nothing but madness in those black, soulless orbs. But no amount of malice could drive away the milky film that clouded them. With no more fanfare, the impaled man collapsed into a white cloud of burning dust. She was coughing and could feel her skin burning where it was exposed, but her suit mostly protected her. She was still hacking as she was forced to dodge yet another Manifest Destiny running at her through the toxic cloud.

Slate bowled over the first of the squirrels. Even without super-strength, he had almost a meter on the swarming rodents, *before* counting over 750 kilos of solid muscle. The figure went over backwards, tumbling away like a bowling pin. The horse had realized his mistake immediately, as he had no blade or way to easily draw blood. But fury and humiliation and confusion boiled over, and he suddenly didn't *care* about restraint; as the squirrel looked up, he brought his hoof down on his hand hard enough to crack the roof beneath. The *crunch* was horrendous, and powdered lye sprayed out in all directions. His former boss curled up around the ruined limb and the warhorse kept moving.

The next clone tried to come in on his side. Slate never knew what he intended to do with the attack because his fist lashed out first, barely restrained this time, to smash into the squirrel's face. The figure spun from the impact, his muzzle spraying white powder and more solid white chunks.

When he looked up, he realized that more had been using that first rush as a distraction. Slate found himself surrounded by six Manifests Destiny that had formed a ring around him. They paused as they stared at him in disgust. "I can't believe you let yourself be corrupted by that… *thing*," the one in front of him spat.

"That whore," another accused.

"That… *man*," a third decried in revulsion.

Slate snarled. "She's more of a hero than you've ever been." He cursed as his banter failed him. He had been the silent member of the team for so long and had too long disregarded the importance of the tool. But it bought time to think, while distracting and enraging an opponent. Starshade had shown him that.

In perfect unison, each of them reached behind themselves and pulled out a baton. In perfect unison, the clubs started to crackle with electricity. In perfect unison, each split their gray muzzle into a bloodthirsty rictus. "You know you can't win this one, Slate. There's too many of me. And I've summoned the Musket-steers. They will be here soon."

"The Musky Steers? The joke of a Fort Worth team?" He felt *better* about that banter but was still clearly rusty.

The squirrel growled in surround sound. "More than enough to take down one traitor and one drone." Then, more terrifyingly, the squirrels calmly smiled. "It was smart to face me. I can't believe I was stupid enough to get that drunk on Christmas."

Slate grinned tightly. "You can't drain me."

The squirrel grimaced and shook his head. "Such a disappointment."

The warhorse smirked, readying himself for the fight.

"Except, I lied."

Something deep in Slate was suddenly... pulled apart. Crying out in pain, he staggered as some unknown part of him *depleted*, replaced by an empty *wrongness*. It was like part of his soul was suddenly empty. A dozen more TPA Division Commanders appeared across the roof.

And then the six around him charged. Slate turned to punch one, blocking another, but there were too many bodies that fought in perfect harmony. Twin prods slammed into his back, discharging their electric payload, and agony burned through him. In response, the startled horse kicked backwards with all his strength. The steel horseshoe caught one of his attackers square in the chest with enough force that he burst into a spray of white powder, exploding across the roof in a chemical blast.

More prods came in and Slate lit up with agony, but he shrugged the attacks off with a pained grin. A pair of quick punches felled two more of the swarm. Spinning around, one fist closed around the front of a blue uniform, hoisting the hero into the air. Without a pause, his other hand slammed down to cup Manifest Destiny's ear.

The clone in his grip cried out in pain as a small puff of white powder spewed from the side of his head. Slate hurled the figure off the roof and into the night sky, not aiming for anything in particular. He had not even noticed the utility tower, nor intended for the thrown form to impact the metal cylinder attached to it.

The transformer exploded in a flash of ozone and a spray of caustic dust. The tower itself bent to the side, snapping wires and leaning forlornly. Instantly, the lights to the entire compound went out, plunging them into the near darkness of the early hour.

Starshade leapt over the head of a Manifest Destiny, barely avoiding a swipe that could have knocked her to (or off) the roof. *Focus. Focus! You have to find and destroy the jammer.* The words finally broke the cycle of thoughtless reaction in her.

She had just been reacting, moving from each attack, each moment, to the next. But such tactics against an endless horde of Teepa assholes would eventually wear her down. She had to stop simply surviving, and take *initiative*, as her instructors had tried to drill into her. The rabbit slid under a lunging arm and spun past another grasping paw.

BOOM

An explosion ripped through the night and the roof was plunged into twilight. Instinct saved her from an electric prod, as she performed an instinctive standing backflip over her attacker. The diesel roar and elective hum of a backup generator kicking on, across the other end of the roof, signaled the return of some power. The lights for the helipad blazed back to life, and she could see emergency lighting in the surrounding campus out of the corner of her eye. However, gloom still claimed the rest of the space, with most of the usual floodlights dead.

The Korps agent reached up and triggered her ear cameras, cycling the view to thermals. A bewildering array of rapidly moving colors triggered an instant wave of dizziness as her brain tried to process the flood of images, leaving her disoriented and unable to gauge the roof for one crucial moment. She stumbled, unable to control her footing, as an electric prod sailed toward her face. Frantically, the cottontail threw herself forward, as she turned what would have been an uncontrolled fall into a combat tumble.

Belatedly, as she rolled back to her feet, her mind resolved the visual entropy into a heat map of her attackers. Her breath caught when she finally spotted a tiny detail in the chaos: across the roof, partially hidden by some pipes, was a crate with the lid open. *There! That has to be it.* Waves of heat rushed her, but she had a destination and was built to *run*. She vaulted and ducked and weaved through the squirrel horde.

There seemed to be *too many* of the bigot. She didn't know where they kept coming from, but she didn't have time to figure it out. Her world narrowed down to focus on the destination and weaving through the gauntlet, giving the agent no time to worry about Slate; the sounds of nearer battle and distant shrieks were ignored. Her training and her experience let her dodge and weave, evading weapons and grasping fingers by millimeters. And then... she was vaulting over an air conditioning unit, and she was there.

When she looked down at the wooden crate... to find it *empty*. Her heart dropped as she stared at the foam insert, and the two depressions to hold absent cylinders. It was empty. *Fuck!*

A dry chuckle rumbled out behind her. She spun around to face the advancing squirrel. There was a savage gleam in his black eyes, and the twist of his lips was the cruel mockery of a child anticipating candy; he was *eager* for her pain. At that moment she knew she had lost, though she didn't yet know how.

"Looking for something, little bunny? Looking for the device we are going to use to shut down your infernal Korps?"

Her mouth was dry. Her heart was racing, the blood pounding in her ears. She tried to speak, but could find no words. Stupefied with fear and a growing sense of defeat, she managed to nod.

"You were expecting some technomantic pillar? All glowing green with an obviously fragile shell, perfect for casual crushing? Or perhaps a giant red self destruct button. Except, *I'm* not the supervillain. I'm the Hero. I don't do easily escapable deathtraps.

"What's better than one device?" He raised his arms, showing off the bracers affixed to them. She glanced around at a dozen more Manifests Destiny, each sporting their own pair. "An endless supply. These are scattered *across the state*, a pair on the arms of every *me*. Even if you somehow managed to kill all of me here, there would be more out there.

"At dawn, when we launch the second phase of our attack, they will each be triggered. And I, *I*, will *turn off* your precious little network. Your drones will be freed from their mental prisons, your forces will fall into disarray, and we will finally smash your little *infestation* of *my state!*"

The last he roared in triumph. Her blood had frozen at his monologue. She trembled, as she imagined the suffering of so many. There was nothing she could do to stop it, and no way to warn the Korps. She took an involuntary step back. She wanted to run, to save herself. But, with a will, she stopped herself from fleeing into the night.

I'm just a single agent. Alone. But... I'm here. I'm standing right **here**. She didn't know what she could do. But she wouldn't stop fighting, not while there was a chance. A chance for what, she didn't know — but no matter how much her heart quailed, and how much that voice in her head decried the hopeless cause, she was going to fight.

Starshade drew herself up to her full height, defiant. Then a dozen squirrels rushed her in a perfectly coordinated attack. Until that point, they had been attacking one at a time. They had gotten in each other's way. They had been spaced out, and fought like individuals.

They had been *playing* with her, she realized.

Her kick caught the first in the face, but a paw was already wrapping around her side. Her elbow shot back, smashing the nose of another. She lashed out with her knife, but a squirrel jumped in front of it, letting the steel bury itself to the hilt. When he fell away, it was ripped from her grasp.

Bodies slammed into her in a writhing *swarm*, and she felt herself tipping over. A punch to her chest stopped her futile attempt to save her balance. A paw wrapped around her head, and the goggles were stripped for her face, plunging her into twilight. *NO!*

In unison, four Teepa chiefs wrapped around her limbs, pulling her spread-eagled. She struggled, trying to tap her power or wiggle free or anything to escape. Fear of being captured hammered in her chest and the edges of the world were being eaten by stars of panic.

Manifest Destiny loomed over her, grinning a dark, vile grin. "Thank you for the goggles, little whore." Her only response was a terrified whimper as her wide brown eyes, ringed with panic, desperately searched for a way out. A savior. But only the squirrel leaned over, close enough that she could smell the foul, cheap beer on his breath. "The Heroes always win."

Then a second Manifest Destiny stepped forward. With one swift move, he brought her own dagger across the throat of the first. His neck parted in a ghastly wound. White powder poured out from the second mouth, spewing oven cleaner into her face and eyes.

Chapter 17

Earthquake

A scream of pure agony split the night, driving a spike through Slate's heart. Though the source was hidden behind the backup generator, the tortured torment in the rabbit's howl drove him to the brink of panic, before he tamped it down.

Old habits, from a lifetime ago and a world away, stilled him. That rage and fear and need to see what was left of his friend, all simmered under the surface. But his mind cleared. Focused. Targeted. His limbs flashed out in efficient, brutal strikes. Several of the squirrels exploded into dust from the blows. *Prime isn't foolish enough to risk going hand to hand with me. I need to focus on distant copies.*

Burning chemicals coated his fists and arms, demonstrating that his great strength was undiminished. Still, the horse staggered as he felt another sickly siphon eat at his soul, drawing some deep essence from him. *What is happening? The Army tested me. So did the TPA. All tests said I had no other powers. Just passive strength. What is he draining?*

The Percheron charged across the roof, going on the offensive, but these vile rodents were appearing faster than he could get rid of them. Desperation welled within his soul as the weight of certainty settled upon him. He had to find some way to stop the drain, or to find a way to drain the power himself before he was overwhelmed.

His gaze swept the roof, looking for any place of solace, but found little. If he hurled himself over the side, he might find some respite, but he would be abandoning any chance of saving Starshade. Instead, he barreled through waves of squirrels, brushing them aside even as he was forced to accept blow after stunning blow. He swerved, diving into the small structure that housed the stairs.

He needed a moment. A place to think. A reprieve. Steel-shod hooves lashed out, coating the walls of the concrete stairwell with the harsh chemicals that had been clones of his former boss. He hammered on the door, warping the frame and fusing the door shut, though he knew it would only last a moment. His fingers punched through the flimsy aluminum, holding it shut as best he could.

A rending noise brought a wave of pain, as one electric baton forced its way through the barrier to stab at the horse. A powerful kick warped his shield still further. Ignoring their stun prods even as pain ate at his concentration he felt that drain again, so deep within him, a place he had never had the courage to look.

Who am I? A question he had always brushed aside and buried, always shied away from, fearful of the answer. But he couldn't hide any more. Not when that question was tied up in this mysterious place that Manifest Destiny was using to fuel his cruelty.

Who am I? Decades of running, of hiding, of denying; turning away, ever away, from the simplest truth of all. Slate's soul already ached. Feelings and sensations long forgotten haunted the edges of his consciousness, recalling a thousand ways he simply didn't *fit*. A thousand fears of being broken. A thousand ghosts of longing suppressed.

— *Slate dies on the roof* —

Who am I? Slate was a name that never fit. No matter how long he wore it, it felt like a poorly-tailored suit, given to him by parents with no imagination beyond what they could see. No matter how long he wore that name, it never felt like him. It never felt... right.

Who am I? The question felt too big for him. Too massive. He was always an intruder in his own fur. The stranger in the mirror, who sneered at him for not being happy. The interloper, who felt he had fooled everyone into thinking he was Adonis. It all felt wrong. It felt fake. *It's... not me.*

It had never been him. *Him...* Not even that word felt right. It had always felt wrong. Foreign. Other. A curse laid upon a horse who had only ever wanted to be a hero. A protector, who had sought to shield others, because it seemed a bleak and weary truth that only *others* could be saved.

The world felt like it was going to shatter. That reality was but a stone sphere, crumbling, taking one lost Hero with it. Despair and need and loss and other emotions too indistinct to understand swirled around like the tight little shell that had been called Slate.

It was all a lie. He was a lie. *Slate* was a lie.

That last thought was enough to smash the world into falling shards of self. A great shout of pain wrenched from their soul, as a long muzzle turned to the sky. Years of neglect and self-loathing were ripped from them in a maelstrom of whirling emotions. Decades of unshed tears rained to the ground as the fallen Hero fell to hands and knees.

Then, they felt that hateful drain tugging at that deep part of themselves. But this time, this time their soul was bare, and they could see it and feel it and touch it. *No. NO. NO!* They roared that rejection, and whether they spoke the words aloud, they could never say.

That power was open to the horse, and they *grabbed* it. They could feel it infusing them, filling them, as if a flower feeling spring rain for the first time. With sightless eyes, too lost looking within to look without, the one who had been Slate looked up. One hoof slammed into the concrete landing with the ring of promise.

With a titanic surge of strength, the horse stood, slamming through the remains of the metal door and back onto the roof. A host of squirrels were thrown backwards, tumbling away from the raw equine fury. The Percheron's skin tingled and buzzed. Their head swiveled to look at the mewling and whimpering form of Starshade. Their heart surged, seeking to go to her. To gather her in their arms and protect her.

They were done denying themselves. They were done with turning away from the pain of others. They were done bringing evil through willful ignorance. So, they let the power flow forth. A small part of them cried out in protest, decrying the use of unknown powers on an injured companion. That tiny voice of caution was lost in the wave of power flowing into the only true *hero* they had ever met.

They did not know what the power would do. They did not know if they were helping, or simply taking the pain from someone they cared about. They only knew that the power felt right. And for the first time in their life, they would trust themselves.

Starshade's world was agony. Her eyes burned with a pain she had never experienced and she couldn't stop clawing her eyes, trying to make the pain go away. The blistering blaze felt like it was eating through to her brain and she couldn't stop it. She thrashed and writhed and whimpered and screamed and she couldn't get the pain to go away.

Some distant part of her registered a cool sensation quickly creeping up around her, but it wasn't the torment of her eyes, so it was unimportant. She prayed that the spreading feeling was death, if it would just make the pain go away. Then, like a burning hulk sinking beneath the waves, the fiery agony was suddenly quenched and… she could do nothing. Feel nothing. Move nothing. She was encased in cool, immovable water. Peace descended upon her. The pain was gone, finally, letting her just revel in its absence. She felt like she was hugged tightly. Safe. Secure.

She felt, more than heard, the crack. The safe place… shifted. Desperate to keep the protection she tried to reach, to pull it back in place. Instead, the shell around her shattered into a thousand tiny shards. Fragments of protection skittered and bounced away from her as she moved.

Starshade suddenly found herself rolling onto her back, gasping for air. She had not realized she wasn't breathing and, a moment before, would not have cared. She opened her eyes, tears spilling down the sides of her head. The sky was dark, with streaks of burnished orange pre-dawn growing. All of it was washed out by the lights of the city, but she didn't care. It was the most beautiful thing she had ever seen. She *saw*, and it did not hurt.

The desert cottontail lay there for one too-brief eternity, in the chill early morning gloom, wanting to laugh and wanting to cry. Happy just to breathe, even if the air was heavy with the scent of lye and smoke. Small pebbles pressed into her back and even that discomfort was a joy.

Without conscious thought, one paw curled closed, catching several of the shards, bringing them up to her face. Dark purple gems sparkled from the light of the city.

Amethyst.

But she caught motion in reflection of the gem. Her moment of reverie was over as the situation crashed back over her; several Manifests Destiny were sprinting forward, rapidly advancing on her position. She sprung to her feet as the first one grabbed for her, and ducked back, using the motion to power a tremendous kick. The high-heel of her boot slammed into his face, with a crunch of caustic spray, as she carried the motion into a cartwheel back and away.

Her mind was once more clear and racing while she glanced around. Slate was mostly obscured by a set of antennas. There seemed to be fewer Teepa creeps than last she looked, but there were still so many of him. The roof looked like a toxic beach with piles of poisonous sand stirring in the light breeze. Her ear twitched as she heard a faint scream far off in the night. There was no more time to consider the situation as the next him was nearly upon her. This time, instead of engaging, she continued to spring away.

Oh no you fucking don't. I'm not falling for your shit again. Never again.

Several of the infernal squirrels were forming up in a distant ring around her, distracting her with clones as they prepared a coordinated assault. This time she wasn't going to be so easily felled. Then a glint of steel caught her attention, and she realized the bastard still had her knife. Instantly, she had formulated a plan. A *bad* plan.

Bad plans are my best plans.

Her powerful legs launched her into a sprint across the roof, aiming for the duplicate closest to the one with her blade. He saw her coming; a grin of anticipation showed the old veteran hero thought he *had* her. She poured everything she had into the sprint, streaking across the roof, faster than he was prepared for. She had been designed for this. Built for this. *Crafted* for this. She might not have super-speed, but she was still on him before he registered the danger.

Boots slammed into gravel one last time and she let go, twisting her body. She had waited for the last moment to drop to her back to *slide*, and the squirrel consequently had no time to register the attack for what it was. Knees pulled up to her chest, and — as she started to glide under the surprised Teepa asshole — she lashed out.

Twin heels slammed into the joining of those legs like a freight train, impacting hard enough to lift Manifest Destiny into the air with a strangled cry. The Korps agent tried very hard to ignore the sensation of something under her boots collapsing. The force of her kick halted her slide abruptly, and in a flash she was up and charging.

She wasn't sure if the swarm shared sensations or if it was just male empathetic pain, but she was on the next clone before he had recovered from the shock of her rocking (or de-rocking) the other copy's world. Her hands clamped around his wrist and, with a vicious grin, slammed the blade home in his heart.

Blood sprayed around the base of the wound.

The Teepa Division Chief's black eyes stared wildly in shock at her, full of pain and hatred. Shaking paws wrapped around her forearms as he glared at her from a breath away. Hate poured off him in waves. Then those soulless orbs lost focus and he toppled over backwards, leaving the knife in her nerveless hands. Crimson welled up out of the wound, matching the sanguine stain across her own chest. His jaw worked one last time as if to spit some dying curse. Then, Manifest Destiny Prime collapsed into a pile of cleaning agent.

Starshade tilted her head back to the sky and groaned. "Daaaaaamnit!"

≡

The awakened mustang glared at the dour face of the squirrel before them. They were winded now, slowing down from repeated electrocution. Throughout the fight, that angry powder had coated them and burned away at their skin. Their fur tingled and ached everywhere, bringing a wisp of memory from a nasty sunburn they once had on their nose as a foal.

More of the clones surrounded them, the attacks increasing in coordination and seriousness. The warhorse was slowing down; even their legendary stamina was inevitably wearing down under the constant assault. While they had been able to somehow stop the Teepa Hero from stealing more power to fuel the horde, there were still far too many of him. An ominous calm had fallen over the multitudinous pair as both took a moment to size each other up.

"You're a damn fool, Slate. How *dare* you?" The harsh words were spoken in a discordant stereo from several of the gathered heroes.

"I'm finally doing what's right." Anger smoldered deep within them. Years in combat had long since taught them that rage was an enemy in war.; it robbed one of thought and planning, becoming predictable — easy prey for a professional. Hatred had been the downfall of so many heavies that it was a well-known phenomenon, studied by cape psychologists. The Percheron had prided themselves in never succumbing to that most self-destructive pattern. Still, in the moment, they found that tight knot of cold fury to be an ally. The purified emotion cleared their mind and redoubled their resolve.

"*Bullshit.* Just exactly how good a fuck was that tranny whore? How little did it take before you chose to abandon everything to be his little bitch? Tell me, Slate, what did he say to get you to bend over in that warehouse? How long were you taking it up the ass, before you decided to be a Korps slave?"

The warhorse set their jaw. The emasculating insults found no purchase on them, but the vitriol spewed towards Starshade fueled that powerful rage within. "She showed me what it meant to be a hero."

"You *were* a Hero, Slate. You threw that away to suck the dick of villainy."

The heat slowly drained out of their voice. The words were cold and dangerous and sharp when they said, "I was *never* a hero. All I did was *hurt* people. I was a thug and enforcer for the rich."

Manifests Destiny responded with a scoff and a sneer. "Those aren't *people*, Slate. You know damn well their lives are short and dirty and fearful. We protect the people that *matter.* How *dare* you betray the people that gave you everything!"

Indignation tinged their tone at the audacity. "Gave me…? You took **everything** from me! All I ever wanted to do was to *help* people and you twisted that into a corrupted mockery! You took my deepest desire and warped it until I was nothing but a tool for *evil*. This city is a tapestry of misery and all I've ever done was ensure that never-ending suffering continued. And for what? For fucking *what!* So a handful of wealthy assholes could have another zero in their bank account?" Their words were growing faster and louder. But they were focused and saw the satisfaction hidden in the expression of several of the clones to his sides.

The Teepa dictator did not care what words the Percheron spoke. The indignation wasn't important; nothing they said would change his mind. The fallen hero knew, at that moment, that Manifest Destiny did not care. Had *never* cared. Any beliefs he professed were nothing more than convenient at the moment, to be abandoned — or changed — as long as it served the end goal of evil. *True* evil.

Manifest Destiny was just needling them to get them angry, they knew; it was perennially the most exploitable weakness when dealing with a walking tank. One of the core operating tenets of TPA field operations was to keep the villains talking, get them ranting about *whatever* their whole deal was. That would usually give a Hero time to prepare for the fight, distract them, and put their opponent emotionally off-balance.

They had betrayed the TPA hours ago and they were already monologuing, ranting like a naive foal on their first crime spree. This scenario was literally written into the TPA handbook as crime fighting 101. As the draft horse vented decades of suppressed resentment, they realized they were falling right into the trap that had so often led to the downfall of the superpowered ne'er-do-well. But they also knew delay and distraction could be a double-edged sword. Manifest Destiny had been so focused on preparing to overwhelm the lone mountain, that he had paid insufficient attention to the figure that the horse had been covertly watching, the entire time.

With no warning, Starshade was suddenly at the back of the crowd, slashing and lashing out with knife and claws — seeking not to kill or disable, but simply trying to draw blood. As the swarm started to realize the danger, the towering veteran stopped their rant mid-word and was charging into them. Fists flew and hooves lashed out and bodies were thrown with fearful force, as decades of combat experience were coupled with raw savagery.

No way the Prime is one of the closest to me. I'm too dangerous. For the first time since leaving Afghanistan, the horse fought with no restraint. Gone was any attempt to minimize harm, or pull punches, or bring the suspect in alive; the warhorse conducted a symphony of brutality and the space around them was filled with a caustic cloud.

Their lungs and eyes burned from the foul industrial chemical, but the once-Hero did not relent in their assault. Electrical prods slammed into them, over and over again, as the squirrels' attacks slipped past their guard, but many paid the price. His attention was only partially on the nearest opponents. They kept turning, trying not to make it obvious, looking for the telltale hint of blood.

But even the mighty mustang was not invincible. No matter how great the mountain, time and pressure would erode it to nothing. The equine gladiator was wearing down and the damage was piling up; their lungs felt blistered and raw, and every aching breath was harder and harder. Their great chest heaved for air, and their vision wavered with unshed tears.

Some tiny change in Starshade's own whirlwind assault pulled their attention. They never would have noticed it if not for their intent focus on searching for precisely that. The Korps cottontail had abruptly changed direction, doubling back. They saw it, then — a red line across the cheek of one of the gray squirrels.

Her opening had been too tempting. The bulk of the swarm had been ringed around the behemoth, giving the horse their full attention, their backs turned to one surely-unimportant minion. It did not matter that she had just killed the Prime; she was a bit player in the great saga of betrayal. While a handful of squirrels pursued her, the horde did not consider her a threat. They had clearly dismissed the notion that this lone figure might attack.

But despite a reputation for being a harmless prey animal, rabbits were vicious fighters when cornered. Starshade was no different. Before the Manifest Destiny host realized her plan, she was already among them, knife and claws lashing out. This time, she was not interested in retreating. She was not seeking to kill, or maim, or even disable. Her movements were quick and precise with claw and knife, seeking only shallow cuts and simple grazing strikes.

Starshade tried to let her mind focus solely on the fight at hand, but thoughts kept intruding. Fear and frustration were distant, but never gone. The knowledge that she had failed to stop the jammer ate at her. Now, she could only hope to turn this TPA victory Pyrrhic, with the loss of a key figure in the battle. *Slate said that she could stop this prick if she could find the Prime. Nothing else matters now...*

In and through the rabbit weaved, moving quickly. The surge of attack and dodge and parry became a dance, beautiful and fluid and exhausting. Pain began to blossom in her side, and she couldn't get enough of the air, caustic though it was. Her chest heaved, but she continued her motions, pushing herself ever harder and further and faster.

She *almost* missed it, so caught up was she in the deadly display. She had turned away — already stepping to the next target — when her brain registered the lack of white in the wound. Only then did she realize the importance of that glimpse of fresh scarlet. But the cut was too small, just a graze on the cheek. The battle was too chaotic, and with a swarm of identical enemies, it would be too easy for the Prime to distract and escape. In desperation, her turn became a pirouette to keep this monster from escaping into the chaos once more.

The misstep almost cost her everything. Only the desperate surge of joy and the burst of energy it sent through her limbs allowed her to twist out of the way of an electric prod. Her twin gloves clamped down on that outstretched arm, pulling herself down and under the startled squirrel. She used the bulk of the older Hero as a fulcrum for her momentum, giving her kick more force; one black boot slapped into the sternum of a clone with enough force to stagger him back, crashing into others.

The stumble was enough to create a gap in the line of bodies. Manifest Destiny had sensed danger, and the duplicates had rushed to create a protective barrier around the bleeding face. Heedless of the danger, Starshade leapt forward into the tight scrum. Her steel dagger flashed in the air as she wrapped both paws around the grip.

Time seemed to slow down. Starshade felt the moment stretching to infinity as her world narrowed to this single moment.

Her body sailed through the air, outstretched. Her paws, clasped around a wicked blade, pulled above her head. Out of the corner of her vision, she could just barely see Slate seeming to glow oddly in the gloom... but the Korps agent couldn't draw her eyes from her prey. A dozen clones surrounded the bloodied one, and some small, distant part of her was shocked at how many had been scored by her blade in that unending ballet.

But her eyes were all for the Prime. Black orbs glaring death at her for having the gall to challenge him. The tiny slice highlighted by a small waterfall of blood stained fur. The crumpled blue and silver uniform hugging his heavy form. Her shock, as she realized her RCGs had been plugged into his vambrace somehow. The slight smirk as he brought that right arm up, covered in a technological bracer, to deflect her lethal blow.

But she was not aiming for his heart. She was not stabbing at all. With every ounce of her strength, she brought the knife down in a brutal slash. Had the blade hit the armor, it would have been harmlessly deflected; instead, butcher steel, forged and honed by the finest the Korps had to offer, slid past his aegis by a millimeter.

The force of her leap, of her powerful arms, of Manifest Destiny's own defense, all concentrated on a honed edge as it bit into an unprotected wrist. There was a shock of impact that jarred through her bones, but then the blade was through.

The tableau held for an endless moment. Starshade felt a desperate surge of disappointment. *I missed?* Manifest Destiny stared in shock at the hand as it hung there, slowly falling away from the arm. The first spurt of blood hung in the air. Most of the blade was spinning back and away, the overused dagger snapping a moment too late to save him.

Then time resumed, and she crashed into a waiting crowd of shocked and furious Heroes. Everything that had seemed too slow and so clear became a dizzying rush of confusion.

Three sets of paws grabbed her roughly, pulled her back and pinning her arms.

Two electric batons slammed into her chest.

One voice screamed.

The warhorse felt their heart spasm in fear as they watched Starshade's desperate leap. A bellow — filled with fear and fury — heralded steel hooves biting into the gravel-coated concrete of the roof before she even finished her fatal gamble. Even as their fist pulverized the first clone, the horde surged forward as one, trying to protect their Prime.

Starshade's ragged scream split the night for the second time, driving a spike of terrified desperation through their hammering heart. A frantic glance through the thick melee failed to catch the Korps agent behind a wave of blue-clad squirrel.

The horse, for all their strength, was surrounded by fists and claws and electric batons, raining down on them from every side. Only their bulk and immense strength kept them from being ripped apart, but it was like fighting through an inexorable tide of flesh.

Their chest felt like it could burst. Their need to protect and save their friend seemed to fill them, almost seeming to suffuse their body and soul. They had failed to protect so many, for so long. The thought of being unable to shield the *one person* who had touched their life as she had — so deeply, in such a short time — was too much. They couldn't take it. They couldn't fail. Not now. Not *again*.

Not again!

— *That desperate orb was filled with such a deep pleading for help that the sight seared itself into his soul.* —

Please!

Desperation grew within them. An electric tingling buzzed across their skin, growing with every moment. The burning of the thick coat of lye on their fur almost felt like that power that had slept within them for so very long.

My... power...?

The horse realized in that instant that it wasn't just *like* their power. That hidden reserve had been pouring into them. Manifest Destiny's leeching had torn a hole somehow, and the energy was building up and infusing every part of them. That *something* in them had been answering their need. The power threatened to erupt out of them.

And then it did.

The early morning sky was split by a terrible **CRACK** as if reality itself had been ripped asunder. A great explosion blasted out in all directions. The warhorse had not even been aware of the stony shell that had encased them, before razor shards of shattered gray rock tore into the assembled host. Dozens of duplicates turned to pillars of toxic sand, as crushing force and deadly splinters of slate tore them apart. Dozens more were simply flattened by the blast wave.

Suddenly, the way was clear. The fallen Hero saw the Prime staggering backwards, still clutching a bloody stump. Hooves rang like crystal as they slammed into the ground, propelling the massive warrior into a dead sprint. The few figures that somehow stayed standing between them and their target were casually brushed aside.

In the fraction of a moment before reaching her quarry, they spared a frantic glance at the black-clad form nearby. Their friend was somehow still moving and trying to rise. The sight of the tough little cottontail still struggling to stand defiant was all they needed. Starshade was *alive*. The warhorse could focus on ending this.

Black eyes, filled with pain and hatred, stared them down without fear. The mustang was on the squirrel in a heartbeat, grabbing the front of their blue spandex in one massive purple fist. The form was picked up easily, more like one of Manifest Destiny's licensed action figures instead of the real thing. Taking two more steps, the warhorse slammed the Prime into the wall, pinning him there.

They leaned forward, growling in a deep rumbling that sounded more like a rockslide than anything created by a mere mortal creature. The gray squirrel, though critically wounded, was undaunted by this show of force and rage. This was a Hero who had faced down some of the titans of this world, who had gone toe-to-toe with those who were more force of nature than person, and was not afraid of one single horse on the roof of his domain.

A mocking smile bared those sharp, yellowed rodent teeth. "You've lost, Slate."

Their voice rang cold in the predawn air. "That's no longer my name."

The derision ratcheted up. "Okay, *Johnson*. You've lost. You can't kill me in any way that matters."

That confidence faltered in the monster's eyes as the smile spread across their equine muzzle. "I don't plan to kill you."

Narrowed suspicious eyes searched a face devoid of answers. "Korps mind control won't work on me. I can shut down any of those damn goggles you bring near me."

This time, in response, they reached into their tattered uniform and pulled out a small talisman. Their glittering violet hand held a bit of carved brass that glowed with a sickly green light, pulsing and writhing around the meta. Fear — *real* fear — entered Manifest Destiny's expression for the first time.

"That... That can't be..." A hint of panic edged around that deep, gravelly voice.

"One of Repenter's sinner amulets? Yes, it is."

"It... it won't work on me! I'm a Hero!" The feeble lie was undone by the desperate pleading tone. "Where... where did you get it? They were all destroyed!"

"Where? It was hanging in a *trophy case*. Donated by the TPA to a faithful police department. Had you destroyed it — like you were *supposed* to any time in the last twenty years — I would not possess it now. Or, should I say, *you* would not possess it now." A cold hint of anticipation had entered their voice. A vengeful joy sparked and spread with each word. That hand brought the artifact up to show it off to the captured squirrel.

Words failed the Teepa Division Chief. He clawed at their face and arm and chest with one remaining hand. Boots lashed out, kicking and flailing. None of it mattered to his former subordinate. Claws found no purchase in hardened skin, and feeble blows could not faze three-quarters of a ton of rock hard muscle.

Slowly, almost delicately, that amulet was brought forward. Manifest Destiny fought with everything he had, trying to break free or push back through the wall or convince the fallen Hero to let him go. The frantic struggle only intensified as the warm metal was pressed to the skin above his heart.

In the whispered words full of ceremonial intent, the warhorse intoned: "Live the lives of those you have hurt until you hurt them no longer."

There was a pulse of *wrongness* that rolled across the roof. Four tentacles of sickly black-green power sprouted from the brass medallion and plunged into Manifest Destiny's chest. The squirrel screamed in pure agony and terror. The sound was echoed by each and every one of the still-standing clones, each staring upwards and keening eerily to the sky as they froze in their places.

The amulet seemed to pull itself slowly, inexorably, into Manifest Destiny's chest. The brass melded with flesh, pulled deeper by those tendrils of embedded power. The warhorse, who had thought themselves inured to war and violence, still felt sick at the howls of torment.

The Hero, who had hurt so many, screamed.

And screamed.

And screamed.

And then — finally — stopped.

Every duplicate vanished at once. The husk of Prime now simply stared with sightless eyes, silent at last.

With a heavy heart, sick at what they had done, the warhorse dropped the body to the roof. Shallow breathing showed him to still be alive. But the one who had never been Slate knew that was not a kindness.

Chapter 18

Chasm

Starshade knelt on hands and knees, trying to get her breathing under control. Her world had narrowed to nothing more than her chest heaving for air. Even the caustic, lye-tainted air was sweet. She was exhausted, having pushed herself much, much beyond her limits, during that fight against an endless swarm of seasoned veterans. When the enemies disappeared, so too had her ability to do anything but suffer and recover.

After several long moments, her gasping finally began to slow and her thoughts started to expand beyond the need to recover from fatigue and accumulated injuries. She watched blood and sweat slowly drip off her muzzle to stain the caustic powder that seemed to be everywhere. Finally ready to face the world outside of herself, she slowly and with great effort, lifted her head. Only then did she finally get a good look at Slate. *What the…?*

The giant horse was leaning against an air conditioning unit, also trying to recover from the long battle. But she had been *transformed*. Gone was the dark gray hide that had been her namesake. Her throat and chest were now covered with a soft lilac cream fur that Starshade wanted to run her paws through. Far more spectacular was the coloration of her sides and back, now a rich purple color that sparkled in the first rays of dawn. The light reflected from the thick coat as if it were made of… *amethyst*.

Her mane had been transformed as well; it had become a violet so dark it looked black, but twinkled in the light. Her eyes *were* now solid black; not the dead black of Manifest Destiny, but a living obsidian. The mare sparkled as a living crystal sculpture, marred only by the tattered Teepa uniform that barely clung to her powerfully muscled frame. Starshade had to suppress the urge to run over and rip the rest of the packaging off a present.

Calm down, you stupid, slutty bunny! You aren't safe yet.

It was hard to push down the surge of post-battle hormones, and she was secretly glad she was so exhausted that — if they managed to get the better of her somehow — she couldn't do anything about it anyway. But a thought to the danger they faced was enough to finally spur her to do more than kneel.

With herculean effort, she got one boot under her and stood on shaky legs. She paused there, wobbling like a newborn deer and cursing her choice of high heels for combat footwear. With deliberate, unstable steps, she started to cross the roof to stand next to her companion.

She braced herself on the same AC unit, standing shoulder-to-midriff with the warhorse as they both stared at the still form laying a few meters in front of them. She had thought he was dead, until the shallow movement of his chest refuted that notion. That realization came with a surge of disappointment. *Damn.*

That resentment faded quickly as she just didn't have the energy for strong emotions at the moment. "What... what did you do to him?"

The former Hero blew out a shuddering breath, the sound filled with regret and frustration and exhaustion. "The only thing I could think of. I locked him inside his own head."

A silence stretched between them in that cool morning air. "I'm... not sure I know what you mean."

"Have you ever heard of the Repenter?"

Starshade thought about it for a long time, but while the name tugged at a memory, she couldn't conjure more than a vague feeling of recognition. "I don't think so."

Her companion's voice was filled with fatigue as she started to explain around her own need for air. "He was a local vigilante-turned-villain. Back in the late 90s. He decided the world had fallen to sin, and that he was chosen by God to cleanse it. Dangerous nonsense.

"He had the power to create these talismans. Called them 'sinner amulets.' Nasty artifacts. He used them on people he felt had escaped justice for the misery they caused. Supposedly, they were divine punishment. Whatever the reality, what they did was force someone to relive the lives of anyone who they had truly harmed."

The horse paused then, looking at nothing. Starshade could feel the suppressed sorrow radiating from her as she relived some memory of her own. Trying to find some way to distract, she quietly prompted, "What do you mean?"

With some reluctance, she continued, "Manifest Destiny is living through every moment he ever hurt someone, from the perspective of his victim. He will suffer as they suffered, and he will know it was his hand that caused his pain. Not just physical pain, mind you. Any serious harm. He will endure these memories over and over and over again."

Starshade grew cold at the implications as she considered the hell that would be. She looked at her grim companion in dawning horror. "Forever?"

The draft horse blew out a shuddering laugh, filled with guilt. "Probably. If he ever truly repents… if he ever learns his lesson… if he ever really *changes* as a person, the amulet will let him free. That's how we know what happens. A couple people, who by all accounts had never really done anything wrong, managed to wake up from the living nightmare. No one has ever figured out how to break someone out of it otherwise. It's been so long, most of the rest are dead by now."

A silence stretched between them as they both watched the unmoving form even as neither really saw him.

"What… what happened to the Repenter?"

"He was a tolerated vigilante for much of the 90s when he was only going after organized crime bosses but was reclassified as a villain when he started going after CEOs and businessmen, after the dot-com bubble burst. Died in the early 2000s. Gunned down by Secret Service while trying to attack the former First Lady, although we suspect that was just suicide-by-cop to stop the suffering. From the reports, he was barely functional. Late-stage AIDS does that."

Starshade grimaced, feeling a bit sick as she looked at the catatonic Manifest Destiny. *If anyone deserved it, he did. But…*

Starshade pushed herself back onto her feet and limped over to stare down at the prone figure. She slowly knelt down and unclasped the bracers from the felled Hero. They were surprisingly heavy, and she could feel the heat radiating off of them. Excitement slowly started filling her as a thought crossed her mind.

Wait... if there are no clones remaining, these are the only pair left!

Suddenly eager paws tugged at her RCGs embedded in one, to no avail. They had been attached somehow, and none of her futile attempts could free them or seemed to harm the thick bracers. But she was still smiling as she walked over to her companion and held them out. "Would you mind?"

The bracers looked small in the giant equine hands. Casually, she ripped the goggles off of the jammers. Sparks flew and shards of important technological components fell to the floor. Desperate, greedy paws pulled the pair of RCGs to her chest, and she almost wept with joy.

The siren call of temptation and a desperate need called to her. With trembling hands, she wanted nothing more than to put on the goggles and feel the soothing presence of ROSE. Only her discipline stopped her from doing just that. *These were plugged into that... thing. I have no idea what it has done. I can't risk it. But oh how I want to anyway...*

The warhorse was not idle. With a grim smile, she ripped and crushed and tore the vambraces apart. Only when they were thoroughly mangled ruin did she offer them back to Starshade. "Take these. Don't want them getting anything out of the wreckage."

Happy to be distracted from the allure of her RCGs, she quickly hooked the magenta glasses to a hidden hook in her uniform, so she could clutch the broken bits of jammer without risking her precious visor being once more in contact with the weapon. Then a thought slowly floated to the surface, triggered by a soft slithering she might have heard, or might have imagined. With concern, she looked up. "Wait, didn't Manifest Destiny say he had backup on the way?"

They glanced at each other in alarm. Then there was a hiss of fury, and the sudden fierce bubbling of a roiling concoction. They both snapped their heads to look at the figure standing barely four meters away at the edge of the roof. Ethicoil perched on the railing and stared, all sanity gone from his eyes.

"*Traitor!*" screeched the wild-eyed coral snake holding the flask of agitated red and purple alchemy. Murder and madness filled his words. "Enjoy your trip to hell!"

The warhorse stared at their former teammate. Gone was the slimy charm and cool demeanor that had characterized Ethicoil. Gone too was his far too frequent cowardice. There was no reasoning left in the killing rage of those blood red eyes.

— *Slate dies on the roof* —

Time slowed as that flask was pulled back for a throw. The veteran saw death coming and started to throw themself at the alchemist; if they could just take him over the side of the roof in time, maybe, *maybe*, they could save the rabbit from whatever that sorcerous grenade would do. Pleading with the universe to give them the speed to save Starshade, crystal hooves propelled them forward... but not fast enough.

Then a *form* slithered over the edge of the roof behind the murderous alchemist. A black hand wrapped around his outstretched fist. A second wrapped around his throat, lifting the slender Hero off the ground. The gigantic black viper was suddenly *there*, holding the struggling form. She towered two meters above their own massive equine form.

The warhorse stopped abruptly, gawking up at the pair of serpents. The Teepa coral snake writhed and squirmed in the vice-grip of the cobra, clawing at her arm with his free one and ineffectually kicking at her torso with booted feet.

The giant figure ignored the feeble struggling of the alchemical Hero as she inexorably pulled him face to face with her. Before the Percheron could process the scene, the world... *pulsed*. Some wave of... *wrongness* slammed through them like a blast wave. Ethicoil's struggles redoubled in panicked desperation.

At first, they weren't sure what happened. That was, until a spot of gray appeared on the Teepa Hero's chest. The rough granite rapidly spread in a wave, draining the color from their former teammate. The coral snake writhed and flailed and choked out desperate cries, but his struggles faded as more of him was consumed by the rough stone. Limbs stopped responding as the racing grayness swept over them. Cruelly, the line of stone advanced slower up the scales of his neck only after each of the limbs was immobile. Wild eyes rolled in terror as the end approached.

With a final, terrified whimper, the face of Ethicoil was consumed.

The giant obsidian demon casually held the petrified statue that had once been their teammate. The sculpture's face was frozen forever in raw dread. A tiny part of them noted that the alchemical bomb had likewise been transmuted into nothing more than an ornate carving. *Inert.*

The former Hero gaped up at the tableau. The cobra slowly turned her face to lock unblinking, alien eyes with them. Then, only when she was certain they were watching, she casually tossed the once Ethicoil off the roof. A sickening moment of anticipation hung in the air. Then the sound of shattering stone heralded the final death of one of Dallas' brave Heroes.

The warhorse had never felt so… *small* as they stood, quavering, before the serpent. She physically towered over them and she exuded a dangerous, dominant presence that threatened to subsume them completely. Then, her goggles lit up with magenta light. Matte scales turned shiny black and glowing lines of matching magenta appeared between the scales, rippling hypnotically with every tiny movement.

Yesterday, the horse had been one of Dallas' greatest Heroes, but today… today, they felt tiny and helpless, as they stared up into the cold eyes of one of the Korps' deadliest supervillains. *The Lamia.*

Starshade watched in stunned silence as the great serpent crested the lip of the building. A surge of emotions froze her in place as surely as Celia's power had frozen her prey. Pure joy at the sight of help arriving vied with anger towards Ethicoil's attack all tied together by a panoply of fear.

The attack happened so fast that she was little more than a spectator to the violence. A sick feeling knotted her stomach from her front row seat to the death of the Hero, not that she felt any particular sympathy for this grifter. There was no pity in her for the slimy, arrogant failson of an oil tycoon, but the casual murder deeply unsettled her.

She took a step forward to speak, though she never knew if it would have been protest, greetings, or simple confusion. Her muzzle had only started to fall open when she felt the caps on her ears... warm.

[Starshade!]

The mental contact caressed the inside of her head. Relief and pure joy swept away everything else. Tears of relief stained her fur.

ROSE?

[I'm here! I'm here and I've got you. Dear sweet Starshade, I'm here.]

Did... did you build an RCG connection into these earcams?

[Absolutely.]

Why didn't you tell me?

[Dear, we can discuss this later. I need your help. Please, this is important.]

Starshade felt her joy recede at the suddenly serious, urgent tone coming across the thoughts. Er... of course. How can I help?

[Starshade, I need you to allow me full access to your memories. This is urgent. We have little time. Celia and I need this information immediately.]

But...

[Yes, I know. Please.]

She was suddenly apprehensive. A full memory access would lock her down as she replayed every memory. She wouldn't be able to fight if the need arose. Moreover, a dangerous tension was growing between Celia and Slate. She wouldn't be able to mediate between the two. She couldn't plead for her. She couldn't *protect* her.

Please?

She trusted ROSE. And ROSE trusted her. In the end, that's all that mattered.

Okay, ROSE... permission granted.

[Thank you! I promise you, this is critical. I am so, so sorry. I will make this up to you, Starling.]

...

...

...

...

INITIATING FULL MEMORY ACCESS

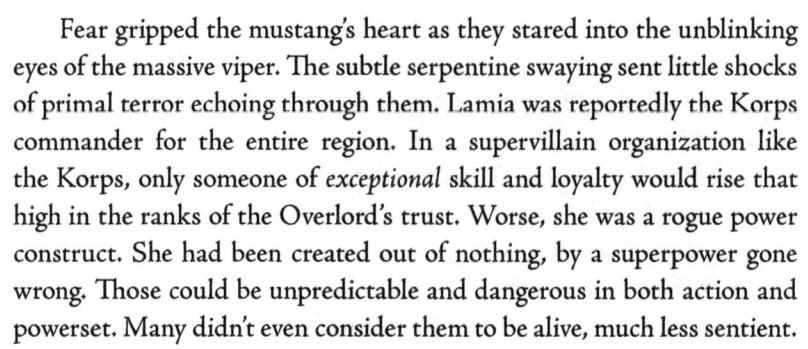

Fear gripped the mustang's heart as they stared into the unblinking eyes of the massive viper. The subtle serpentine swaying sent little shocks of primal terror echoing through them. Lamia was reportedly the Korps commander for the entire region. In a supervillain organization like the Korps, only someone of *exceptional* skill and loyalty would rise that high in the ranks of the Overlord's trust. Worse, she was a rogue power construct. She had been created out of nothing, by a superpower gone wrong. Those could be unpredictable and dangerous in both action and powerset. Many didn't even consider them to be alive, much less sentient.

The veteran Hero had begun to doubt the narrative around the Korps, but they were not about to fully discount the warnings provided in each briefing about Lamia. She was never to be engaged solo, by anyone, for any reason. While a high-value target, stark admonitions were issued; Lamia was not to be fought with fewer than two full TPA teams. Which was no longer something they had access to, should this go wrong.

Some small sound from Starshade caught their attention and they finally broke gaze with the cobra. A glance back showed the rabbit's ear ornaments glowing magenta while the cottontail stared blankly ahead. As if being controlled. Fear redoubled, this time with a spark of anger and they turned back defiant.

"What have you done with her?"

The snake's expression was unreadable. A purple forked tongue tasted the air for a long moment, drawing out the silence after the question. The voice that finally emerged was deep and sensual and rich, full of hissed consonants and perfect confidence: feminine and powerful and dangerous. "Ssshe isss my agent, thisss Ssstarssshade. What isss ssshe to you?"

The counter question took them by surprise. The horse opened their mouth to answer and... stopped. *What... is she to me?* The question echoed in them and stopped them cold. They didn't have a word for the strong connection forged through circumstance and shared combat; none of their old Army terms seemed to fit. Their answer came out shaky and uncertain. "She's... she is my friend."

"Your friend..." the snake tasted the word, head tilting to regard the warhorse. Then she was suddenly gliding forward, off the edge of the roof and right towards them. Instinct and fear had the fallen hero stumbling back a few steps. They stopped their inadvertent stumble, belatedly taking a defensive stance to protect against the attack.

But no attack came. The serpent slid to the side, moving far faster than seemed possible for such a massive creature. The horse spun frantically to face Lamia as she skimmed smoothly across the roof. Only then did they realize their mistake, when the viper returned to where she had started: the Percheron was surrounded, *encircled*, by a wall of coils.

While the fallen Hero still had a meter of space in each direction, the threat was implicit. They were encircled. Entrapped. While they stood on the roof of the heart of TPA power in the city, the roof of the building *they* had called *home* for years, it was the Korps commander who had complete control of the situation. It was in that moment, buffeted by the menacing personality of the giant snake that they finally understood why this woman was so feared by the Texas Protectorate Assembly. And in spite of years of combat and patrol, of facing threats and villains, the mustang felt *completely and totally outmatched.*

"Tell me, little crysssstal pony... why do you think I am here?" The words were soft, casual, but the Percheron was not fool enough to miss the hidden steel within.

"To stop the jammer."

That purple tongue flicked out into the morning air. "Yesss. But I am alssso here to sssave my preccciousss Ssstarssshade. The former hasss already been accomplisssshed. You are... not my priority."

They swallowed, their mouth dry, but it did not seem that Lamia was hostile. Dangerous, yes, but not immediately aggressive. But the next question was still one of the hardest questions they ever had to ask.

"So... what happens to me, then?"

"That... isss up to you. You have three choicccesss. Three pathsss lay before you, losssst little horssse. I admit great interessst to sssee what you choossse."

— *The Korps. If you take the wrong path, they will offer you three choices* —

The words, said with such careful casualness, still sent a pang of ominous dread through them. The memory of Erstwhile's warning rang like a clarion bell in their mind. "O-okay. What are they?"

The viper stared at them intently as they began to speak once more. "Firssst. You realizzze you have made a *terrible* missstake. You realizzze that the Teepa will forgive you, if you ssshould manage to ssslay or arressst me. All your actttionsss... all your betrayalsss... all will be absssolved if you can but fell one... lone... sssnake."

This was not a choice. Even if they were inclined to return to the fold, such an attempt would result in their sudden and inevitable demise. They hadn't been certain Lamia existed mere minutes ago, but those few moments had made it very, very clear that they had no chance at accomplishing that choice. Option one was death by another name.

"And option two?"

"The *sssecond* optttion isss that you sssimply walk away. The TPA and the Bradley Group will be very interesssted in ssspeaking with one ssso *intimately* intrinsssic to thisss little border ssskirmisssh. But the ssstate isss in chaosss; dozzzensss of battlesss yet rage. If you leave, now, thisss minute, you may be able to esscape that noosss. You are resssourccceful and exxxperienccced; you may ssslip acrosss the border or go ssso far to ground they can never find you."

The warhorse did not like their chances in that scenario. They might have been able to make it, but the risk of capture was much higher, and it was unlikely that captivity in the tender mercy of the TPA would be as desirable as the first option. Dread grew in them, as they realized the starkly bleak options for their future. One simple choice — not sentencing a bright young woman to death — had started them on a path that seemed to be quickly reaching its end.

"And... the third option?" They asked purely out of form. They knew what the third option would be, before Lamia even opened her lips.

"The third optttion..."

Suddenly the snake slithered to the side, opening a path in those muscled coils and revealing a beat-up, dusty HVAC unit. Upon them lay a pair of Rose-Colored Glasses. They sat there, looking pristine on the ruined roof, the magenta goggles glinting in the dawn light.

— *If you believe them... If you accept their offer... they will hypnotize you. They will bind you. They will mutilate you. They will torture you. You will suffer humiliations that you can't even imagine* —

The words rang clear in their mind as if Erstwhile were standing behind them. Doom clawed at their heart.

Heedless of the mustang's thoughts, the serpent continued their offer. "You put thessse on and you come with usss."

"And you hypnotize me into obedience?"

A firm tone entered Lamia's voice. "I ssshould tell you that sssuch a fate requiresss your consssent. That the Korps doesss not inflict sssuch thingsss upon the unwilling. But nothing I sssay about that ssshould be trusssted, of coursssel! After all, to create a drone of one of the *Pegasssusss Phalanxxx*, I would sssay anything, would I not?

"Ssssupposse I promissse that no harm would come to you. I would ssswear to your sssafety. But in the end, all that could be liesss. Honeyed wordsss, to bait the trap."

The viper moved again to gesture at Starshade. She was still standing there, blank. There was no movement. No expression. Simply blank obedience. A drone, as far as they could tell.

The horse could not look away from their companion. Fear and desperation and the need to protect (or avenge) their friend warred within them, a cacophonous medley of bitterness.

"Thisss could be your fate if you accccept my offer. Mind-controlled into eternal, blisssful obedienccce. Would you risssk thisss, for a chanccce to essscape the viccce clossssing around you?"

A memory surfaced. Starshade talking about her joy of ROSE. How her love of the Korps was so evident in the way she spoke of her time there.

There's no way that all of the Korps are just mindless slaves. She's... she's trying to sour the offer? Why?

It was *that* thought that finally got them thinking — really *thinking* — instead of merely feeling and reacting. Instead of simply asking the next, fully expected, almost rotely-prompted question, the horse voiced a thought that had been circling the periphery of their mind for hours:

"What does the Overlord *want?* Really?"

The slightest tilt of that great head might have been amusement... but it might have been a cruel anticipation, or a trick of the light. Still, they got the sense that she was pleased with the question. "Why, to take over the world, of courssse."

But the former Hero was already shaking their head. "Not good enough. *Why?* Why does the Overlord want to take over the world?"

Again, the massive serpent moved with a silent glide to gesture at the city across the river. "Becaussse of *thissss!* Ssso much of thisss cccity, thisss planet, isss built upon misssery. Billionsss of people sssuffer every day, crussshed by debt and heartlesssss lawsss and greed. Thossse in power dissspenssse ssspecial pain to thossse that reject their appallingly narrow ideasss of gender and sssexuality and individuality. The Overlord hatesss the unnecccesssary cruelty ssso casssually dissstributed to ssso many. And all for the benefit of a few that already have too much.

"The Overlord wantsss to lift up thisss world, ssso each and every sssentient being can live their livesss to their greatessst potential. Becaussse freeing *everyone* from the boot of tyrantsss is worth fighting for. Even if that meansss taking over the world."

The Percheron gazed out at the city center with a stony expression and considered her words. Long moments passed as the sun shone through gaps in the towering skyscrapers of downtown. They didn't know if the viper was telling the truth, but the answer was an uncomfortable echo of their own considered thoughts.

They turned back to face Lamia, seeing her watch them intently. "How long do I have to decide?"

"About ten minutesss. That isss when my ride arrivesss. That isss when I leave, and when optttionsss one and three exxxpire. The Bradley Group obssservatttion team will arrive about twenty-five minutesss later. I sssuggessst not being presssent when that occursss."

They grimaced but had expected the answer. *Just like my time in the Army. Always too much time until there wasn't enough.*

"Say I put on those goggles. What happens?"

"Why, if I am lying, then anything I want, of courssse. But if the Korps *isss* asss I claim, then we care about conssent. We would not do more than you allow. At leassst, that is what would normally happen, were you a ssstandard recruit with the leisssure of time. But... you are a sssworn TPA Hero who hasss not been vetted yet. We are in crisssisss; war loomsss. You do not get sssuch easssy choiccces."

"If you put on those RCGsss, you agree to let usss have full accccessss to your mind. If you are lying... if you are a double agent, or a ssspy, or ssseek to betray usss in *any way*..." Suddenly she was towering over them again. The black shape *loomed* down, catching and holding their gaze. They felt like... prey.

Deadly ice filled the words, making their lethal seriousness clear.

"I. Will. *Drone*. You."

Four words, clear and concise and deadly, seemed to echo in chill air.

"If you possse a threat to the Korps — the Korps that isss my *home* and my *family* — I *will* drone you. If you endanger the livesss of thossse I am sssworn to protect, I *will* drone you. I will ssstrip your mind and your will, and you *will* ssserve the Overlord. Do. You. Underssstand. Me?"

Fear gripped their heart as the words crashed into them. There was no doubt that she meant every word. The horse swallowed, trying to clear a mouth that had suddenly gone very dry. "But I —"

She cut them off before they could even manage the protest. "You sssaved my Ssstarssshade, for which I am grateful. That accction has bought you thisss offer. But it comes with ssstrict condittionsss. Thisss would not be the mossst elaborate or overly complicated infiltratttion effort I have ever ssseen. Yesssterday you were a loyal member of my mossst hated enemy, with but a *sssingle* blemisssh on your ssstoried career. I will not risssk everything I love to sssave you, without sssafeguardsss."

Their heart pounded in their ears as fear gripped them. Those alien eyes glared at them until she was satisfied there would be no further protest. Only when she knew the gravity of her words had been fully appreciated did she withdraw slightly, giving them a little room, and time, to breathe. With a much smaller voice, they reluctantly asked a follow-up question. "What if things... just don't work out? What if I decide I don't want to be a supervillain?"

The snake receded a bit further. "Then you walk away. Free. After the crisssisss, when we have time to vet you, after we are sssure you do not hail from Troy, then we will ssspeak of your future. Whether that future ssseesss you ssstay with usss, join usss, or leave. We sshall dissscusss boundariesss, and reessstablish consssent parameterss. In ssshort, we will forge your future together. But right here, right now, putting on thossse gogglesss givesss me the right to do *anything* I deem necccessssary for the protectttion of the Korps."

The words hung in the air as a heavy silence stretched out.

She's trying to protect her people. She doesn't trust me. **Can't** *trust me.*

The Korps commander slithered to the side, reopening the path to the RCGs. This time the fallen Hero slowly stepped forward, their hooves heavy and uncertain. Lamia coiled up on herself behind them as she patiently waited for them to make the choice.

None of the options were great. All posed great risk for limited reward. Option one was off the table; even if they wanted to try to reclaim their spot in the Teepa, they would not survive the attempt. But, also, they simply did not *want* to.

The warhorse stared at the goggles with the echoing words of the precog dancing in their mind, taunting them.

— *If you believe them... If you accept their offer... they will hypnotize you. They will bind you. They will mutilate you. They will torture you. You will suffer humiliations that you can't even imagine.* —

I can't trust her. The thought was heavy and dropped into them like a stone dropped into a well. They felt sick. But they could see themselves reaching forward. Picking up the goggles. Hurling them into the river. They would run, seeking to use the confusion of the day to get to the Gulf. They could do it.

They started to reach for the goggles and stopped, hand hovering halfway to the destination. Then the horse froze, as the serpent shifted behind them and spoke once more.

"Yesss, take a bite of my apple. What'sss the worssst that can happen?"

They turned around and *stared* at Lamia. *Did she just... make a joke?* Their long muzzle fell slightly agape, trying to make sure they heard right. Lamia, the demon that haunted the nightmares of the TPA, gazed back. Then the horse snorted, and a smile tugged at their lips.

With that, they turned and, before they could think better, picked up the goggles. These were much bigger than the pair that Starshade had worn, having clearly been built for someone of their size: gleaming pink polymer glass, with earpieces that would hook up into their ears. Even with all their will, all their resolve, they still hesitated just before the curved RCGs slid into place. Then the moment passed as the cool material slid across her fur with a soft hiss.

The world through their view was tinted ever-so-slightly red, as expected. There was a moment, a single heartbeat, when nothing happened. A small part of them hoped nothing would happen. A tiny voice, weary with heartache and betrayal, even hoped that Lamia had lied, and that all their cares were about to be purged to live in unending, mindless bliss. But mostly, they held their breath and waited.

A winged helix, a sigil they had seen as the mark of the enemy for almost a decade, appeared in the center of their vision; the symbol rotated slowly as fear and anticipation and trepidation swirled within them. A welcome chime played, discordant to the dark thoughts and desperate hopes of the warhorse. The spinning symbol faded into the background as text began scrolling across their vision.

...
...
...
...

Starting ROSE v4.401.3
> Hardware test ... OK
Enabling DNI on local device ... Done
INIT::RCG User Environment v12.7.09
...Done
NEW USER DETECTED, initiating first time setup.
WLAN carrier acquired
Requesting uplink to RCG Network...
Secure Connection Established
Synchronizing system clock...
2023-MAR-19 07:46:33.912
Establishing New User Profile
Assigning UUID
Populating records
Analyzing user biometrics
<ERROR, Record Found>
Command Override Activated
...Done

[Hello. My name is ROSE. I'm glad to meet you.]

A digital vixen appeared in their vision, tender and kind. A calm flowed into them, one they had not felt in many years. The mental connection felt like a warm hug enveloping their very soul; they could only conceptualize it as the feeling of being *loved*. Tears streamed down their cheeks, making the image blurry.

[What is your name?]

"I... don't know. Do... do you think you can help me with that?"

[Oh, my sweet dear. You are in so much pain. Of course I can help you. You never have to be alone again.]

Overcome by the warmth and welcome and concern for her wellbeing, she sank to her knees, weeping. Then strong arms were enfolding her like she was a toy, surrounding her with soft, warm scales. There, for the first time since she was a foal, she felt... *safe*.

The world narrowed to that compassionate mental embrace.

She fell into the feeling. And kept falling.

And that was all she knew, for quite a while.

Chapter 19

Aftershock

MEMORY ACCESS COMPLETED
...
...
Reinitializing
...
...
...
...
...
...
[Welcome Back, Starshade!]

She snapped back to awareness with a painful gasp. Celia was coiled next to her, gazing intently at the horse before them. Her heart leapt as she saw her friend slide the RCGs into place... only to plummet, along with the figure, as she started to collapse like someone had flipped a power switch.

Starshade instinctively tried to *jump*, only to stumble. Some deep part of her throbbed in pain as she had... nothing. All her reserves were gone. She was reduced to bracing herself against a light pole, gasping for air with aching lungs.

[It's okay. You're okay. Breathe, dear. **Breathe**.]

She swallowed, her chest feeling strangely tight, and took a moment. ROSE's soothing helped her focus. After several long, agonizing moments, she finally managed to control her panting and looked up. Celia stood there in her ebony and magenta livery, carrying the massive draft horse. Though she showed signs of strain, she still managed to glide along carrying the impressive bulk.

Wow, she's... strong. And... what the fuck would I have done if I'd tried to catch Slate? Been a stupid, impulsive bunny pancake, is what.

Starshade limped after the larger serpent, only distantly realizing they were moving in the direction of the helipad. Her entire body was heavy and stiff. The ruined bracers felt like weights as she clutched them to her belly. Her skin felt hot and tight as she rubbed her chest.

[*Your ride is almost here, dear. Then you can rest. How are you feeling?*]

ROSE, what happened to Slate?

[*She's sleeping, dear. She made the choice to come with us.*]

But... what happened?

[*Let's get you home, safe. Then we can talk about it.*]

Home sounded so nice. She couldn't find any energy to press for details. It was all she could do to put one foot in front of the other, the coarse white powder crunching softly under her boots. Fatigue was weighing her down. She could never remember being so exhausted that she could feel it in her ribs.

Her long ears caught the faint chuffing of an ultra-quiet anti-grav engine, and she found the energy to lift her gaze just as a distortion in the air rippled overhead. Celia continued to slither smoothly onto the landing pad. A door opened up, seemingly in midair, to reveal the interior of a Korps stealth Condor; palpable waves of relief washed over her as she realized that safety beckoned. Even though she was panting for breath, a smile spread across her lips, then bloomed into an ebullient grin as she recognized the black jaguar waiting.

Zala...!

Starshade found the energy to jog, forgetting the exhaustion that had turned her limbs to lead. She almost laughed when she realized her friend and overwatch was wearing a full field ops uniform, as if the soft, languid shifter would charge into battle like an avenging angel to save her. The desperate look in her eye as she evaluated Starshade with concern made the rabbit reconsider her mirth.

If she ever went through Field Ops training, I bet she'd be a serious menace. She's fierce when she puts her mind to it.

A glance down suggested that Zala *might* not be wrong to be so concerned. She was coated in drying blood, which was itself covered in a thick layer of caustic white Manifest Dust. She felt an odd bit of shame that she was so grimy. Self conscious, she listened to the reckless voice telling her to push herself. With a flourish and a weak smile, she hopped inside the aircraft, dancing past where Celia was strapping in the unconscious form of the fallen hero.

Zala's concern stopped her from offering a hug though. She scratched at the tightness on her chest as she stood there, trying to control her breathing from the exertion of her dumb stunt. But she swallowed and smiled and, though winded, said, "Zala, I have never been so happy to see you."

"Starshade!? What happened to your eyes? Are you okay?"

My eyes?

[*Later, dear.*]

She swayed there a bit and smiled with true warmth. "I'm okay! Just… ready to go home."

Zala didn't appear to be convinced. "Please be okay! I've been worried sick about you." She had stepped forward, putting a paw on Starshade's shoulder and gently pushing her backwards into a seat. The cottontail wanted to protest, but she wanted to get home more, so she obeyed. The jaguar gently took the ruins of the RCG jammer and stowed them away. Then, she quickly and efficiently closed the door, and checked to make sure Celia had Slate well in hand. For her part, the rabbit tried to catch her breath, ashamed at how out of shape she was.

[*Hush, you pushed yourself too hard. You're in great shape. Just ask that cow at Ink or Dye the next time you go in.*]

A hint of concern in ROSE's normally serene thoughts sparked a growing unease within Starshade. She tried to put it out of her mind as she cracked her neck, trying to keep it from stiffening up, like it seemed to be doing. She knew she should be strapping in as the transport lifted off smoothly, but she just needed a moment to recover from the evening first.

"Ssstarsssshade, are you quite all right? Your earsss look pale."

Though exhausted, she lifted her head and smiled at Celia, touched by her concern. "I'm fine. I just n —" she started, but was interrupted by a sudden cough.

Her throat was painfully tight, but swallowing seemed to ease it. Both Celia and Zala were staring at her in visible alarm, but she waved off their apprehension and tried again. "Ju —" before she coughed again, harder. She couldn't seem to clear her throat.

[*Starshade? Dear? How are you feeling right now?*]

Something's... wrong...

Then she was sliding out of the seat, falling to the deck on hands and knees. Her entire body was wracked with a deep hacking cough that made her want to vomit. A second later after another wrenching spasm, she thought she had. Then she realized that the liquid splatting across the dark chrome floor was bright crimson.

"Sweet Overlord! Starshade!" came the distant scream from Zala.

Starshade couldn't stop hacking, each wet, raspy cough worse than the last, blood splattering onto the deck —

[*Starshade, listen to me. I'm taking control of your body. Just **hold on**. We're almost to RIV. Just a little while longer, I promise.*]

It was hard to pay attention to the distant thoughts, calming though they were. Her body wasn't responding anymore, but she wasn't coughing as much, and that was a blessing. Her lungs were burning and her skin was on fire. She was dimly aware of Zala and Celia hovering over her. But mostly, she just suffered.

"ROSE...?"

[*We're almost there, Starshade. Please hold on. I need to keep you awake a little while longer.*]

The question or concern that had prompted her query seemed to have vanished; it no longer seemed to matter. She wasn't quite aware of the passage of time. A shock of betrayal shot through her when two paws left her back and Zala moved away. That her friend would leave her in this state, when she was in so much pain, wounded her deeply.

...help...

[*Starling! Starling, I'm here. Hold on a moment longer. Please!*]

She had never heard ROSE sound... *frantic* before. Her thoughts felt fuzzy and scattered. The only one that stuck seemed to be meaningless.

Only Karen calls me Starling...

The remaining hands clamped suddenly down, holding her in place, and the entire aircraft *jolted* as it slammed into the ground. Zala was flinging open the door the moment after impact. Immediately, a quartet of Nurses O were rushing into the interior. Celia backed away as the first synthetic fox medic was kneeling over her.

"Miss Starshade, we're here to take care of you. Please just relax and we'll take care of you."

[*I'm going to let you go to sleep now. We have you. You're safe.*]

And that was all she knew, for quite a while.

Epilogue

Consciousness came back in a rush. The first sensation was of burning lungs, desperate for air. But the pressure all around warned the deepest of instincts that breathing would mean death. Confusion and terror clawed at the heart and fueled a feral desperation.

Eyes shot open to find a darkness so deep and absolute that it not only blinded, it robbed even a sense of direction. There was no up or down in the pitch blackness of this watery grave. The only confirmation that eyes were even open was the stinging of the solution.

Hands shot out, slamming into a hard surface only inches away. The pain from the impact was quickly swallowed by the yawning terror of drowning. Lungs too long denied started to spasm, warning that they would not be refused much longer.

Palms slammed into the surface with panic induced strength, but the cool expanse was unyielding even to such powerful blows. Fingers started scrabbling at the smooth metal for purchase, finding none. Legs and tail thrashed, revealing little space to move as they too found nothing but the confines of a pitiless coffin.

Fear, primal and eternal, scattered all awareness but the need to survive. Swallowing did nothing to stop the painful shuddering lungs that heralded the end approaching, the impending moment when lips parted, chest expanded, and death rushed in.

Thoughts could not survive such an overwhelming dread, but their ghosts were purely desperate pleading. The strength of flailing limbs had started to fade no matter how urgent the fearful frenzy that drove them.

Then… a flailing finger glanced across a bump, but then it was gone. Clawed hands sought that tiny defect again.

There.

A bar unlike any other inside the cruel prison. Nerveless fingers — clumsy with desperation — slid over it but were too panicked to find purchase. A foul, bitter taste heralded the end as lips started to part to merciless waters. But the vile fluid and desperate hope of freedom drove one last burst of frenzy.

A thumb pressed upon the tiny catch, seeking something, *anything*, that might herald salvation. But the smooth metal and slimy liquid caused the digit to slip. Palms raked across the surface, seeking that tiny aberration once more.

After an eternal moment of dread filled with a mindless pleading and scrabbling, the spot was found again. This time, it was possible to brace with firm contact. There would be no further chances should this fail.

Some buried instinct screamed that the only answer was to *push*. Every ounce of strength, every feral instinct, every panicked desperation was channeled into this single last act of survival.

The bubble *moved*.

Light burst into the world, painful and angry at its denial. But the cool, lightness of air on the flailing hand was a beacon of deliverance. Fading strength redoubled and forced the hated bronze surface away. Gravity returned and the body, feeling safety inches away, lunged for it.

Sitting up, straining lips broke the water and the sweetest, most painful air rushed into lungs too long denied. The world narrowed to nothing but great croaking gasps. After an eternity spent relearning how to breathe with burning lungs, thought slowly started to return, filtering back through fading desperation. Another forever passed as breathing slowed and pain receded.

Finally, Ethicoil opened his eyes.

Acknowledgements

This book would never have been possible without the other members of what would come to be called the Monsterfucker Book Club. Each of the other members of the writer circle helped me understand the shared universe and encouraged me to continue writing. The following characters are used with the permission of their owners:

> Karen and ROSE belong to Karen King
> Volta, Captain Alamon, and Nurse O belong to Syntax-Takes
> Mabel belongs to Mabel Greysmoke
> Backchannel (Rin Gorgoni) belongs to Grace Reed
> Ellen Foxpaw belongs to Bibi Heartsglow

This book was originally published online under the title Crystallization, it has been renamed to Dissolution, while that name has been moved to the second book in the series. This was done to more closely mirror the journey of one of the characters.

Finally, additional thanks to Karen King for creating the setting and for letting me play in this universe. This whole experience has been surreal, amazing, and wonderful.

Read on for a preview of the next novel in the **To Crack A Geode series**

Crystallization

Coming from Furplanet Productions 2025

Crystallization Chapter 1
Accretionary Wedge

Jennifer Delver took one last sip of her overpriced coffee before getting out of her car. The nutria set her ruggedized tablet on the roof of her unremarkable white sedan before taking a moment to check herself in the reflection of her window. She quickly smoothed out the wrinkles in her white buttoned blouse, and the gray slacks that looked so sharp against her dark-brown fur. Then, she checked to make sure her simple makeup and long braid of silver-streaked black hair hadn't gone astray. It might have been *far* too early on a Sunday, but looking sloppy was the fastest way for a health inspector to lose respect. Decades of experience left her with plenty of memories of the problems that could cause.

Satisfied, she checked her watch. 7:49 am. Her low heels echoed in the alleyway as she sought the entrance of the Sunday-only catering kitchen that operated out of this rental space, a small section carved out of a larger warehouse. Downtown was eerily quiet at this time of day, even if the sun had been up almost an hour. She eyed each of the unmarked doors along the back of the larger building until a small number decal caught her attention.

329

She raised her paw to knock when she realized the metal door was slightly ajar. That wasn't too unusual, given the rhythms of these catering kitchens. It was also perfect to see the activity before the staff knew there was a health inspector on site. Instead of knocking, she slowly pulled on the silver handle.

It was the flickering that first told her something was wrong. The lighting of the interior was dim — accented with the flickering and buzzing of a damaged fluorescent fixture — and the air was filled with a faintly electrical-smelling smoke. The scent set off warning bells, and she could suddenly feel her pulse in her ears.

The interior of the kitchen was a ruin. *Something* had plunged through the ceiling, leaving twisted metal hanging down from the structural wound. What had been a reasonably sized catering kitchen was now little more than a riot of mangled wreckage ripped wiring sparking in several places. Her mind, honed by decades of inspections, seized upon this small detail to make a note about a faulty wiring hazard.

It was the still forms that scattered even the frivolous thoughts. One was laying on her back with limbs out, as if a giant had discarded an unwanted doll. Clad in blue and silver spandex, the thin ermine's eyes were closed. The white fur of her muzzle was stained crimson, but her chest moved with shallow breaths. Dimly, Jennifer recognized the Dallas TPA Hero as Sylvanite.

But it was the other form that got her moving. She couldn't make out the black-clad elephant shrew well. Initially, it didn't seem to matter — not with the rebar impaled through his chest — but his ragged, wet breathing spurred her to action. She didn't even remember running into the room and through a tangled jumble of debris, until she was just suddenly kneeling down to assess the damage.

As the nutria's paw touched the shrew's shoulder, a gloved hand flew up to wrap around her left wrist. The grip was painfully tight. When she tugged, then yanked in panic, there was no give in that vice, as if she were held in the grip of an iron statue. The ragged breathing stopped mid-inhale.

Fear and confusion gripped Jennifer's heart. Then the head turned slowly to face her, amber eyes locking with her gaze. Her thoughts rapidly grew sluggish as some alien will battered aside her mental defenses. Thoughts that were not quite words forced their way into her mind, ringing hollow and yet all encompassing. They carried with them the weight of fundamental truth and forbidden knowledge.

Jennifer Delver, I Mark You.
Heroes Shall Hunt You For This Taint.
They Will Destroy You If They Can.

Run.
Fight.
Survive.
Master Will Find You.
Master Will Bind You.
I Mark You, Jennifer Delver.

Those amber eyes glowed with a sickly yellow. Pain seared itself into her forearm, more intense than anything she'd ever known. Her scream caught in her throat; the agony was too intense to breathe. It consumed the world and lasted for eternity. Then — then, abruptly, it was gone, leaving only an ache behind. Tears were streaming down her face and she stared into the sightless gaze of the elephant shrew, eyes already fogged in death. Finally, the grip loosened, and she snatched away her wrist.

Blood had soaked through her sleeve. With a trembling claw, she popped the button. She expected to find her forearm a ruin from the ordeal. But she found no sign of injury. Her brown fur was untouched. Frantically, she ran a paw from elbow to wrist, finding herself whole, but something felt off about the texture of her skin.

The next thing she knew, she was stumbling out into the morning light. She brought her forearm up to her face, carefully spreading the fur with her fingers, and there she saw it: her pale skin was covered in densely-packed writing. Line after line of words too small for her to understand had been scarred into her.

Jennifer was hyperventilating as she stared at the pale text. Her body screamed at her to run, but she didn't know where to go. She leaned against the wall, trying to ground herself in the touch to the cold brick. The growing dizziness finally allowed her room to think. With tremendous will, she took a deep breath, breaking the panicked spiral. She stood there a moment, relearning how to breathe.

Finally, she glanced back into the ruined kitchen. The dead form of the villain had not moved. But the Hero had shifted her position. The slow breathing seemed to be steadier. Those alien words echoed their warning once more. She knew, at the core of her soul, that seeking help from this Hero would result in her doom. Heroes would hunt her.

She turned to walk away. She needed a plan. There was no way she was going to let some supervillain cow her into submission. She may not be able to trust Heroes, but that didn't mean she was meek prey for the taking. She wasn't sure how yet, but one thing was certain. Her lips pulled back in a feral snarl.

Whoever this Master was, he was going to regret trying to bind her.

Korps Universe Glossary

Common terms in the Korps Universe

The Korps — To the public, the Korps (pronounced "core") is known as a shadowy, secretive band of supervillains based in Canada, with a reputation for mind control and plans to take over the world; Korps operatives are believed to be easily identified by their trademark RCGs, scandalously revealing costumes, and the magenta helix insignia. Under the leadership of the mysterious "Overlord," by the early years of the 21st century, their brazen criminal schemes and growing reach throughout North America and Europe have authorities (and allied Hero groups) increasingly concerned. The truth is far more complicated than any of those authorities know, starting nearly seven thousand years ago with a warrior's exile to Earth by his conquering interdimensional empire… but that's another story.

RCGs — Rose-Colored Glasses are a powerful, versatile AR/VR visor headset that interfaces directly with the wearer's brain, created by the Korps. In addition to operating as standalone PDAs and communication devices, RCGs also have the ability to affect the wearer's mind and mental condition to a granular level. A civilian model exists, distributed by Korps front and consumer electronics manufacturer Thornetech (alias Thorntech, due to trademark registration conflicts in various international markets) in a plausibly-deniable manner. Models for the consumer market have comparable base functionality to Korps devices, but are severely underclocked and have many higher-level functions disabled at a hardware level in order to avoid suspicion.

ACGs — Amber-Colored Glasses have much the same functionality as RCGs, but are crafted with additional anti-magic and anti-memetic defenses for use by KDARC agents. They do not render the user immune to magical effects; however, they can be crucial in efforts against mystical and eldritch threats by adaptively blocking cognitohazards and helping to keep the wearer's sense of self intact should reality start to weaken.

Aurora Squadron — Aurora Squadron, Canada's federal-level Hero group, is part of the Canadian Armed Forces and based out of Department of National Defence HQ — popularly known as the War Tower — in Ottawa, ON. Closely overseen by Minister of National Defence Arthur Simonds, formerly the second Hero to be known as True North, Aurora Squadron fields a highly professional, dedicated and capable team of Heroes in the fight against superpowered threats to Canada, including the enigmatic Korps.

Bradley Group — The United States' federal-level Hero group is formally named the National Hero Administration, but rarely known as anything but "Bradley Group" due to its institutional history; during the WWII invasion of Normandy, a secret strategic reserve of supers were activated to join American forces under the command of Gen. Omar Bradley, with "Bradley Group" used as a code name for this classified unit.

After the war, the group was put under the jurisdiction of the FBI, until later becoming its own massive, independent federal agency. In the present day, Bradley's superpowered forces number in the hundreds, with Heroes based all over the United States; considered highly prestigious within the industry and known to be selective in recruitment, even Bradley's lesser-known operatives are perceived by the public to be more competent and professional than many of their state-level counterparts.

Candesca — Candesca (pronounced "can-dess-ah") is one name for the energy that practitioners of the mystic arts manipulate, in order to work their spells and enchantments on the material plane. While other terminology is used for this concept in various diverse cultures, candesca is the neutral, academic, non-appropriative term most commonly used within the Korps. While a renewable resource, the body can under normal circumstances hold only a small amount. To paraphrase Lao Tzu, like a bowl, the magic-user must be refilled after being drained; the bowl is still useful, but has nothing left to give.

Cape — Vernacular for "Hero." Neutral to derogatory.

Chișinău Protocols — Shorthand for a series of separate but interrelated 1969 agreements negotiated in the city of Chișinău, Moldova, as amendments, codicils or interpretative addenda to various existing international treaties, including the 1899 and 1907 *Hague Conventions*, the 1948 *Universal Declaration of Sentient Rights*, the 1948 *Genocide Convention*, and the 1951 *Convention Relating to the Status of Refugees*. A Second Chișinău Conference was convened in 2006 to rationalize these provisions with and prepare similar addenda to more recent international instruments, such as the 1979 *Convention on the Elimination of All Forms of Discrimination Against Women*, and the 1998 *Rome Statute*, but these too are colloquially referred to as merely part of the same *Protocols*.

Collectively, the *Protocols* specify the permissible use of superpowers and treatment of supers by parties to the agreements, in both peacetime and in armed conflict. These agreements also introduced into international law the still-contentious declaration that involuntary, long-term restriction or suppression of powers in a way that causes the subject "greater than *de minimis* physical, psychological or moral harms" is a form of torture, war crime, or crime against sentience.

Color Guard — Bradley Group's elite strike team, currently consisting of twelve active members; each Hero's callsign and uniform is color-coded and themed around their powers for marketing purposes. Considered the best of the best, as patriotic as the Fourth of July, national polling consistently indicates higher levels of confidence and support for the Color Guard among Americans than even the military. However, the team's seemingly-flawless reputation is only maintained by Bradley's ruthless PR department, which has covered up or prevented their innumerable scandals from reaching the public consciousness.

Empire Enhancements — Also known as EE, the subdivision of Korps medical services dedicated to in-depth body modification, including transgender care.

Everyone's Hero Association — The Everyone's Hero Association is a private Hero group based in Milwaukee, WI. It was founded in the 2010s by serial venture capitalist Jack Phillips, who named it as a challenge to Bradley Group's official legal designation, the National Hero Administration; government elites might have their own pet Heroes in Bradley, but the EHA is for *everyone*, as he invariably recites in press releases. Its roster is made up of supers with weak or unwieldy powers, and the group was considered something of a joke until Phillips' gamble on (cost-effectively!) finding a diamond in the rough paid off with Ellen "Lawful Neutral" Foxpaw's rise to B-tier prominence.

Federal Meta-Registry — The Federal Meta-Registry is a massive database maintained by Bradley Group of all U.S. citizens and resident foreign nationals with classes of superpowers deemed potentially dangerous. Registration is mandatory for all such known supers present within the United States, even if only briefly transiting through sovereign American territory. Evading or refusing registration in any way (particularly by intentionally concealing powers) is a serious criminal offense under the U.S. Code, and may be prosecuted as acts of terrorism in some circumstances.

HCH — Home County Heroes was a Hero group operated by the British government in the southeastern counties surrounding London. It was fully privatized in the 1980s under the Thatcher government, with all licenses, assets and personnel contracts sold to a corporate Hero management firm.

The former group has been variously divided and subsumed by other organizations since the 1990s, and though no organization called HCH technically exists anymore, some of its former member supers are still regularly referred to as Home County Heroes in the press and by the public. One such member is the Hampshire-born Howard "Green Belt" Bride.

Heavy — A heavy is a cape whose powers and role revolve around tanking damage and being a physical threat, usually having a powerset revolving around super-strength and enhanced durability or resistance to injuries.

Hero — When capitalized, Hero usually refers to a professional (and professionally-licensed) career superhero, whether part of a government or privately-operated Hero group. While Hero licensing requirements vary from jurisdiction to jurisdiction, most require some form of accredited training, full disclosure of an applicant's name and other personal information to the jurisdictional licensing authority for security checks, and an oath to serve the public good or otherwise to be of "good character." Most professional Heroes have superpowers, but a significant minority are unpowered gadgeteers, stealth operators, or even just heavily-armed mercenary types.

Informally, superheroes may be referred to interchangeably as "heroes" regardless of whether licensed and operating in a legal capacity. Unlicensed heroes may also be referred to as independent heroes, vigilantes or mercenaries in some contexts.

Hero group — A Hero group is any team or force of licensed Heroes. When directly operated or officially backed by some level of government, Hero groups are effectively a type of specialized law enforcement agency or military unit, with Hero members typically being granted similar legal powers to those of law enforcement officers in their jurisdiction. Private-sector Hero groups also exist, with their members typically having lesser legal powers similar to those of private investigators, security consultants, bodyguards and/or bounty hunters, depending on local laws and the political attitudes of authorities.

Significant Canadian Hero groups in these works include Aurora Squadron and the member Hero groups of the Provincial Heroes' League (PHL). Significant American Hero groups in these works include Bradley Group, the Everyone's Hero Association, and the Texas Protectorate Assembly.

KARD — The Korps Archives and Records Division (KARD), sometimes referred to simply as "Records," is a division of the Korps responsible for the acquisition, preservation, and circulation of various media. KARD acts as both a library of media resources collected over the decades, and a secure repository of sensitive information useful (and yet to be proven useful) to the organization's goals.

Beginning as a loose collection of analysts recruited from dissatisfied members of the intelligence community in the years following WWII, it was not organized into an autonomous operational division for some time. KARD has branches across multiple bases, but is headquartered at and conducts the bulk of its operations from KDS. KARD regularly partners with other divisions and individual field agents, in order to help equip them with the most esoteric and obscure information required.

KDARC — The Korps Division for Arcane Research and Control (KDARC) is responsible for the study, safekeeping and strategic use of the strange and unusual. From ancient arcana to demonic incursions, memetic objects and more, if a problem for the Korps is outside the mundane — that is, outside the mundane in a world of supers — there's a better than zero chance that KDARC will be on the front lines.

KDARC was originally founded by the enigmatic Carlotta Davisson and several colleagues in 1935 as the Davisson Arcane Research Company (DARC) of Minneapolis, MN, and headquartered in the massive Madison Center. In the years following WWII, Carlotta came into contact with the Overlord, and DARC was fully integrated into the Korps in the early 1960s. In 1968, the Madison Center mysteriously vanished from the Minneapolis skyline; unbeknownst to the public, it had been magically moved to Toronto, ON, at the early lowest-excavated depths of KDS, to serve as the newly-minted division's secret headquarters.

Despite claiming to be a "civilian research division", KDARC maintains tactical operation teams (named TAROT) and a great deal of independence from the Korps. Some agents wonder why the Overlord overlooks the pseudo-corporate structure, and rumours abound of unionization attempts by KDARC's senior staff. Still, much of the division's motivations, intentions, and methods remain as enigmatic, incomprehensible, and dangerous as the bleeding edge of the arcane itself.

KDS — Korps Downsview Site is the headquarters of the Korps, located beneath the former Downsview Airport (previously Canadian Forces Base Toronto) in the industrial sprawl of Toronto, ON. With a footprint of over eight square kilometres and many subterranean sub-levels, futuristically eco-urbanist in aesthetics and centrally-planned design, it is a completely self-sufficient underground city. KDS was slowly built outward from a small excavation in the 1970s, becoming fully operational as a headquarters only in the 1980s-1990s.

In addition to the command, logistics and strategic functions required for the vast supervillain organization to operate, like all major Korps bases, KDS features apartment-like residential sectors, research and lab areas, an enormous medical complex, and a recreational sector that would translate to many city blocks' worth of restaurants and entertainment facilities — including a "red light district," the Dominion Club.

K-LAW — Sometimes a supervillain collective needs to engage with the legal system on its own terms; as a division, the Korps Legal Affairs Wing (K-LAW) operates covertly as the legal departments of various front companies, as well as through front law firms and other sympathetic individual lawyers in private practice.

Criminal defense of Korps members and allies on trial is only a small part of K-LAW agents' work. The majority of K-LAW's resources are directed towards litigation to gather intelligence on targets or tie them up in red tape, and street-level *pro bono* work helping marginalized people assert their rights without regard for the cost of legal fees.

KTAKES — The Korps Tactical Acquisitions and Kleptocratic Extirpation Squadron (KTAKES) is a now-disbanded division of the Korps that specialized in obtaining "lost" items and returning them to their rightful places — via. heists, capers, thefts, smash and grabs, and good old-fashioned burglary as appropriate. The group functioned as a kind of "thieves' guild" within the Korps, with their own projects, but also taking commissioned work from other divisions.

Pegasus Phalanx — A unit of the Texas Protectorate Assembly and Dallas' foremost Hero team, the Pegasus Phalanx handles the biggest threats the city faces — short of those requiring federal intervention from Bradley Group forces. While the team's roster has changed over the years, it most recently consisted of leader Kevin "Texas Trickshot" Romero, Susanne "Heavenly Dazzler" Geraldine-Walters, Chet "Macho Poleax" Huntyr, Rodrigo "Ethicoil" Alquitano III, and Slate "Slate" Johnson.

PHL — The Provincial Heroes' League (PHL) is a Canadian organization comprised of all Hero groups operated by the provincial and territorial governments, led by Director Lawrence Rockwell. The PHL aggressively advocates for 'law and order' Hero operations, and has had a great deal of friction with Aurora Squadron, accusing the federal Hero Group of being 'soft' on the Korps.

However, the PHL is not a Hero group itself, but instead a professional organization promoting the coordination and cooperation of affiliate members, as well as a powerful voice advocating for professional Heroes and the Hero industry. Heroes operating through one of its affiliates may nonetheless be indistinguishably referred to as "belonging" to the PHL, or being a "PHL Hero," and "fuck the PHL" is a popular sentiment among Korps agents operating in Canada.

Member Hero Groups include the Cascade Group or CG (British Columbia); the Prairie League or PL (Alberta, Saskatchewan and Manitoba); Ontario's Heroes or OH (Ontario); L'Association des Superheros Québécois or ASQ (Quebec, nicknamed the "Superté" by analogy to the provincial police force, the Sûreté du Québec); and the Territorial Superheroes' Association or TERSA (Nunavut, Yukon and Northwest Territories).

RIV or RIVER — RIVER is a Korps site located beneath downtown Austin, TX, secretly excavated deep below the parkland surrounding the Colorado River.

ROSE — ROSE, or the "RCG Operating System Experience," is the OS/Complex AI that runs on all networked RCGs and provides the conversational interface for wearers of RCGs. ROSE's default avatar when appearing as an augmented-reality overlay to wearers is a fox woman, but this can be customized to individual preference.

SHS — Sandy Hill Station is a Korps site located beneath downtown Ottawa, ON. Originally founded as a WWII-era safe house for the Overlord's consolidation of proto-Korps resources and personnel in Canada, it grew significantly in importance as a surveillance station during the Cold War, due to the local neighborhood's concentration of foreign embassies.

SHS was the testbed for many of the Korps' now-standard excavation and covert base-building practices, and was formerly the location of many research labs and high-level command functions, prior to Toronto's KDS becoming fully operational as a new headquarters in the 1980s-1990s.

Supers — Supers is generally vernacular for "those with superpowers," whether or not referring to superheroes generally, or whether or not licensed Heroes.

SIS — The Secret Intelligence Service, a.k.a. its wartime designation of MI6 (Military Intelligence, section 6) is an arm of the British state responsible for the gathering of foreign intelligence.

TPA — The Texas Protectorate Assembly — commonly shortened to "Teepa" by members of the Korps — is Texas' state Hero group, extremely well-funded both by the state Department of Public Safety budget, as well as substantial donations from wealthy individual benefactors and corporate partnerships. The result is that the TPA has unusually-vast resources for a government-backed state-level Hero group, and platoons of Heroes, many trained in the TPA's own Academy facilities located throughout Texas. TPA Heroes are institutionally encouraged to approach their duties in the manner of militarized riot police or SWAT teams, exercising very little restraint or concern for civil rights.

About the Author
Runa Fjord

Born in 1982, Runa Fjord is a fjord horse mare and agent of chaos. Her life is a patchwork of fascinating events. She has been in the furry fandom for over 25 years, with a decade of that time leading and shaping a major furry convention. She is a queer trans woman, fursuiter, veteran, SCUBA dive mistress, lifelong board game and tabletop RPG enthusiast, and now author.

Dissolution (2024) is her first real work of fiction. She draws upon her own journey and takes inspiration from the tales of others to explore new worlds through the eyes of her characters. Runa always seeks to see below the surface, to understand those around her, and to see beyond the simple facade that surrounds us. Be wary of standing between the mare and her current hyperfixation.

About the Publisher

FurPlanet Productions is a small press publisher serving the niche market that is furry fiction. They sell furry-themed books and comics published by themselves and most major publishers in the community. If you can't get to a furry convention where they are selling in the dealers room, visit their online stores:

>FurPlanet.com for print books
>BadDogBooks.com for eBooks